PUSHKIN PRESS CLASSICS

AND TIME WAS NO MORE

ESSENTIAL STORIES AND MEMORIES

'Pushkin Press deserves our thanks for bringing Teffi to a much wider audience'

SPECTATOR

'A writer who deserves her seat at the top table of Russian authors'

SARA WHEELER, WALL STREET JOURNAL

'The translucent surface of her writing gives sight of the depths of the human spirit: its raging and yearning, its dark nights and joyous awakenings'

NEW YORK REVIEW OF BOOKS

TEFFI (pseudonym of Nadezhda Lokhvitskaya) was born in St Petersburg, in 1872, into a distinguished family that treasured literature; she and three of her four sisters all became writers. Teffi wrote in many styles and genres: political feuilletons published in a Bolshevik newspaper during her brief period of radical fervour after the 1905 Revolution; Symbolist poems that she declaimed or sang in Petersburg literary salons; a crime novel titled *Adventure Novel*; and a number of mostly satirical short plays including "The Woman Question". Her finest works are her short stories and *Memories*, a witty yet tragic account of her last journey across Russia and what is now Ukraine, before going by boat to Istanbul in summer 1919.

Teffi was widely read; her admirers included not only Ivan Bunin, Mikhail Bulgakov and Mikhail Zoshchenko, but also Lenin and Tsar Nicholas II. In pre-revolutionary Russia, candies and perfumes were named after her; after the 1917 Revolution, her stories were published and her plays performed throughout the Russian diaspora. During the first decades after her death in Paris in 1952, however, she was almost forgotten. This was probably because of prejudice against women; because she was thought lightweight (critics had always focused more on her wit more than on her depth of emotional understanding); and because both Western and Soviet scholars tended to ignore émigré literature. Her work is now being published widely in Russia, as well as being translated into many languages.

ROBERT CHANDLER's translations from Russian include works by Alexander Pushkin, Andrey Platonov, Vasily Grossman and Hamid Ismailov. He is the editor and main translator of *Russian Short Stories from Pushkin to Buida* and *Russian Magic Tales from Pushkin to Platonov*; together with Boris Dralyuk and Irina Mashinski, he has co-edited *The Penguin Book of Russian Poetry*. He has run regular translation workshops in London and worked as a mentor for the British Centre for Literary Translation.

AND TIME WAS NO MORE

ESSENTIAL STORIES AND MEMORIES

TEFFI

TRANSLATED FROM THE RUSSIAN
BY ROBERT AND ELIZABETH CHANDLER

WITH MICHELE BERDY, ROSE FRANCE,
ANNE MARIE JACKSON AND CLARE KITSON;
AND WITH CONTRIBUTIONS FROM BEE BENTALL,
MARIA EVANS, IRINA STEINBERG AND SIÂN VALVIS

PUSHKIN PRESS CLASSICS

Pushkin Press
Somerset House, Strand
London WC2R 1LA

This new selection first published by Pushkin Press in 2024

1 3 5 7 9 8 6 4 2

ISBN 13: 978-1-80533-042-4

Designed and typeset by Tetragon, London

Printed and bound in the United Kingdom by Clays Ltd, Elcograf S.p.A.

www.pushkinpress.com

Contents

Introductory Note

There are writers who muddy their own water, to make it seem deeper. Teffi could not be more different: the water is entirely transparent, yet the bottom is barely visible.

—GEORGY ADAMOVICH[1]

Teffi had a rare gift for establishing a sense of intimacy between herself and her readers. Nicholas Lezard, for example, began his review of *Subtly Worded* (our first selection of Teffi's stories and memoirs), with the words, "Pushkin Press has done it again: made me fall in love with a writer I'd never heard of. [...] I wish she were still alive, and I could have met her."[2] And Erica Wagner, in a review of *Memories*, wrote, "Teffi is a courageous companion for anyone's life."[3] Other reviewers and readers have responded in a similar vein.

This sense of intimacy is to some extent an artistic construct; Teffi's "memories" are not precise historical records and there are crucial turning points in her life about which she is startlingly reticent. Nevertheless, the clear-eyed goodwill that informs her writing was evidently characteristic of the real person. Leo Tolstoy wrote, "The poet takes the best things out of his life and puts them into his work. Hence his work is beautiful and his life bad."[4] This could not be said of Teffi: she was kind, tolerant and courageous. Few, if any, members of the fractious Russian émigré community in Paris, where she spent the last thirty years of her life, were so generally liked and admired.

Teffi's life is emblematic of many of the most important aspects of twentieth-century history. She was one of a liberal, optimistic generation whose hopes were shattered by the advent of totalitarianism. *Memories*—her account of her last journey across Russia and Ukraine during the Civil War—is a vivid evocation of life as a refugee, of its tragedies, absurdities and unexpected moments of joy. Teffi is also central to the history of women's writing. In about 1898, probably on the edge of an emotional breakdown, she left her husband and three small children and returned to Petersburg to begin a career as a professional writer. A letter written nearly fifty years later to her elder daughter Valeria is both a self-justification and a confession of guilt. After saying she had been a bad mother, she backtracks, "In essence I was good, but circumstances drove me from home, where, had I remained, I would have perished." It should be no surprise that Teffi seldom spoke of a sacrifice that must have been almost unbearable.[5]

Our aim here has been not only to represent Teffi's best work, but also to give an impressionistic account of her life. This collection begins with stories about her early childhood and moves on through her accounts of revolution, civil war and exile. It ends with stories and articles about her experience of old age. She suffered from poor health throughout her life and was close to death at least three times. Nevertheless, she lived to the age of eighty.

Teffi's work is extremely varied—both in tone and in subject matter. It is not unusual for a writer to be pigeonholed, but few great writers have suffered from this to such a degree; many Russians still know only the light satirical sketches she wrote during the very first years of her career. Like Chekhov, she fuses wit, tragedy and a remarkable perceptiveness; there are few human weaknesses she did not relate to with compassion and understanding. And like her close friend Ivan Bunin and many other great Russian prose writers, Teffi was a poet who turned to prose but continued to write with a poet's sensitivity to melody and rhythm.

If anyone wishes to read more about Teffi, I wholeheartedly recommend Edythe Haber's exemplary biography: *Teffi: A Life of Letters and of Laughter.*

PART ONE
Childhood

Like the Impressionist painter Berthe Morisot—another great woman artist who was famous in her lifetime but then largely forgotten for several decades—Teffi portrays children without the least hint of sentimentality. She is aware of the complexity of children's emotions and of the intensity with which they can feel not only love and joy, but also rage, jealousy and despair. Her psychological understanding is profound yet unobtrusive. She herself wrote:

> During those years of my distant childhood, we used to spend the summer in a wonderful, blessed country—at my mother's estate in Volhynia province.[1] I was very little. I had only just begun to learn to read and write—so I must have been about five. [...] What slipped quickly through the lives of adults was for us a matter of complex and turbulent experience, entering our games and our dreams, inserting itself like a brightly coloured thread into the pattern of our life, into that first firm foundation that psychoanalysts now investigate with such art and diligence, seeing it as the prime cause of many of the madnesses of the human soul.[2]

The first story in this section is taken from the collection *Witch* (1936), which Teffi particularly valued. In a letter sent to a historian friend in 1943, she wrote, "In *Witch* you find our ancient Slav gods, how they still live on in the soul of the people, in legends, superstitions and customs. Everything as I encountered it in the Russian provinces, as a child."[3]

Most of Teffi's stories about her childhood are written in the first person. When she writes about herself in the third person, she usually calls herself either Katya or Lisa.

RUSALKA

WE HAD MANY SERVANTS in our large country house. They lived with us for a long time, especially the most important of them: the coachman, who so astonished us little ones when we once saw him eat an entire black radish; Panas, who was our head gardener and the village wise man; our elderly cook; the housekeeper; Bartek the footman; and Kornelia the chambermaid. These were all a part of the household, and they stayed with us for many years.

Bartek was a rather picturesque figure. Short, with a distinctive forelock. His walk and some of his other mannerisms were very like Charlie Chaplin's, and he too was something of a comedian. I think he must have been with us a good ten years, since he appears in every one of my childhood memories. Yes, at least ten years, even though he was fired every year, always on Whit Monday.

"It's his *journée fatale*," my elder sister liked to pronounce.

Bartek could never get through this fateful day without running into trouble.

Much was expected of servants in those stricter times. Some of the transgressions for which poor Bartek was dismissed can hardly be described as serious.

I remember one occasion when he let a dish of rissoles crash to the floor. And there was the evening when he spilled a whole gravy boat down an elegant lady's collar. I also remember him serving chicken to a particularly stout and self-important gentleman. Evidently not someone who liked to rush at things, this gentleman studied the pieces of chicken for a long time, wondering which to choose. All of a sudden, Bartek—who was wearing white cotton gloves—pointed daintily with his middle finger at a morsel he thought particularly tasty.

The gentleman looked up in some indignation.

"Blockhead! How dare you?"

It was Whit Monday, and Bartek was duly dismissed.

But I don't think he was ever dismissed for long. He may, perhaps, have gone on living in some little shed behind the wing. Then he would come and ask for forgiveness and everything would go smoothly until the next Whitsun.

He was also famous for having once shot, plucked, roasted and eaten a whole crow. All purely out of scientific interest.

He loved telling our old *nyanya* about this,[1] probably because the story really did make her feel very queasy.

"There's nowt quite like it, my dear Nyanya. No, there's no flesh so full o' goodness like that of a crow. Brimful of satiety, and how! The ribs be a little sour, mind, the loins a little like human flesh. But the thighs—so rich, so dripping wi juice they are… After a meal of crow, it be a whole month till you next feel hunger. Aye, it's three weeks nah since I last put food in me mouth."

Nyanya gasped. "So you really… You well and truly ate a crow?" she would ask.

"That I did, Nyanya—and washed it dahn wi good strong water."

The heroine of this tale, Kornelia the chambermaid, was another of these important, long-term servants. She was from a family of Polish gentry and some of her elegant mannerisms seemed affected. She was, therefore, known as the "Pannochka"—the Polish for "Mademoiselle".

She had a plump, very pale face and bulging eyes. The eyes of a fish—yellow with black rims. Her fine eyebrows were like an arrow, cutting across her forehead and giving her a look of severity.

Kornelia's hair was extraordinary. She had long plaits that hung down below her knees but which she piled up in a tight crown. All rather ugly and strange, especially since her hair was a pale, lacklustre brown.

Kornelia was slow and taciturn, secretly proud. She spoke little, but she was always humming to herself, through closed lips.

"Kornelia sings through her nose," Lena and I used to say.

In the mornings she came to the nursery to comb our hair. Why she had assumed this responsibility was unclear. But she wielded the comb like a weapon.

"Ouch!" her victim would squeal. "Stop! Kornelia! That hurts!"

Calm and deliberate as ever, Kornelia just carried on, humming away, her nostrils flared and her lips pursed.

I remember Nyanya once saying to her, "What a slowpoke you are! For all I know, you could be asleep. You working or not?"

Kornelia looked at Nyanya with her usual severe expression and said in Polish, "Still waters break banks."

She then turned on her heels and left the room.

Nyanya probably couldn't make head or tail of these words, but she took offence all the same.

"Thinks she can scare me, does she? Coming out with gobbledygook like that—the woman's just plain workshy!"

On Sundays, after an early lunch, Kornelia would put on her best woollen dress—always decorated with all kinds of frills and bows—and a little green necktie. She would slowly and carefully comb her hair, pin it up, throw a faded lace kerchief over her shoulders, tie a black velvet ribbon with a little silver icon around her neck, take her prayer book and rosary and go to a bench near the ice house. She would then solemnly sit down, straighten her skirt and begin to pray.

Lena and I were intrigued by Kornelia's way of praying. We always followed her to the ice house and observed her for a long time, unabashed as only children and dogs can be.

She would whisper away to herself, telling the long oval beads of her rosary with her short, podgy fingers and looking piously up at the heavens. We could see the whites of her bulging eyes.

The hens bustled about and clucked. The cock pecked away crossly, right next to the Pannochka's fine Sunday shoes. Rattling her keys and clattering her jugs, the housekeeper went in and out of the ice house. Aloof as ever, her pale, plump face plastered with face-cream, Kornelia seemed not to notice any of this. Her beads clicked quietly, her lips moved silently, and her eyes seemed to be contemplating something unearthly.

She ate her meals apart from the other servants, fetching a plateful of food from the kitchen and taking it to the maids' room. Arching her neck like a trace horse, she always put her spoon into the right-hand corner of her mouth.

One summer, we arrived from Moscow to find all our servants present as usual, except that Kornelia was now living not in the maids' room but in the little white annexe beside the laundry, right by the pond. We were told that she had married and was living with her husband, Pan Perkawski, who did not yet have a position on the estate.

Kornelia still came to do battle with our hair in the mornings and she still prayed on Sundays, now sitting outside her new home, where there was a sprawling old willow. One of its two trunks leaned over the pond; the other grew almost horizontally along its banks. It was on this second trunk that Kornelia now sat, her prayer book in her hands, her velvet ribbon around her neck and her skirt spread out decorously beneath her.

Her husband was nothing to write home about. Dull, pock-marked and—like Bartek—rather short. Most of the day he just hung about smoking. He'd acquired a chicken that he used to bathe in the pond. The chicken would struggle to get free, letting out heart-rending squawks and spattering him with water—but he was unflinching. Grunting and grimacing, with the air of a man who has sworn to fulfil his duty no matter what, he would plunge the chicken into the water. In other respects Pan Perkawski had little to distinguish him.

It was a rowdy and merry summer. There was a regiment of hussars stationed in the nearest town. The officers were frequent visitors to our house, which was always full of young ladies—my elder sisters, our girl cousins and a great many friends who had come to stay. There were picnics, expeditions on horseback, games and dances.

Lena and I did not take part in all this and we were always being sent away just as things were getting interesting. Nevertheless, we entirely agreed with the housekeeper that the squadron commander was a splendid fellow. He was short and bow-legged, and he had a moustache, a topknot and whiskers just like Alexander II. He would arrive in a carriage drawn by three frisky grey horses, caparisoned with long, colourful ribbons. On each side of the painted shaft bow was an inscription. On the front: "Rejoice, ladies—here comes your suitor!" On the back: "Weep—he is already married."

The squadron commander was, in reality, a long way from being married. He was in a state of permanent infatuation, but with no one in particular. He offered his hand and his heart to each young lady in turn, took their refusals in his stride, entirely without resentment, and sped on to his next choice.

And he was not the only one to be in love. Love was the prevailing mood. Young officers sighed, brought bouquets and sheets of music, sang songs, recited poems and, narrowing their eyes, reproached the young ladies for their "be-eastly cruelty". For some reason, they always pronounced the word "beastly" with a particularly long "e". As for the young ladies, they grew more mysterious by the day. They laughed for no reason, spoke only in hints, went for walks in the moonlight and refused to eat anything for supper.

It was a shame that we kept being packed off to the nursery at the most interesting moment. Some of those moments have stayed with me to this day.

I remember a tall, pockmarked adjutant translating some English poem for one of my cousins:

> Clouds bow down to kiss mountains…
> Why should I not bow to kiss you?[2]

"What do you make of the poem's last line?" he then asked, bowing every bit as impressively as the clouds.

The cousin turned around, caught sight of me and said, "Nadya, go to the nursery!"

Even though I too might have been interested in her opinion.

Other enigmatic dialogues were no less intriguing.

She (pulling the petals off a daisy): "Loves me, loves me not. Loves me, loves me not, loves me. Loves me not! Loves me not!"

He: "Don't trust flowers! Flowers lie."

She (glumly): "I fear that non-flowers lie still more artfully."

At this point she noticed me. Her look of poetic melancholy changed to one of more commonplace irritation. "Nadezhda Alexandrovna, it's high time you were in your nursery. Please go on your way."

But this didn't matter. What I'd already heard was enough. And in the evening, when little Lena bragged that she could stand on one leg for three days on end, I deftly cut her down to size: "That's a lie. You just lie and lie, like a non-flower."

That summer's favourite entertainment was riding. There were a lot of horses, and the young ladies were constantly running out to the stables, bearing gifts of sugar for their favourites.

It was around this time that everyone became aware of the exceptional good looks of Fedko the groom.

"He has the head of Saint Sebastian!" enthused one of my sister's student friends. "What a complexion! I really must find out what he washes with, to have skin like that."

I can still remember this Fedko. He couldn't have been more than eighteen. Creamy pink cheeks, bright, lively eyes, dark hair cut in a fringe and eyebrows so defined they could have been drawn with a brush. All in all, handsome as handsome can be. And he seemed well aware of his charms: he arched his eyebrows, gave little shrugs and smiled contemptuously. He could have been a society beauty.

And so the young ladies began plaguing Fedko with questions, wanting to elicit from him the secret of his good looks.

"Tell me, Fedko," said my sister's friend. "What do you wash with, to have such a fine complexion?"

He did not seem in the least taken aback. "With ear-r-rth, Pannochka. Ear-r-r-th."

"What do you mean?" squeaked the young ladies. "Earth isn't liquid!"

"So what?" replied Fedko, preening himself. "I rub some ear-r-rth on me face, wipe it away—an' I'm set."

Probably he would have liked to top this with something still more startling. But since nothing came to mind, he just said, "Aye, that's how I am."

The young ladies realized they'd forgotten to bring any sugar. So I was sent to Kornelia.

Kornelia must have been halfway through her elaborate coiffure. She finished it in a hurry and, just as she got to the stables, her hair cascaded down to her knees.

"Jesus Mary!" she exclaimed affectedly.

"Kornelia!" my sister's friend exclaimed in astonishment. "You're a *rusalka*—a real Russian mermaid! Isn't her hair remarkable, Fedko?"

"Her 'air? There be enough on 'er for four mares' tails."

Sensing that these words had not gone down particularly well, he added, with a languid sigh, "Beauty—our world be not without beauty!"

Probably, though, it was his own beauty that he had in mind.

At this point I turned to look at Kornelia. Her jaw had dropped, her cheeks had gone pale and her bulging, fishlike eyes were fixed on Fedko. It was as if her whole being had frozen in some intense, astonished question. Then she gasped and dropped the plate of sugar. Without picking it up, she turned around and walked slowly out of the stable.

"Kornelia's upset," whispered the young ladies.

"Silly girl! What's there to get upset about? On the contrary."

There are moments when the line of our fate suddenly fractures. And moments of this kind are not always noticeable. Sometimes they bear no sign or seal and are lost among our ordinary routines. We watch without interest as they slip by, and only later, when we look back after some train of events has reached its conclusion, does their fateful impact become clear.

Kornelia still came every morning to yank at our hair. She was still as quiet and slow as ever. She would still sit every Sunday on the bough of her old willow. Only, instead of reading her prayer book and telling her rosary, she'd be combing her hair with a large comb. And instead of singing "through her nose", she'd be singing aloud. One and the same Polish song.

"Golden plaits, golden braids…"

She sang quietly and with poor articulation. Apart from these golden plaits and braids, there was barely a word we could make out.

"She's singing about the Lorelei!" my eldest sister said in surprise. "The fool really does seem to fancy she's some kind of *rusalka*!"

One evening, Lena and I went out with Nyanya to water the flowers. First we went down to the pond to fill our watering cans. We heard a lot of splashing, which turned out to be Kornelia and Marya the washerwoman bathing. Kornelia's hair was like a long cloak, floating behind her. When she raised her head, however, it seemed more like the skin of a walrus, fitting perfectly over her strong, gleaming shoulders.

Loud shouts rang out from somewhere off to one side: "Hey there! Rusa-a-alka!"

Fedko and another man were bathing the horses.

Marya screamed and plunged down deeper. All we could see of her was the top of her head.

But Kornelia quickly turned her whole body away from us, towards the shouting. She stretched out her arms and began to shake with hysterical, staccato laughter. Then she began to leap up and down, her whole upper half rising out of the water. Her nostrils flared and her eyes opened wider than ever—round, yellow and full of wild animal joy. With the fingers of her outstretched hands, she seemed to be beckoning.

"The horses! Kornelia's luring the horses!" cried Lena.

This startled Kornelia. She shot up higher still, then sank out of sight, deep into the pond.

Then came more shouting, "Hey, Rusa-a-alka!"

Nyanya grabbed us crossly by the hand and led us away.

Autumn was approaching.

Like a noisy flock of birds, the love-sick officers took off and left. Their regiment was being posted elsewhere.

The young ladies quietened down and grew less interested in riding. They ate more, dressed worse and ceased to speak in subtle hints.

Those who were studying talked more often about the exams they had to retake. Or rather, other people began to mention these exams more often. It was not a subject the girls were keen to bring up themselves.

Soon we would all be leaving. This was sad and unsettling.

One evening, after supper, Nyanya decided to go down to the laundry to ask about a missing pillowcase.

I trotted along at her heels.

The laundry was in the annexe, next to where Kornelia now lived with her husband. Just by the pond.

Water, damp, slime. The square orange window looked out onto the path, close to the water. Through the murky glass I could see a table. On it were a small lamp and a plate of food. And a quiet, dark figure was sitting there, barely moving. Who was it? Kornelia's husband—her Pan?

Marya met us on the threshold and at once started whispering to Nyanya.

"Lord have mercy!" sighed Nyanya. "Anyone else would have chased her away with a stick."

More whispering. And then, once again, I made out a few words of Nyanya's: "So, he just sits there, does he?"

She must have been asking about the still, silent figure at the table.

"Bathing at night! The housekeeper said she'd speak to that priest of theirs."

"Her sort shouldn't be allowed communion. And there's no getting away from it—she smells of perch. We should speak to the mistress, really—but do our masters ever believe us?"

Whisper, whisper, whisper.

"Are you all right here, Marya? You don't feel frightened? Sleeping here, I mean?"

Yet more whispering.

"Does she still wear her cross?"

As we left, Nyanya took my hand and didn't let go of it until we were back inside the house.

We heard a low moan from the pond. Was someone singing? Or crying?

Nyanya stopped for a moment and listened. "Howl all you like!" she said fiercely. "But wait till he grabs you by the legs and drags you down under—that'll put an end to your howls!"

When she came to the nursery the following morning, Kornelia's eyes were red from crying.

Nyanya didn't allow her into the room.

"Get out!" she said sternly. "This nursery's no place for your sort. Go plait the beard of the pond sprite. Tie him a tithe of harvest wheat."[3]

Kornelia did not seem in the least surprised. She turned round and left without a word.

"Fish tail!" hissed Nyanya. "Slimy and slippery."

"Nyanya," asked Lena, "is Kornelia crying?"

"Crying! Her sort are always crying. But don't you go pitying her—every tear will cost you dear. Why, oh why, has the mistress not noticed? But do our masters ever believe us? More foolish than fools, they are. God help us."[4]

And that was the last we saw of Kornelia in the nursery.

I recall that day clearly. I'd had a headache all morning and the bright sun hurt my eyes. And little Lena was whimpering, stumbling and knocking against my shoulder. Her eyes looked murky, bleary, and we were both feeling sick. In the blur around us we could hear a tambourine and the squeals of a violin—a village wedding.

The bridegroom turned out to be Fedko. He was red-faced, sweating and a little drunk. He was dressed in white—in a new Ukrainian smock. Around his neck was the little green tie that Kornelia used to wear on Sundays, when she sat outside and prayed.

The bride was young, but startlingly ugly. Her long pockmarked nose poked out from beneath the white linen cloth that, in those parts, took the place of a Russian bridal headdress.

Together with Fedko, she threw herself down several times at Mama's feet, offering her the wedding *karavay*—a round loaf of pimply, sour-smelling rye bread.[5]

It was strange to see a woman with pockmarks like hers beside the handsome Fedko.

People began to dance in the huge hall, from which our two giant tables of Karelian birch had been temporarily removed. Young boys and girls whirled around, stamping grimly away in their heavy boots. Bartek the footman, sticking out his lower lip with a look of contempt, wandered about with a tray of boiled sweets and small glasses of vodka. The violin continued its plaintive squeals.

Lena and I huddled in a corner of the sofa. Nobody paid any attention to us. Lena was quietly crying.

"Why are you crying, Lena?"

"I'm sc-a-ared."

All around us were rough, scary people we didn't know. Stamping and leaping.

"Look, there's another wedding going on over there!"

"Where?"

"There."

"But that's a mirror!"

"No, it's a door. Another wedding!"

And I too begin to think that it's not a mirror but a door, and that beyond it are other guests, celebrating another wedding.

"Look! Kornelia! She's dancing!"

Lena closes her eyes and lays her head on my shoulder.

I half get to my feet. I'm looking for Kornelia. The people in this other wedding are all rather green—cloudy and murky.

"Lena! Where is Kornelia?"

"There!" she gestures, not opening her eyes. "Kornelia's weeping."

"What did you say? Weeping? Or leaping?"

"Don't know," Lena mutters. "I don't know what I'm saying."

I look again. My head whirls. And green evil people are whirling around, stamping stubbornly, as if trampling someone into the ground. And isn't that Kornelia, all dark and blurry? With huge, staring, fishy eyes? And then she leaps up, like that time in the pond, naked down to the waist. She stretches out her arms and beckons, beckons. Below her breast, she is all fish scales. Her mouth is wide open and she half sings, half cries, "O-o-ee-o-o!"

In a frenzy, trembling all over, I shout back, "O-o-ee-o-o!"

Then came a whole string of long days and nights. Heavy and murky. Strangers came and went. There was an old man, a water spirit, who tapped on my chest with a little hammer and pronounced, "Scarlatina, scarlatina. Yes, they've both got scarlatina."

Spiteful old women kept whispering about Kornelia, "I don't believe it! How could she? Some evil spirit must have dragged her down."

I had no idea who these old women were.

Apparently, the pond was drained.

"They searched and they searched, but they found nothing."

"Not till they looked in the river, behind the mill."

That is all I know about Kornelia's life. And only many years later did I realize what it was they found in the river. Nobody ever said anything more in our presence. And when I got over my scarlet fever and began to ask questions, all I ever heard was, "She died." And on another occasion, "She's gone."

Once we had recovered, we were taken back to Moscow.

What are we to make of this story? Did Kornelia love this Fedko? It's not impossible… Fedko in his white kaftan, with her little green tie… Kornelia dying on the very day of the wedding…

Or did love have nothing to do with it? Did Kornelia simply go mad and slip away, like a *rusalka*, into the water?

But if I'm ill, or lying half-asleep in the small hours, and if among the clouded memories of childhood I glimpse her strange, distant image, then I believe that the real truth is the truth we two little sick children saw in the mirror.

1931

TRANSLATED BY ROBERT AND ELIZABETH CHANDLER

THE LIFELESS BEAST

THE CHRISTMAS PARTY WAS FUN. There were crowds of guests, big and small. There was even one boy who had been flogged that day—so Katya's *nyanya* told her in a whisper. This was so intriguing that Katya barely left the boy's side all evening; she kept thinking he would say something special, and she watched him with respect and even fear. But the flogged boy behaved in the most ordinary manner; he kept begging for gingerbread, blowing a toy trumpet and pulling crackers. In the end, bitter though this was for her, Katya had to admit defeat and move away from the boy.

The evening was already drawing to a close, and the very smallest, loudly howling children were being got ready to go home, when Katya was given her main present—a large woolly ram. He was all soft, with a long, meek face and eyes that were quite human. He smelled of sour wool and, if you pulled his head down, he bleated affectionately and persistently: "Ba-a-a!"

Katya was so struck by the ram, by the way he looked, smelled and talked, that she even, to ease her conscience, asked, "Mama, are you sure he's not alive?"

Her mother turned her little bird-like face away and said nothing. She had long ago stopped answering Katya's questions—she never had time. Katya sighed and went to the dining room to give the ram some milk. She stuck the ram's face right into the milk jug, wetting it right up to the eyes. Then a young lady she didn't know came up to her, shaking her head: "Oh, dearie me, what are you doing? Really, giving living milk to a creature that isn't alive! It'll be the end of him. You need to give him pretend milk. Like this."

She scooped up some air in an empty cup, held it to the ram's mouth and smacked her lips.

"See?"

"Yes. But why does a cat get real milk?"

"That's just the way it is. Each according to its own. Live milk for the living. Pretend milk for the unliving."

The woollen ram at once made his home in the nursery, in the corner, behind Nyanya's trunk. Katya loved him, and because of her love he got grubbier by the day. His fur got all clumpy and knotted and his affectionate "Ba-a-a" became quieter and quieter. And because he was so very grubby, Mama would no longer allow him to sit with Katya at lunch. Lunchtimes became very gloomy. Papa didn't say anything; Mama didn't say anything. Nobody even looked round when, after eating her pastry, Katya curtsied and said, in the thin little voice of a clever little girl, "*Merci*, Papa! *Merci*, Mama!"

Once they began lunch without Mama being there at all; by the time she got back, they'd already finished their soup. Mama shouted out from the hall that there had been an awful lot of people at the skating rink. But when she came to the table, Papa took one look at her, then hurled a decanter down onto the floor.

"Why did you do that?" shouted Mama.

"Why's your blouse undone at the back?" shouted Papa. He shouted something else, too, but Nyanya snatched Katya from her chair and dragged her off to the nursery.

After that there were many days when Katya didn't so much as glimpse Papa or Mama; nothing in her life seemed real any longer. She was having the same lunch as the servants—it was brought up from the kitchen. The cook would come in and start whispering to Nyanya, "And he said… And then she said… And as for you!… You've got to go! And he said… And then she said…"

There was no end to this whispering.

Old women with foxy faces began coming in from the kitchen, winking at Katya, asking Nyanya questions, whispering, murmuring, hissing: "And then he said… You've got to go! And she said…"

Nyanya often disappeared completely. Then the foxy women would make their way into the nursery, poking around in corners and wagging their knobbly fingers at Katya.

But when they weren't there it was even worse. It was terrifying.

Going into the big rooms was out of the question: they were empty and echoing. The door curtains billowed; the clock over the fireplace ticked on severely. And there was no getting away from the endless "And he said… And then she said…"

The corners of the nursery started to get dark before lunch. They seemed to be moving. And the little stove—the big stove's daughter—crackled away in the corner. She kept clicking her damper, baring her red teeth and gobbling up firewood. You couldn't go near her. She was vicious. Once she bit Katya's finger. No, you wouldn't catch Katya going near that little stove again.

Everything was restless; everything was different.

The only safe place was behind the trunk—the home of the woollen ram, the lifeless beast. The ram lived on pencils, old ribbons, Nyanya's glasses—whatever the good Lord sent his way. He always looked at Katya with gentle affection. He never made any complaints or reproaches and he understood everything.

Once Katya was very naughty—and the ram joined in too. He was looking the other way, but she could see he was laughing.

Another time, when he was ill and Katya bandaged his neck with an old rag, he looked so pitiful that Katya quietly began to cry.

It was worst of all at night. There was scampering and squealing everywhere, all kinds of commotion. Katya kept waking up and calling out.

"Shh!" said Nyanya, when she came in. "Go back to sleep! It's only rats. But you watch out—or they'll bite your nose off!"

Katya would draw the blanket over her head. She would think about the woollen ram, and when she sensed him there, dear and lifeless, she would fall peacefully asleep.

One morning she and the ram were looking out of the window when they suddenly saw someone brown and hairless trotting across the yard. He looked like a cat, only he had a very long tail.

"Nyanya, Nyanya! Look! What a nasty cat!" Nyanya came to the window too.

"That's not a cat—it's a rat! And it isn't half big! A rat like that could make mincemeat of any cat. Yes, some rat!"

She spat out the last word so horribly, grimacing and baring her teeth as if she herself were an old cat, that Katya felt frightened and disgusted. She felt sick to the pit of her stomach.

Meanwhile, the rat, belly swaying, trotted up, in a businesslike, proprietorial way, to a nearby shed and, crouching down, crawled under a slat and into the cellar.

The cook came in and said there were so many rats now that soon they'd be eating your head off. "Down in the storeroom they've gnawed away all the corners of the master's suitcase. The cheek of them! When I come in they just sit there. They don't stir an inch."

In the evening the foxy women came, bringing a bottle of something and some stinking fish. Along with Nyanya, they took swigs from the bottle, swallowed down mouthfuls of fish and then started laughing at something or other.

"You still with that ram of yours?" a rather stout woman asked Katya. "He's only fit for the knacker's yard. He's going bald—and look at that leg of his! It's hanging on by a thread. I'd say he's had it."

"Stop teasing her," said Nyanya. "Don't pick on a poor orphan!"

"I'm not teasing her. Just telling it how it is. The stuffing will all fall out and that'll be the end of him. A live body eats and drinks—and that's how it stays alive. You can mollycoddle a rag all you like but it'll always fall apart in the end. Anyway, the girl's not an orphan. For all we know, her mother drives past the house laughing into her sleeve: Tee-hee-hee!"

The women had worked up quite a sweat with laughing so much. Nyanya dipped a lump of sugar in her glass and gave it to Katya to suck. The sugar lump clawed at Katya's throat and there was a ringing in her ears. She tugged at the ram's head.

"He's special. I tell you—he really bleats!"

"Tee-hee! You are a silly girl," said the stout woman, with more sniggering. "Even a door squeaks if you push it. A real ram squeals all by itself. You don't need to pull its head."

The women drank some more and went back to whispering the same old words: "And he said… You've got to go!… And then she said…"

Along with the ram, Katya went behind the trunk in the nursery, to be well and truly miserable.

The ram wasn't very alive. He was going to die soon. His stuffing would all fall out—and that would be the end of him. If only she could get him to eat—if only she could find a way to get him to eat even the very littlest of little nibbles. She took a baked rusk from the window sill, held it to the ram's mouth and looked the other way, in case he felt shy. Maybe he would bite a little bit off… She waited, then turned round again: no, the rusk was untouched.

"I'll nibble a little bit off myself. Maybe that'll encourage him."

She bit off a tiny corner, held the rusk out to the ram again, turned away and waited. And once again the ram did not touch the rusk.

"No? You can't? You can't 'cause you're not alive?"

And the woollen ram, the lifeless beast, answered with the whole of his meek, sad face, "I can't! I'm not a living beast. I can't!"

"Call out to me then! By yourself! Say 'Ba-a-a!' Go on: 'Ba-a-a!' You can't? You can't?"

And Katya's soul overflowed with pity and love for the poor lifeless one. She went straight to sleep, face pressed to her tear-soaked pillow—and found she was walking down a green path, and the ram was running along beside her, nibbling the grass, calling to her, shouting "Ba-a-a!" all by himself and laughing out loud. How strong and healthy he was. Yes, he would outlive the lot of them!

Morning came—dismal, dark and anxious—and suddenly there was Papa. He was looking grey and angry, his beard all shaggy, and he was scowling like a goat. He poked his hand out so Katya could kiss it, and he told Nyanya to tidy everything up because a lady teacher would be coming soon. And off he went.

The next day there was a ring at the front door.

Nyanya rushed out. She came back and started bustling around.

"Your teacher's arrived. To look at the face on her, you'd think she was some great dog. Just you wait!"

The teacher clicked her heels together and held out her hand to Katya. She really did look like an intelligent old watchdog; she even had some kind of yellow blotches around her eyes. And she had a way of turning her head very quickly and snapping her teeth, like a dog catching a fly. She looked round the nursery and said to Nyanya, "You're the nyanya, are you? I want you to take all these toys, please. Put them somewhere well out of the way, so the child can't see them. All these donkeys and rams must go. It's important to be truly rational and scientifical about toys. Otherwise we end up with morbidity of imagination and all the damage that ensues from that. Katya, come here!"

She took from her pocket a ball attached to a long rubber string. Snapping her teeth and rotating the ball on the string, she began singing out, "Hop, jump, up and down, bound and bounce! Repeat after me: hop, jump… Oh, what a backward child!"

Katya said nothing and smiled forlornly, to keep from crying. Nyanya was carrying away the toys, and the ram let out a "Ba-a-a!" in the doorway.

Pay attention to the surface of this ball! What do you see? You see that it is two-coloured. One side is light blue, the other white. Point to the light-blue side. Try to concentrate."

And off she went, holding out her hand to Katya and saying, "Tomorrow we're going to weave baskets!"

Katya was shaking all evening long. She couldn't eat anything. She was thinking about the ram, but she didn't dare say a word.

"It's hard being lifeless. What can he do? He can't say anything and he can't call out to me. And she said, 'He's got to go!'"

The words "got to go" made her whole soul turn cold. The foxy women came, eating and drinking, whispering, "And he said… And she said…" And again: "Go! Just got to go!"

Katya woke at dawn, feeling a fear and anguish the likes of which she had never known before. It was as if someone had called out to her. She sat up in bed, listening.

"Ba-a-a! Ba-a-a!"

The ram's call was pitiful and insistent. The lifeless beast was shouting.

All cold now, she leapt out of bed, clenching her hands and pressing them to her chest, listening. There it was again:

"Ba-a-a! Ba-a-a!"

From somewhere out in the corridor. He must be out there.

She opened the door. "Ba-a-a!"

He was in the storeroom.

She pushed the door open. It wasn't locked. It was a dim, murky dawn, but there was enough light to see. The room was full of boxes and bundles.

"Ba-a-a! Ba-a-a!"

Just by the window was a flurry of dark shapes. The ram was over there too. Something dark jumped out, seized him by the head and began dragging him along.

"Ba-a-a! Ba-a-a!"

And then—two more of the dark shapes, tearing at his flanks, splitting open his skin.

"Rats!" thought Katya. "Rats!" She remembered how Nyanya had bared her teeth. She trembled all over, clenching her fists still tighter. But the ram was no longer shouting. He was no more. A big fat rat was silently dragging some grey scraps of cloth, pulling at some soft bits and pieces, tossing the ram's stuffing about.

Katya hid away in her bed, pulling the blankets up over her head. She didn't say anything and she didn't cry. She was afraid Nyanya would wake up, bare her teeth like a cat and laugh with the foxy women over the woollen death of the lifeless beast.

She went quite silent; she curled up into a little ball. From now on she was going to be a quiet little girl, oh so quiet, so that no one would ever find out.

1916

TRANSLATED BY ANNE MARIE JACKSON

JEALOUSY

THAT MORNING she felt uneasy from the very first.

It began when instead of her usual white stockings she was given a pair of murky blue stockings, and Nyanya grumbled that the laundress had put too much blue in the wash. "I ask you, how can she give us the laundry in a state like that! And all these airs and graces. If she's going to call herself 'Matryona Karpovna', she should know her business and do things proper!"

Liza sat on the bed and examined the long, skinny legs on which she had walked about the great world for seven years. She looked at the pale-blue stockings and thought, "This is bad. They look like death. Something's going to happen to me!"

Then, instead of Nyanya, Kornelka the chambermaid came into the room—Kornelka with the oily head, oily hands and cunning, oily eyes—and began combing Liza's hair.

Kornelka yanked so hard with the comb that it hurt, but Lisa considered it beneath her dignity to complain in the maid's presence and so she just grunted instead. "What makes your hands so oily?" she asked.

Kornelka turned one short red hand this way and that, as though admiring it. "It's work makes me hands shine. I work hard, that's why me hands shine so."

Out on the terrace, under the old lime tree, Nyanya was making jam on a small clay stove. The cook's little daughter, Stioshka, was helping out, feeding wood chips into the little stove, fetching a spoon, fetching a plate, then fanning away flies.

Nyanya was encouraging the little girl, saying, "Very good, Stioshka! Oh, what a smart little girl Stioshka is. Now she's going to go and fetch me some cold water. Run along, Stioshka, go fetch me some water. Little Stioshka is more precious than gold buttons!"

Liza went round the lime tree, scrambling over its stout roots. There was plenty among the roots to catch the eye. In one little corner lived a dead beetle. Its wings were like the dried husks inside a cedar nut. Liza flipped the beetle onto its back with a twig, and then onto its front, but it wasn't afraid and didn't run away. It was completely dead and living a peaceful life.

Across another corner stretched a little web, with a tiny fly reclining in it. The web was obviously a hammock for flies.

In a third corner sat a ladybird, minding her own business.

Liza lifted her up with a twig. She wanted to introduce her to the fly. But along the way the ladybird suddenly split down the middle, spread her wings and took flight.

Nyanya was rapping a spoon against a plate and skimming the foam off the jam.

"Nyanya! Give me the foam!" said Liza.

Nyanya was all red and cross. She was trying to blow a fly off her upper lip, but the fly seemed to be stuck to her damp skin. It kept trying to creep across either her nose or her cheek.

"Go away! Go away now! There's nothing for you here! How can you have the foam when it hasn't even boiled yet? Any other child would have stayed in the nursery and looked at picture books. Can't you see Nyanya's busy? What a fidget! Stioshka, my little love, get some more wood chips. Oh, what a good girl you are!"

Liza watched Stioshka mincing along on her bare feet, fetching the wood chips and diligently feeding them into the stove.

Stioshka had a scrawny pigtail tied with a dirty pale-blue ribbon, and under the pigtail her neck was dark and as thin as a stick.

"She's trying very hard," thought Liza. "And all for show. The girl really *does* think she's clever. But Nyanya's just trying to be kind."

Stioshka got up and Nyanya stroked her head, saying, "Thank you, little Stioshka. Soon there'll be some foam for you."

Liza's temples began to pound, very loudly. She lay face down on the bench, kicking her legs about—in their "deathly" stockings. With a furious smile and trembling lips, she said, "I won't! I won't go anywhere! I don't want to and I won't!"

Nyanya turned and threw up her hands. "Lord have mercy! What have I done to deserve this? I put a fresh dress on the girl this morning, and look at her now, rolling around on that dirty bench—she's filthy! Well, are you going or not?"

"I don't want to and I won't!"

Nyanya was about to say something else, but just then a layer of thick white foam appeared on top of the jam.

"Good heavens! The jam's boiling over."

Nyanya rushed over to the pan, and Liza got to her feet and began singing defiantly. And off she hopped.

As she emerged from under the lime tree, she met Stioshka carrying a dish of berries.

Stioshka was stepping along very carefully. All for show. To show Liza what a clever girl she was. Liza went up to her and whispered in a strangled voice, "Go away! Go away, stupid!"

Stioshka put on a frightened face, for show, so Nyanya would see. Now walking a bit faster, she went over to the lime tree.

Liza ran off into a thicket of gooseberry bushes, collapsed onto the grass and burst into loud sobs.

Her entire life was in ruins.

She lay there with her eyes closed, picturing Stioshka's scrawny pigtail, her soiled pale-blue rag of a ribbon and her thin neck, dark as a stick.

Nyanya would be petting her and saying, "What a clever girl you are, Stioshka! Soon there'll be some foam for you!"

"Fo-oam! Fo-oam! Fo-oam!" Liza moaned, and each time the very sound of the word was so painful, so bitter, that tears trickled from her eyes straight down into her ears.

"Fo-oam! But maybe something will happen, maybe Stioshka will suddenly drop dead as she's fetching the wood chips! Then everything will be all right again!"

But it wouldn't be all right again. Nyanya would be sad. She'd say, "Once there was this smart little girl, but she went and died. If only Liza had died instead." And once again the tears trickled down into Liza's ears.

"A very smart little girl. A little girl who doesn't even go to school. While I'm learning French. I know how to say *zhai*, *tu ah*, *eel ah*, *voozahvay*, *noozahvay*... I'll grow up and marry a general. Then I'll come back here and say, 'Who's this girl? Send her packing! She stole my blue rag for her pigtail.'"

Liza began to feel a little better, but then she remembered the foam.

"No!" she said to herself. "It won't be like that at all."

Her life was over now. She wouldn't go back inside ever again. Why should she?

Just like Marya the old laundress, she would lie on her back and die. She would close her eyes and lie perfectly still.

God would see her and send His angels to fetch her sweet young soul.

The angels would come, their wings rustling—flutter, flutter, flutter—and carry her soul way up on high.

And at home everyone would sit down to dinner and wonder, "What's wrong with Liza?" "Why isn't Liza eating?" "Why's our Liza gone so pale?" But she would go all quiet and wouldn't say a word.

And suddenly Mama would guess!

"Can't you see?" she would say. "Look at her! She's dead!"

Liza was now sitting quite still, sighing heavily and looking at her thin legs in their deathly blue stockings. That was it. She was dead. Dead.

But something was buzzing, buzzing, closer and closer… and then—bop!—it flew right into Liza's forehead. A fat May-bug, drunk on sunshine, had crashed into Lisa's forehead and fallen to the ground.

Liza jumped up and broke into a run.

"Nyanya! Nyanya! A bug hit me! A bug attacked me!"

Nyanya took fright, then gave her an affectionate look. "What's the matter, you silly little goose? There isn't even the least little mark on you. You just thought it was attacking you. Now sit down, my clever little thing, and I'll give you some foam, some lovely foam. Wouldn't you like that? Ahh?"

"Fo-oam! Fo-oam!" Deep in her soul, which God's angels hadn't yet had time to carry away, she could hear joyful laughter.

"Nyanya, I won't ever die, will I? I'll have lots of soup, and drink lots of milk, and I'll never die. That's right, isn't it?"

1916

TRANSLATED BY ANNE MARIE JACKSON

KISHMISH

LENT. Moscow.

In the distance, the muffled sound—between a hum and a boom—of a church bell. The clapper's even strokes merge into a single, oppressive moan.

An open door, into murky predawn gloom, allows a glimpse of a dim shape, rustling stealthily about the room. Now it stands out, a dense patch of grey; now it dissolves, merging into the surrounding dark. The rustling quietens. The creak of a floorboard—and of a second floorboard, further away. Silence. Nyanya has left—on her way to the early morning service.

She is observing Lent.[1]

Now things get frightening.

Barely breathing, the little girl lying in bed curls into a small ball. She listens and watches, listens and watches.

The distant hum is becoming sinister. The little girl is all alone and defenceless. If she calls, no one will come. But what can happen? Night must be ending now. Probably the cocks have greeted the dawn and the ghosts are all back where they belong.

And they belong in cemeteries, in bogs, in lonely graves under simple crosses or by forsaken crossroads on the outskirts of forests.

Not one of them will dare touch a human being now; the liturgy is being celebrated and prayers are being said for all Orthodox Christians. What is there to be frightened of?

But an eight-year-old soul does not believe the arguments of reason. It shrinks into itself, quietly trembling and whimpering. An eight-year-old soul does not believe that this is the sound of a bell. Later, in daytime, it will believe this, but now, alone, defenceless and in anguish, it does not know that this is a bell calling people to church. Who knows what this sound might not be? It is sinister. If anguish and fear could be translated into sound, this is the sound they would make. If anguish and fear could be translated into colour, it would be this uncertain, murky grey.

And the impression made by this predawn anguish will remain with this little creature for many years, for her whole life. This creature will continue to be woken at dawn by a fear and anguish beyond understanding. Doctors will prescribe sedatives; they will advise her to take evening walks, or to give up smoking, or to sleep in an unheated room, or with the window open, or with a hot water bottle on her liver. They will counsel many, many things—but nothing will erase from her soul the imprint of that predawn despair.

The little girl's nickname was "Kishmish"—a word for a kind of very small raisin from the Caucasus. This was, no doubt, because she was so very small, with a small nose and small hands. Small fry, of little importance. Towards the age of thirteen she would suddenly shoot up. Her legs would grow long and everyone would forget that she had ever been a kishmish.

But while she still was a little kishmish, this hurtful nickname caused her a great deal of pain. She was proud and she longed to distinguish herself in some way; she wanted, above all, to do something grand and unusual. To become, say, a famous strongman, someone who could bend horseshoes with their bare hands or stop a runaway troika in its tracks. She liked the idea of becoming a brigand or—still better—an executioner. An executioner is more powerful than a brigand since it is he who has the last word. And could any of the grown-ups have imagined, as they looked at this skinny little girl with shorn, flaxen hair, quietly threading beads into a finger-ring—could any of them have imagined what terrible dreams of power were seething inside her head? There was, by the way, yet another dream—of becoming a dreadful monster. Not just any old monster, but the kind of monster that really frightens people. Kishmish would go and stand by the mirror, cross her eyes, pull the corners of her mouth apart and thrust her tongue out to one side. But first she would say in a deep voice, acting the part of an unknown gentleman standing behind her, unable to see her face and addressing the back of her head: "Do me the honour, Madam, of this quadrille."

She would then put on her special face, spin round on her heels and reply, "Very well—but first you must kiss my twisted cheek."

The gentleman would run away in horror. "Hah!" she would call after him. "Scared, are you?"

Kishmish had begun her studies. To start with—Scripture and Handwriting.

Every task one undertook, she learned, should be prefaced with a prayer.

This was an idea she liked. But since she was still, among other things, considering the career of brigand, it also caused her alarm.

"What about brigands?" she asked. "Must they say a prayer before they go out briganding?"

No one gave her a clear answer. All people said was, "Don't be silly." And Kishmish did not understand. Did this mean that brigands don't need to pray—or that it is essential for them to pray, and that this is so obvious that it was silly even to ask about it?

When Kishmish grew a little bigger and was preparing to make her first confession, she underwent a spiritual crisis. Gone now were the terrible dreams of power.

"Lord, Hear our Prayer" was, that year, being sung very beautifully.

Three young boys would step forward, stand beside the altar and sing in angelic voices. Listening to them, a soul grew humble and tender. These blessed sounds made a soul wish to be light, white, ethereal and transparent, to fly away in sounds and incense, right up to the cupola, to where the white dove of the Holy Spirit had spread its wings.

This was no place for a brigand. Nor was it the right place for an executioner, or even a strongman. As for the monster, it would stand outside the door and cover its terrible face. A church was certainly no place to be frightening people. Oh, if only she could get to be a saint. How marvellous that would be! So beautiful, so fine and sweet. To be a saint was above everything and everyone. More important than any teacher, headmistress or even provincial governor.

But how could she become a saint? She would have to work miracles—and Kishmish had not the slightest idea how to go about this. Still, miracles were not where you started. First, you had to lead a saintly life. You had to make yourself meek and kind, to give everything to the poor, to devote yourself to fasting and abstinence.

So, how would she give everything to the poor? She had a new spring coat. That was what she should give away first.

But how furious Mama would be. There would be a most unholy row, the kind of row that didn't bear thinking about. And Mama would be upset, and saints were not supposed to hurt other people and make them upset. What if she gave her coat to a poor person but told Mama it had simply been stolen? But saints were not supposed to tell lies. What a predicament. Life was a lot easier for a brigand. A brigand could lie all he wanted—and just laugh his sly laugh. How, then, did these saints ever get to be saints? Simply, it seemed, because they were old—none of them under sixteen, and many of them real oldies. No question of any of them having to obey Mama. They could give away all their worldly goods just like that. No, this clearly wasn't the place to start—it was something to keep till the end. She should start with meekness and obedience. And abstinence. She should eat only black bread and salt, and drink only water straight from the tap. But here too lay trouble. Cook would tell on her. She would tell Mama that Kishmish had been drinking water that hadn't been boiled. There was typhus in the city and Mama did not allow her to drink water from the tap. But then, once Mama understood that Kishmish was a saint, perhaps she would stop putting obstacles in her path.

And then, how marvellous to be a saint. There were so few of them these days. Everyone she knew would be astonished.

"Why's there a halo over Kishmish?"

"What, didn't you know? She's been a saint for some time now."

"Heavens! I don't believe it!"

"There she is. See for yourself!"

And she would smile meekly, as she went on eating her black bread and salt.

Her mother's visitors would feel envious. Not one of them had saintly children.

"Are you sure she's not just pretending?"

Fools! Couldn't they see her halo?

She wondered how soon the halo would begin. Probably in a few months. It would be fully present by autumn. God, how marvellous all this was. Next year she'd go along to confession. The priest would say in a severe voice, "What sins have you committed? You must repent."

And she would reply, "None at all. I'm a saint."

"No, no!" he would exclaim. "Surely not!"

"Ask Mama. Ask her friends. Everyone knows."

The priest would question her. Maybe there had, after all, been some tiny little sin?

"No, none at all!" she would repeat. "Search all you like!"

She also wondered if she would still have to do her homework. If so, this too might prove awkward. Because saints can't be lazy. And they can't be disobedient. If she were told to study, then she'd have to do as they said. If only she could learn miracles straight away! One miracle—and her teacher would take fright, fall to her knees and never mention homework again.

Next she imagined her face. She went up to the mirror, sucked in her cheeks, flared her nostrils and rolled her eyes heavenward. Kishmish really liked the look of this face. A true saint's face. A little nauseating, but entirely saintly. No one else had a face anything like it. And so—off to the kitchen for some black bread!

As always before breakfast, Cook was cross and preoccupied. Kishmish's visit was an unwelcome surprise. "And what's a young lady like you doing here in the kitchen? There'll be words from your mama!"

There was an enticing smell of Lenten fare: fish, onions and mushrooms. Kishmish's nostrils twitched involuntarily. She wanted to retort, "That's none of your business!", but she remembered that she was a saint and said in a quiet voice, "Varvara, please cut me a morsel of black bread."

She thought for a moment, then added, "A large morsel."

Cook cut her some bread.

"And will you sprinkle a little salt on it," she continued, looking up as if to the heavens.

She would have to eat the bread then and there. If she went anywhere else with it, there would be misunderstandings. With unpleasant consequences.

The bread was particularly tasty and Kishmish regretted having only asked for one slice. Then she filled a jug from the tap and drank some water. Just then the maid came in.

"I'll be telling your mama," she exclaimed in horror, "that you've been drinking tap water!"

"She's just eaten a great chunk of bread," said Cook. "Bread and salt. So what do you expect? She's a growing girl."

The family was called in to breakfast. Kishmish couldn't not go. So she decided to go but not eat anything. She would be very meek.

For breakfast there was fish soup and pies. She sat there, looking blankly at the little pie on her plate.

"Why aren't you eating?"

In answer she smiled meekly and once more put on her saintly face—the face she had been practising before the mirror.

"Heavens, what's got into her?" exclaimed her astonished aunt. "Why's she pulling such a dreadful face?"

"And she's just eaten a great big chunk of black bread," said the telltale maid. "Just before breakfast—and she washed it down with water straight from the tap."

"Whoever said you could go and eat bread in the kitchen?" shouted Mama. "And why were you drinking tap water?"

Kishmish rolled her eyes and flared her nostrils, once and for all perfecting her saintly face.

"What's got into her?"

"She's making fun of me!" squealed the aunt—and let out a sob.

"Out you go, you vile little girl!" Mama exclaimed furiously. "Off to the nursery with you—and you can stay there on your own for the rest of the day!"

"And the sooner she's packed off to boarding school, the better," said the aunt, still sobbing. "My nerves, my poor nerves. Literally, my every last nerve..."

Poor Kishmish.

And so she remained a sinner.

1940

TRANSLATED BY ROBERT AND ELIZABETH CHANDLER

LOVE

IT WAS THE WONDERFUL DAYS of my ninth spring—days that were long and full to the brim, saturated with life.

Everything in those days was interesting, important and full of meaning. Objects were new. And people were wise; they knew an astonishing amount and were keeping their great dark secrets until some unknown day in the future.

The morning of each long day began joyfully: thousands of small rainbows in the soapy foam of the wash bowl; a new, brightly coloured light dress; a prayer before the icon, behind which the stems of pussy willow were still fresh; tea on a terrace shaded by lemon trees that had been carried out from the orangery in their tubs; my elder sisters, black-browed and with long plaits, only just back from boarding school for the holidays and still unfamiliar to me; the slap of washing bats from the pond beyond the flower garden, where the women doing the laundry were calling out to one another in ringing voices; the languid clucking of hens behind a clump of young, still small-leaved lilac. Not only was everything new and joyful in itself, but it was, moreover, a promise of something still more new and joyful.

And it was during this spring, the ninth of my life, that my first love came, revealed itself and left—in all its fullness, with rapture and pain and disenchantment, with all that is to be expected of any true love.

*

Four peasant girls, Khodoska, Paraska, Pidorka and Khovra—all wearing coin necklaces, Ukrainian wraparound skirts and linen shirts with embroidered shoulders—were weeding the garden paths. They scraped and hacked at the fresh black earth with their spades, turning over thick, oily sods and tearing away crackly, tenacious rootlets as fine as nerves.

For hours on end, until I was called, I would stand and watch, and breathe in the heavy damp smell of the earth.

Necklaces dangled and clinked, arms red from the year's first strong sun slid lightly and gaily up and down the spades' wooden handles.

And then one day, instead of Khovra, who was fair and stocky, with a thin red band around her head, I saw a new girl—tall and lithe, with narrow hips.

"Hey, new girl, what's your name?" I asked.

A dark head encircled by thick four-stranded plaits and with a narrow white parting down the centre turned towards me, and dark, mischievous eyes looked at me from beneath curved eyebrows that met in the middle, and a merry red mouth smiled at me.

"Ganka!"

And her teeth gleamed—even, white and large.

She said her name and laughed, and the other girls all laughed, and I felt merry too.

This Ganka was astonishing. Why was she laughing? And what was it about her that made me feel so merry? She was not as well dressed as smart Paraska, but her thick striped skirt was wound so deftly round her shapely hips, her red woollen sash gripped her waist so firmly and vibrantly and her bright green ribbon fluttered so arrestingly by the collar of her shirt that it was hard to imagine anything prettier.

I looked at her, and every move, every turn of her supple dark neck sang like a song in my soul. And her eyes flashed again, mischievous, as if tickling me; they laughed, then looked down.

I also felt astonished by Paraska, Khodoska and Pidorka—how could they keep their eyes off her? How did they dare behave as if they were her equals? Were they blind? But then even she herself seemed to think she was no different from the others.

I looked at her fixedly, without thoughts, as if dreaming.

From far away a voice called my name. I knew I was being called to my music lesson, but I didn't answer.

Then I saw Mama going down a nearby avenue with two smartly dressed ladies I didn't know. Mama called to me. I had to go and drop a curtsy to them. One of the ladies lifted my chin with a little hand sheathed in a perfumed white glove. She was gentle, all in white, all in lace. Looking at her, I suddenly felt Ganka was coarse and rough.

"No, Ganka's not nice," I thought.

I wandered quietly back to the house.

Placid, merry and carefree, I went out the following morning to see where the girls were weeding now.

Those sweet dark eyes met me as gaily and affectionately as if nothing had happened, as if I had never betrayed them for a perfumed lady in lace. And again the singing music of the movements of her slender body took over, began to enchant.

The conversation at breakfast was about yesterday's guest, Countess Mionchinskaya. My elder brother was sincerely enraptured by her. He was straightforward and kind but, since he was being educated at the lycée, he felt it necessary to lisp and drawl and slightly drag his right foot as he walked.[1] And, doubtless afraid that a summer deep in the country might erase these stigmata of the dandy, he greatly surprised us younger ones with his strange mannerisms.

"The countess is divi-i-inely beau-utiful!" he said. "She was the to-oast of the se-ea-son."

My other brother, a cadet at the military academy, did not agree. "I don't see anything so special about her. She may put on airs, but she's got the mitts of a peasant—the mitts of a *baba* who's been soaking neckweed."[2]

The first brother poured scorn on this: "Qu'est-ce que c'est mitt? Qu'est-ce que c'est *baba*? Qu'est-ce que c'est neckweed?"

"But I'll tell you who really is a beauty," the second brother continued, "and that's Ganka who works in the garden."

"Hah!"

"She's badly dressed, of course, but give her a lace gown and gloves and she'll beat your countess hands down."

My heart started beating so fast I had to close my eyes.

"How can you talk such rubbish?" said my sister Vera, taking offence on the countess's behalf. "Ganka's coarse, and she has no manners. She probably eats fish with a knife."

I was in torment. It seemed as if something, some secret of mine, was about to be revealed—but what this secret was I did not even know myself.

"Although that, I think we can say, has nothing to do with it," said the first brother. "Helen of Troy didn't have French governesses, and she ate fish with her fingers—not even with a knife—yet her renown as a world beauty remains unchallenged. What's the matter, Kishmish? Why have you gone so red?"

"Kishmish" was my nickname. I answered in a trembling voice, "Leave me in peace. I'm not doing you any harm. But you… you're always picking on me."

In the evening, lying on the sofa in the dark drawing room, I heard my mother in the hall; she was playing a piece I loved, the cavatina from the opera *Martha*.[3] Something in the soft, tender melody evoked—called up within me—the same singing languor that I had seen in Ganka's movements. And this sweet torment, and the music, and my sadness and happiness made me cry, burying my face in a cushion.

It was a grey morning, and I was afraid it would rain and I wouldn't be allowed out into the garden.

I wasn't allowed out.

I sat down sadly at the piano and began playing exercises, stumbling each time in the same place.

But later that morning the sun appeared, and I raced out into the garden.

The girls had just thrown down their spades and sat down for their midday meal. They got out pots and jugs wrapped in cloths and began to eat. One was eating buckwheat kasha, another had some soured milk. Ganka unwrapped her own little bundle, took out a thick crust of bread and a bulb of garlic, rubbed the bread with the garlic and began to eat, shining her mischievous eyes at me.

I took fright and went away. How terrible that Ganka ate such filth. It was as if the garlic had thrust her away from me. She had become alien and incomprehensible. Better if she'd eaten fish with a knife.

I remembered what my brother had said about Yelena the Beautiful,[4] but this brought me no consolation and I plodded back to the house.

Nyanya was sitting by the back door, knitting a stocking and listening to the housekeeper.

I heard the name "Ganka" and froze. I knew only too well that if I went up to them, they'd either shoo me away or stop talking.

"She worked for the steward's wife all winter. She's a hard-working girl. But not an evening went by—the steward's wife noticed—without this soldier coming to see her. The steward's wife packed him off once and she packed him off twice—but what could the good woman do? She couldn't be packing him off night after night."

"Indeed!" said Nyanya. "How could she?"

"So she scolded her now and again, of course, but Ganka just laughed—it was water off a duck's back. Then, just before Twelfth Night, the steward's wife hears noises in the kitchen—as if Ganka were endlessly pushing something about the room. And then, first thing in the morning, she hears tiny squeals. She hurries into the kitchen: there's not a sign of Ganka—just a baby wrapped up in pieces of cloth, lying on some bedding and letting out little squeals. She takes fright. She looks everywhere: where was Ganka? Had something very bad happened? She looks out through the window—and there she is. Standing by the hole in the ice, barefoot, washing out her linen and singing away. The steward's wife wanted to dismiss her, but how could she manage without her? It's not easy to find such a sturdy, hard-working lass."

I slipped off quietly.

So Ganka was friends with a common, uneducated soldier. This was horrible, horrible. And then she had tormented some little baby. This really was something dark and terrible. She had stolen it from somewhere and wrapped it up in rags—and when it began to squeal, she ran off to the ice hole and sang songs there.

All evening I was in misery. That night I had a dream from which I awoke in tears. But my dream was neither sad nor frightening, and I was crying not from grief but from rapture. When I woke, I could barely remember it. I could only say, "I dreamed of a boat. It was quite transparent, light blue. It floated through the wall, straight into silver rushes. Everything was poetry and music."

"So why all the howling?" asked Nyanya. "It's only a boat! Maybe this boat of yours will bring you something good."

I could see she didn't understand, but there was nothing more I could say or explain. And my soul was ringing, singing, weeping in ecstasy. A light blue boat, silver rushes, poetry and music.

I didn't go out into the garden. I was afraid I'd see Ganka and begin thinking about the soldier and the little baby wrapped up in cloth, and everything would once again become frightening and incomprehensible.

The day dragged restlessly on. It was blustery outside and the wind was bending the trees. The branches shook; the leaves made a dry, boiling sound, like sea surf.

In the corridor, outside the storeroom, was a surprise: on the table stood an opened crate of oranges. It must have been brought from town that morning; after lunch they'd be handed out to us.

I adore oranges. They are round and golden, like the sun, and beneath their peel are thousands of tiny pockets bursting with sweet, fragrant juice. An orange is a joy. An orange is a thing of beauty.

And suddenly I thought of Ganka. She didn't know about oranges. Warm tenderness and pity filled my heart.

Poor Ganka! She didn't know. I must give her one. But how? To take one without asking was unthinkable. But if I did ask, I'd be told to wait until after lunch. And then I wouldn't be able to take the orange away from table. I wouldn't be allowed to, or they'd ask questions—someone might even guess. I'd be laughed at. Better just to take one without asking. I'd be punished, I wouldn't be given any more—but so what? What was I afraid of?

Round, cool and perfect, the orange lay in my hand.

How could I? Thief! Thief! Never mind. There'd be time enough for all that—what mattered now was to find Ganka.

The girls turned out to be weeding right by the house, near the back door.

"Ganka! This is for you, for you! Try it—it's for you."

Her red mouth laughed.

"What is it?"

"It's an orange. It's for you."

She turned it round and round in her hand. I mustn't embarrass her.

I ran back inside and, sticking my head out of the corridor window, waited to see what would happen. I wanted to share in Ganka's delight.

She bit off a piece together with the peel (Oh, why hadn't I peeled it first?), then suddenly opened her mouth wide, made a horrible face, spat everything out and hurled the orange far into the bushes. The other girls stood around her, laughing. And she was still screwing up her face, shaking her head, spitting, and wiping her mouth with the cuff of her embroidered shirt.

I climbed down from the window sill and went quickly to the dark end of the corridor. Squeezing behind a large chest covered with a dusty carpet, I sat on the floor and began to weep.

Everything was over. I had become a thief in order to give her the best thing I knew in all the world. And she hadn't understood, and she had spat it out.

How would I ever survive this grief and this hurt?

I wept till I had no more tears. Then a new thought came into my head: "What if there are mice here behind the chest?"

This fear entered my soul, grew in strength, scared away my previous feelings and returned me to life.

In the corridor I bumped into Nyanya. She threw up her hands in horror.

"Your dress! Your dress! You're covered in muck, head to toe! And don't tell me you're crying again, are you?"

I said nothing. This morning humanity had failed to understand my silver rushes, which I had so longed to explain. And "this"—this was beyond telling. "This" was something I had to be alone with.

But humanity wanted an answer. It was shaking me by the shoulder. And I fended it off as best I could.

"I'm not crying. I... my... I've just got toothache."

1924

TRANSLATED BY ROBERT AND ELIZABETH CHANDLER

MY FIRST TOLSTOY

I REMEMBER... I'm nine years old.

I'm reading *Childhood* and *Boyhood* by Tolstoy. Over and over again.

Everything in this book is dear to me.

Volodya, Nikolenka and Lubochka are all living with me; they're all just like me and my brothers and sisters. And their home in Moscow with their grandmother is our Moscow home; when I read about their drawing room, morning room or classroom, I don't have to imagine anything—these are all our own rooms.

I know Natalya Savishna too. She's our old Avdotya Matveyevna, Grandmother's former serf. Avdotya too has a trunk with pictures glued to the top. Only she's not as good-natured as Natalya Savishna. She likes to grumble. My older brother used to sum her up by quoting a line from Pushkin's "The Demon", "Nor was there anything in nature he ever wished to praise."

Nevertheless, the resemblance is so pronounced that every time I read about Natalya Savishna, I picture Avdotya Matveyevna.

Every one of these people is near and dear to me.

Even the grandmother—peering with stern, questioning eyes from under the ruching of her cap, a bottle of eau de cologne on the little table beside her chair—even the grandmother is near and dear to me.

The only alien element is the tutor, Saint-Jérôme, whom Nikolenka and I both hate. Oh, how I hate him! I hate him even more and longer than Nikolenka himself, it seems, because Nikolenka eventually buries the hatchet, but I go on hating him for the rest of my life.

Childhood and *Boyhood* became part of my own childhood and girlhood, merging with it seamlessly, as though I weren't just reading but truly living them.

But what pierced my heart in its first flowering, what pierced it like a red arrow was another work by Tolstoy—*War and Peace.*

I remember…

I'm thirteen years old.

Every evening, at the expense of my homework, I'm reading one and the same book—*War and Peace.* Over and over again.

I'm in love with Prince Andrei Bolkonsky. I hate Natasha, first, because I'm jealous, second, because she betrayed him.

"You know what?" I tell my sister, "I think Tolstoy got it wrong when he was writing about her. How could anyone possibly like her? How could they? Her braid was 'thin and short', her lips were puffy. No, I don't think anyone could have liked her. And if Prince Andrei was going to marry her, it was because he felt sorry for her."

It also bothered me that Prince Andrei always shrieked when he was angry. I thought Tolstoy had got it wrong here, too. I felt certain the prince didn't shriek.

And so every evening I was reading *War and Peace.*

The pages leading up to the death of Prince Andrei were torture to me.

I think I always nursed a little hope of some miracle. I must have done, because each time he lay dying I felt overcome by the same despair.

Lying in bed at night, I would try to save him. I would make him throw himself to the ground along with everyone else when the grenade was about to explode. Why couldn't just one soldier think to push him out of harm's way? That's what I'd have done. I'd have pushed him out of the way all right.

Then I would have sent him the very best doctors and surgeons of the time.

Every week I would read that he was dying, and I would hope and pray for a miracle. I would hope and pray that maybe this time he wouldn't die.

But he did. He died. And died again.

A living person dies once, but Prince Andrei was dying forever, forever.

My heart ached. I couldn't do my homework. And in the morning… Well, you know what it's like in the morning when you haven't done your homework!

Finally, I hit upon an idea. I decided to go and see Tolstoy and ask him to save Prince Andrei. I would even allow him to marry the prince to Natasha. Yes, I was even prepared to agree to that—anything to save him from dying!

I asked my governess whether a writer could change something in a work he had already published. She said she thought he probably could—sometimes writers make amendments in later editions.

I conferred with my sister. She said that when you call on a writer you have to bring a small photograph of him and ask him to autograph it, or else he won't even talk to you. Then she said that writers don't talk to juveniles anyway.

It was all very intimidating.

Gradually I worked out where Tolstoy lived. People were telling me different things—one person said he lived in Khamovniki, another said he'd left Moscow and someone else said he would be leaving any day now.

I bought the photograph and started to think about what to say. I was afraid I might just start crying. I didn't let anyone in the house know about my plans—they would have laughed at me.

Finally, I took the plunge. Some relatives had come for a visit and the household was a flurry of activity—it seemed a good moment. I asked my elderly *nyanya* to walk me "to a friend's house to do some homework" and we set off.

Tolstoy was at home. The few minutes I spent waiting in his foyer were too short to orchestrate a getaway. And with my *nyanya* there it would have been awkward.

I remember a stout lady humming as she walked by. I certainly wasn't expecting that. She walked by entirely naturally. She wasn't afraid, and she was even humming. I had thought everyone in Tolstoy's house would walk on tiptoe and speak in whispers.

Finally he appeared. He was shorter than I'd expected. He looked at Nyanya, then at me. I held out the photograph and, too scared to speak clearly, I mumbled, "Would you pwease sign your photogwaph?"

He took it out of my hand and went into the next room.

At this point I understood that I couldn't possibly ask him for anything and that I didn't dare say why I'd come. With my "pwease" and "photogwaph" I had brought shame on myself. Never, in his eyes, would I be able to redeem myself. Only by the grace of God would I get out of here in one piece.

He came back and gave me the photograph. I curtsied.

"What can I do for you, Madam?" he asked Nyanya.

"Nothing, sir, I'm here with the young lady, that's all."

Later, lying in bed, I remembered my "pwease" and "photogwaph" and cried into my pillow.

*

At school I had a rival named Yulenka Arsheva. She, too, was in love with Prince Andrei, but so passionately that the whole class knew about it. She, too, was angry with Natasha Rostova and she, too, could not believe that the prince shrieked.

I was taking great care to hide my own feelings. Whenever Yulenka grew agitated, I tried to keep my distance and not listen to her so that I wouldn't betray myself.

And then, one day, during literature class, our teacher was analysing various literary characters. When he came to Prince Bolkonsky, the class turned as one to Yulenka. There she sat, red-faced, a strained smile on her lips and her ears so suffused with blood that they looked swollen.

Their names were now linked. Their romance evoked mockery, curiosity, censure, intense personal involvement—the whole gamut of attitudes with which society always responds to any romance.

I alone did not smile—I alone, with my secret, "illicit" feeling, did not acknowledge Yulenka or even dare look at her.

In the evening I sat down to read about his death. But now I read without hope. I was no longer praying for a miracle.

I read with feelings of grief and suffering, but without protest. I lowered my head in submission, kissed the book and closed it.

There once was a life. It was lived out, and it ended.

1920

TRANSLATED BY ANNE MARIE JACKSON

PART TWO

Other Worlds

Throughout her life, from early childhood to her last days, Teffi was acutely aware of aspects of life beyond our rational understanding. Both Orthodox Christianity and folk religion, with its poetic evocation of the spiritual and the irrational, were important to her. Our previous collection of Teffi's work, *Other Worlds*, is devoted to stories inspired by these themes. Here we include just three of them.

"The Book of June" and "Shapeshifter" evoke experiences of the natural world so intense that the natural and the supernatural are hard to distinguish. The two stories are opposites; the former evokes the overwhelming richness of a midsummer evening, the latter the terrifying emptiness of a midwinter day in the open country. The heroine of "The Book of June" is Teffi as an adolescent, on the threshold of the bewildering world of adult sexuality. "Shapeshifter" may represent her fantasy of a different course her life might have followed: a stranger's chance intervention prompts the Teffi figure to decide *against* marriage to a man who has much in common with Buchinsky, the lawyer whom she married in 1892 and with whom she spent six deeply unhappy years in small provincial towns and at his remote country estate.

"Solovki"—an almost Bruegelesque account of the then-widespread practice of mass pilgrimage to holy sites—was inspired by Teffi's own visit in 1916 to the Solovetsky Monastery on an island in the White Sea. After the Pechersk Lavra cave monastery in Kyiv, this was the most important pilgrimage site in the Russian Empire. Teffi's visit clearly meant a great deal to her; she bought a small cypresswood cross in the monastery shop, kept it with her till her last days and ordered it to be placed with her in her coffin.[1]

THE BOOK OF JUNE

A VAST COUNTRY HOUSE, a large extended family, the spaciousness of the clear, bracing air—it could hardly have been more different from her quiet Petersburg apartment stuffed with carpets and furniture. Katya at once felt exhausted. She had been ill for a long time and had come to the country to convalesce.

Katya was staying with one of her aunts. This aunt was hard of hearing and so the whole house was constantly shouting. The high-ceilinged rooms reverberated, dogs barked, cats meowed, maids from the village clattered plates, and the children shouted and squabbled.

There were four children in all: fifteen-year-old Vasya, a bully and a tattletale studying in a Novgorod *gymnasium*,[1] and two small girls, home from boarding school for the summer. And then there was the eldest, Grisha, who was the same age as Katya but was staying with a school friend in Novgorod. He would be back home soon.

They all talked about Grisha a great deal. He seemed to be a general favourite, even something of a hero.

The head of the family, Uncle Tyoma, who was plump and had grey whiskers, looked rather like a large cat. He was constantly teasing Katya. "What's the matter, my little goose? Are you bored?" he would ask with a smirk. "Just you wait, young Grisha will be here soon. He'll really turn your head!"

"Nonsense!" the aunt would shout (like all deaf people, she spoke louder than anyone else). "Katya is from Petersburg—she'll hardly be impressed by a mere Novgorod student. Katya, my dear, I'm sure you have throngs of admirers. Come on now, admit it!"

And she would then wink at everyone. Knowing that all this was meant to be funny, Katya would attempt a smile, with trembling lips.

The two girls, Manya and Lubochka, gave her a warm welcome and reverentially inspected her wardrobe: a blue sailor jacket, a smart dress (starched piqué) and some white blouses.

"Ooh! Ooh!" repeated eleven-year-old Lubochka, sounding like a wind-up doll.

"I love Petersburg fashions," said Manya.

"All so shiny, like silk," Lubochka chimed in.

They took Katya for walks. Beyond the garden lay a marshy river dense with forget-me-nots. A calf had drowned there.

"He was sucked under. The bog sucked him under and that was it. We never saw him again—not even a bone. We're forbidden to swim here."

They swung Katya on the swing. But when Katya was no longer a novelty, things changed. The two girls even began to snigger at her behind her back. Vasya made fun of her, too, coming out with all kinds of stupidities. He would walk up to her, perform an exaggerated bow and say, "Mademoiselle Catrine, please be so good as to explain to me how you would say 'gulch' in French?"

All very tedious, unpleasant and wearying.

"Why is everything so ugly here?" Katya kept asking herself.

They ate suckling pig, carp with sour cream and pies with burbot. A far cry from the crisp, delicate grouse wings she enjoyed at home.

It was the housemaids who milked the cows. If you called them, they yelled back, "Wot?"

The girl who served them at table was huge. She had a moustache and looked like a soldier squeezed into a woman's blouse. Katya was astonished to discover that this gigantic creature was only eighteen.

It was a relief to escape to the small garden. Clutching a slim volume of Alexey Tolstoy with an embossed cover, she would read aloud:

> It isn't he who holds you spellbound;
> It's not his own perfection that attracts you.
> He's nothing more than an occasion
> For secret dreams of torment, bliss and rapture.[2]

Every time she came to the last words, her heart skipped a beat. Tears would have been sweet.

"Coo-ee, Katya! Tea-ea time!"

Once again, the shouting, the clamour, the general din. Excited dogs flailing hard tails against your leg. A cat suddenly up on the table, its tail flicking across your face. Animal heads. Animal snouts and tails.

Grisha returned shortly before Midsummer Day.

Katya was out when he arrived. Later, as she was going through the dining room, she glimpsed Vasya through the window. He was talking to a tall young man in a white naval jacket and with a very long nose.

"Auntie Zhenya's invited a cousin to stay," she heard Vasya say.

"What's she like?"

"A blue-ish idiot."

Katya moved quickly back from the window.

"Blue-ish? Or did he say 'foolish'? How very strange."

She went outside.

Long-nosed Grisha greeted her cheerily, stepped up into the porch and peered out at her through the small porch window. Screwing up his eyes, he made a show of twirling imaginary moustache.

"What a dolt," Katya said to herself. She sighed and walked on into the garden.

At dinner Grisha was rather boisterous. He kept picking on Varvara, the huge girl with the moustache, telling her she had no idea how to wait at table.

"Enough of that!" said Uncle Tyoma. "Just look at you—that great beak of yours just keeps growing and growing."

And Vasya, always the bully and troublemaker, declaimed in a sing-song voice:

> Monstrous nose, awful nose
> With room inside its flaring holes
> For fields and farms and villages,
> For cupolas and palace halls.

"Such great big boys," yelled the deaf aunt, "and they still keep on squabbling!" Turning to Auntie Zhenya, she went on, "Two years ago I took them with me to Pskov. It's a historic city and I wanted them to see something of it. I had things to do in the morning, so I went out early. Before I left, I said, 'Ring down for some coffee and then go and have a look round. I'll be back for lunch.' I get back at two—and guess what! The blinds are still down—and they're both still lying there in bed. 'What's the matter with you?' I ask. 'Why are you still in bed? Have you had your coffee?' 'No.' 'Why on earth not?' 'Because this blockhead wouldn't ring for it.' 'So why didn't you ring yourself?' 'Me? Why? Why should he lie in bed while I run around at his beck and call?' 'But why should

I have to do all the work!' says the other blockhead. And so the two of them just lay there until two o'clock in the afternoon."

The days went by, noisy as ever. With Grisha back home there was, if anything, even more shouting and arguing.

Vasya had an air of constant grievance. He seemed full of spite and was rude to everyone.

One evening at dinner, Uncle Tyoma, who in his youth had greatly admired Alexander II, showed Katya his huge gold watch with a miniature of the tsar and tsaritsa inside its lid. He told her how he'd made a special trip to Petersburg in the hope of somehow getting a glimpse of His Majesty. "He wouldn't have travelled that far just to see me," Vasya muttered crossly. "That's for sure."

Grisha grew ever more indignant about Varvara and her moustache. "She comes bantering on my door in the morning with those great fists of hers—and that's my whole day ruined."

Vasya shrieked with laughter. "Bantering! I ask you! I think he's trying to say battering!"

"She's no maid, she's a bloke. A peasant bloke. I'm telling you, I don't want to wake up to the sight of her. End of story."

"He's upset because they've got rid of Pasha," Vasya shouted. "Pasha was very pretty."

Grisha leapt to his feet, red as a beetroot. "I'm sorry," he said, looking at his parents but pointing at Vasya. "I cannot sit at the same table as this relative of yours."

Grisha took no notice of Katya at all—except once, when he saw her in the garden with a book in her hands. "May I enquire what you're reading?" he asked with exaggerated politeness. He then went on his way before she could answer.

Varvara happened to be passing by, too. Bristling like an angry cat and glaring at Katya with eyes that seemed almost white, she said, "So young ladies from Petersburg like good-looking boys, do they?"

Katya did not understand this, but she felt scared by the look in Varvara's eyes.

That evening Katya spent a long time with Auntie Zhenya making pastries. It was the eve of Saint Artyom's day—the name-day of her Uncle Tyoma. When they'd finished, she went out into the yard to look at the moon. Not far away, in the wing, she could see a light in one of the windows. Standing on a log she must have just put there herself, Varvara was gazing into the room.

Hearing Katya's footsteps, she beckoned and hissed, "Here!" Seizing her by the arm, Varvara pulled her up onto the log.

"Look!"

Vasya was lying fast asleep on a small sofa. Grisha was lying on the floor, on a straw mattress. He was reading, his face very close to the book, and the book very close to the candle.

"What is it?" Katya asked in surprise. "What are you looking at?"

Varvara hushed her.

Varvara's face was both tense and vacant. Her mouth was half open and her eyes were staring. She seemed bewildered, transfixed.

Katya managed to free her arm and get away. Varvara really was very strange.

The following day the house was full of guests. There were merchants, other landowners and the abbot of the nearby monastery—a huge, broad-browed man who looked like one of Vasnetsov's warriors.[3] He arrived in a two-wheeled carriage and talked all through the meal about crops and haymaking. Uncle Tyoma kept complimenting him on his management of the land.

"What weather!" said the abbot. "What meadows! What fields! June! Wherever I go, it's as if a book of untold wonders is being opened before me. June!"

These words made an impression on Katya. She listened to the abbot for some time, hoping he'd say more in this vein. But he spoke only of the price of fodder and the purchase of a small area of woodland.

That evening, Katya sat in front of the mirror in her chintz dressing gown. She lit a candle and studied her thin, freckled face.

"I'm boring," she said to herself. "Everything's boring, so boring."

She remembered the word that had upset her: Blue-ish. It was true. She was blue-ish.

She sighed.

"Tomorrow's Saint John's day. We'll be going to the monastery."

Everyone was still up and about. Behind the wall she could hear Grisha, playing billiards in the games room.

Suddenly the door burst open. Varvara tore in, red-faced, her teeth bared in a wild grin.

"Not asleep yet—an' why not? What ye waiting for, eh? I'll put you to bed meself. Aye, I'll put you to bed right now."

She grabbed hold of Katya, held her tightly and began to tickle her, laughing loudly as she ran her fingers over the girl's thin ribs. "Not asleep yet?" she kept repeating. "An' why not?"

Katya could hardly breathe. Letting out little shrieks, she tried to escape, but Varvara's strong hands held her fast, fingering her, twisting and turning her.

"Let go! I'm going to die! Let go of me!"

Her heart was pounding. She was choking. Her whole body was screaming, struggling, writhing.

And then she glimpsed Varvara's bared teeth and white, glaring eyes. This was no joke and no game. Varvara was out to harm her, perhaps to kill her. Varvara was unable to stop herself.

"Grisha! Grisha!" Katya yelled desperately.

Varvara at once let her go. Grisha was there, standing in the doorway.

"Get out, you fool. Have you gone mad?"

"Can't I 'ave a little fun?" Varvara said feebly. Everything about her—her face, her arms—had gone limp and droopy. She staggered out of the room.

"Grisha! Grisha!"

Katya had no idea what made her keep on screaming like this. Some kind of lump seemed to be filling her throat, making her gasp and wheeze and scream out Grisha's name.

Still screaming, her legs still jerking convulsively, she reached out to Grisha, flung her arms around his neck and pressed her face to his cheek. Wanting protection, she was still calling out, "Grisha! Grisha!"

Grisha sat her down on the sofa and knelt beside her, gently stroking her shoulders through her chintz gown.

Katya looked into his face, saw the embarrassment and confusion in his eyes and wept still more bitterly.

"You're a kind man, Grisha. You're very kind."

Grisha looked away a little. A thin little arm was fiercely embracing his neck and his lips were somehow brushing against it. Timidly, he kissed Katya in the crook of her elbow.

Katya was now still. Grisha's lips were strangely warm. This warmth was spreading beneath her skin, ringing sweetly in her ears and suffusing her eyelids with a heaviness that made them slowly close.

Then she herself moved her arm to his lips, and Grisha kissed the very same spot once again. Again Katya heard the sweet ringing, and felt the same warmth, and the heavy, blissful languor that closed her eyes.

"Don't be frightened, Katenka," said Grisha, his voice faltering. "She won't dare come back now. If you like, I can stay in the billiard room. And you can bolt your door."

His face looked both kind and guilty. A vein stood out in the middle of his forehead. Somehow, the guilt in his eyes was frightening.

"You must go now, Grisha! Go!"

He gave her a scared look and got to his feet.

"Go!"

She pushed him towards the door and bolted it after him.

"Oh God! Oh God! This is awful."

She raised her arm and cautiously put her lips to the spot Grisha had kissed. It felt warm and silky. She could taste vanilla.

Her strength failed her. She began to tremble and moan.

"Oh… oh… oh… How can I go on living? Lord help me."

The candle on the table trembled and guttered, swaying its black flame.

"Lord help me. I am a sinner."

Katya put her face to the dark rectangle of the icon and joined her hands in prayer.

"Our Father who art…"

But these weren't the right words. She did not know what words would allow her to ask God for she did not know what, and to speak to him about what she did not understand.

She closed her eyes tight and crossed herself.

"God forgive me," she began.

And again she felt that these weren't the right words.

The candle went out, but the room only seemed brighter.

Dawn was drawing near. This white night would soon be over.

"Lord, Lord," Katya repeated and pushed open the door to the garden.

She dared not move. She was afraid of clacking a heel or rustling her dressing gown, so ineffable was the silvery blue silence around her. The magnificent groves of trees were still and silent, as only living, sentient beings can be still and silent.

"What's going on? What on earth's going on?" thought Katya, almost paralysed with fear. "No, I've never known anything like this." Everything was breaking down. The trees, the still air, the invisible light—everything was overflowing with some sort of extreme power, something insuperable and beyond our ken, for which we possess no sensory organ and for which there are no words in our language.

Katya was startled by a burst of sound. It was quiet, yet so sudden that it seemed loud. At once strong and delicate, there was no knowing where it sprang from. It flowed from goodness knows where and spilled over, bouncing back up like the most delicate of silver peas. Then it broke off.

A nightingale?

After this, the voices—"their" voices—grew still quieter, yet still more intense.

And "they" were all as one, all in concert. Only this little human creature, rapt and terrified, was alien. "They" all knew something. While this little human creature could only think.

June. She remembered the book of untold wonders. June.

And her small soul tossed about in anguish.

"Lord! Lord! To be in Your world is terrifying. What am I to do? And what is this? What is all this?"

And she kept searching for words, kept thinking that words would soothe and resolve.

She crossed her arms over her thin little shoulders, as if she were not herself, as if wanting to protect the fragile little body entrusted to her and to bear it away from the chaos of bestial and divine mysteries that had engulfed it.

She bowed her head in obedient despair and spoke the only words that are one and the same for all souls, great and small, blind and wise:

"Our Father… Hallowed be Thy Name… Thy Will be Done."

1930

TRANSLATED BY ROBERT AND ELIZABETH CHANDLER WITH KATHRYN THOMPSON

SHAPESHIFTER

IT WASN'T BY CHANCE that I found myself in that snow-swept small town. Nor was it because I wanted to see my country aunt. I was there for romantic reasons; I'd taken rather a liking to Alexey Nikolaevich.

He had spent the whole autumn in Petersburg—visiting us on occasion, dancing with me at every party and "bumping into me" at exhibitions. And as he was about to leave (having just been appointed a magistrate in that unprepossessing small town), he had told me he loved me, and asked me to be his wife.

I asked him to give me time to consider his proposal—which is how we left things.

Most of my relatives seemed to think well of him.

My granny said, "Well, *ma chère*, he has impeccable manners. And he's a lawyer to boot."

One of my aunts said, "No flies on you! Barely out of college—and you've already landed yourself a husband!"

Another aunt said, "He seems rather dim, and he's got money too. What more could you ask for?"

He wrote me letters—long ones—and the passages about me were quite interesting. But for the main part, he wrote about himself and the complexities of his soul. He even described his dreams, which were full of esoteric visions. Awfully tedious.

And then came the invitation to visit this country aunt, and so I decided to go and test out my feelings.

This little town was sixty *versts*[1] from the nearest railway station, and as godforsaken as they come. The buildings were all of wood, the river was blanketed with snow, and on the far bank stood a monastery.

I happened to come at a time when the place was unusually lively—because of a meeting of the local *zemstvo*.[2]

My suitor, however, was out of town, investigating a case somewhere far away, in the village of The Lakes, near his own estate.

For something to do, my aunt took me along to the meeting, introduced me to the other women, sat me down and told me to listen.

The hall was fairly large and full of people. In the middle was a group of local doctors and other dignitaries, sitting around a table covered in green felt. They all had thick whiskers and bushy eyebrows and were wearing frockcoats that looked like something out of the previous century.

They were talking loudly, arguing with one another. A little old man with a lisp was getting very worked up, constantly repeating, "I'm an old man and I can no longer make eloquent speeches." It sounded, though, as if he were saying, "make elegant peaches".

Then someone embarked on a lengthy speech about the importance of restructuring the hospital, since it was wrong for the lavatory to be located next to the operating theatre. A lady sitting beside me giggled, nudged me with her elbow and said, "What piquant details—whatever next!"

A little apart from the others, just beyond the shaggy doctors, was a strange man. His face was oddly thin, with a small, shapeless beard. He looked, if such a thing is possible, dazzlingly pale. Sitting there with his eyes closed, he could have been dead. I stared at him for a long time. Suddenly, as though sensing my gaze, he opened his eyes, looked straight at me and then closed them again. He looked at me like that several times, always somewhat questioningly, as if in surprise.

"What are you doing, making eyes at that young doctor?" asked my neighbour, the genteel lady who had just been giggling and nudging me. "I wouldn't bother with him. No one here gives him the time of day. They say he's some sort of were-creature."

In the evening, my aunt had visitors. Among them was the most prominent of the town ladies—a widow. Her carriage was drawn by two white horses—and because of these horses she was known as "the priestess". She was the town's chief gossip, and so she already knew that the pale doctor had caught my eye.

"You could do better than that, my dear!" she said. "No one round here can stand him. The peasants say he's a shapeshifter. Where his eyes fall, they say, crops fail."

She went on to say that this doctor—Oglanov by name—had not lived in these parts long, only a little over a year. His grandfathers and great-grandfathers had all lived here and been rich and well known, but the family house was now almost falling down. Nevertheless, that was where the doctor now lived—although his own father had never been seen in these parts.

It was a big stone house, a frightening place with all sorts of legends attached to it; some of them had even been written down. A troublesome serf girl, apparently, was once immured alive—in one of the walls of the main hall. And there had once been a large cellar; the great-grandfather of the current Oglanov had secretly kept ten Jews there, forging banknotes; he'd smuggled these Jews in from somewhere in Austria. The authorities somehow caught wind of all this and the great-grandfather heard that there was likely to be an official investigation. Without saying a word to his Jews, he ordered piles of bricks to be placed in the courtyard, beside each of the air vents to the cellar. Meanwhile the Jews just carried on working, with no idea what lay in store for them.

Soon Oglanov's men reported that the district court was on its way. In those days the legal authorities simply went straight to the place in question, just like that. Oglanov summoned his masonry serfs and ordered them to seal up every last air vent. When the court arrived, Oglanov gave them a splendid welcome. For five days on end they all feasted, while the unfortunate Jews down below suffocated to death. And since the house appeared to have no cellar at all, no one suspected a thing. And then off the court went.

After that, Oglanov never so much as unsealed the cellar. He went on living in that dreadful house as if none of this had ever happened. And his son lived there too; they were both fantastically wealthy. But the grandson—our doctor's father—was brought up in Petersburg, where he squandered the family fortune. And then, years later, this degenerate—the current Oglanov—had shown up out of the blue, to work as a doctor.

A letter arrived from my suitor, inviting me to The Lakes. He wanted to introduce me to his family.

My aunt made no objections. "Only you can't go all that way on your own," she said. "We must find you a travelling companion."

In small towns, such things are arranged quickly. Somebody was sent somewhere, somebody else then knocked on our door, and so on. We were told that, since the *zemstvo* meeting was now over, the delegates were now going their separate ways—so there was sure to be someone who could take me to The Lakes. After a few more exchanges, I learned that Doctor Oglanov would be coming round for me after breakfast. He too was going to The

Lakes, and—as it happened—he would be joining my Alexey Nikolaevich there to attend a post-mortem.

I would be travelling with the Shapeshifter.

"Who knows?" I said to myself. "It might even be rather entertaining."

I waited a long time. By the time the doctor called, it was getting dark. He didn't come up for me, though; he stayed outside.

Felt boots were pulled onto my feet. I put on my fur coat and—on top of that—I was bundled into one of my aunt's old travelling cloaks. I must have looked quite a sight!

Out on the street, instead of the elegant troika I was expecting, I found two rather unkempt horses, harnessed in tandem to a shabby old sleigh.

The doctor greeted me morosely, not even looking up. I could barely see his face behind the collar of his fur coat. He covered my legs in a blanket that smelled of rancid sheepskin.

"This'll keep you warm," he muttered. "It's a wonderful blanket."

That was all he said.

He truly did have a dark presence: where his eyes fell, crops might well fail.

For a long time, we travelled in silence. I began to doze off. It was all very boring: the long white road, a cold, lilac sky and the squeal of the runners.

"… is that so?"

The Shapeshifter was speaking.

"What?"

"I've heard you're going to marry this magistrate—is that so?"

His pale, thin-lipped face was turned towards me, but he was looking down at the ground.

"I don't know," I said.

I felt confused.

He fell silent again. And then: "Oh, well. He's rich and stupid. A good catch, I suppose."

"What's it to do with you?" I asked.

"Just bear in mind," he said, after another long silence, "that his wealth won't mask his stupidity forever. One way or another, his evil stupidity will make itself felt. Not that it's any concern of mine, of course."

"Why say such things then?"

He turned sharply towards me—as if to meet my eye—but then buried his face in his collar again.

"Yes, yes… it is a little strange of me," he muttered. "You're right."

After that, we both fell silent again. There remained a long, long way to go. The white anguish of the boundless snows, the monotonous jingle of our bell, the motionless, evil figure beside me—all this made my heart ache. The driver swayed silently in his seat, as if dead. Ahead loomed the dead of night. I wanted to ask if we'd be arriving soon, yet somehow I lacked the strength to speak.

It was particularly disgusting to have that "wonderful" blanket of his over my legs. Yes, everything about this journey felt wrong! Why had I agreed to travel with the first person who came along? My stupid aunt should never have let me.

I fell asleep.

I woke to the sound of barking. We were approaching a large house.

"I have to pick up my medical instruments," said the Shapeshifter. "This is my home. Come inside. Warm up a bit while we wait for fresh horses."

I didn't want to go in. Why hadn't he told me we'd be stopping at his home? But I had no choice.

A huge stone house. Boarded-up windows—all except three or four. A grand main entrance, flanked by columns—but we stopped outside one of the wings. A man in a sheepskin coat, holding a small tin lamp, let us in and led us rather nervously down a long corridor and through an echoing hall. Patches of damp made strange shapes on the walls. And huge shadows raced along beside us, one overtaking another.

Heavens! This was the house where people had been walled up alive.

"Here we are!" said the Shapeshifter, who had been walking behind me.

The room was almost empty. A sagging sofa, a leather chair and a small table. It could have been a prison cell.

The Shapeshifter put his hand to the stove and said something to the man in the sheepskin. They both went out.

I sat on the chair. The room felt cold and damp. I sat there in my fur coat.

The man in the sheepskin brought in an armful of firewood and thrust it into the stove. He blew and wheezed over it for a long time, filling the room with smoke. Then he brought me a glass of tea and a few sugar lumps on a saucer. After that, he disappeared, eventually coming back with some fried eggs in a pan, a slice of bread and an old iron fork. The giant frying pan could have fed five people. Then, to my surprise, he brought in a jug of water, a chipped wooden basin, a bucket and a rough towel. He placed the basin on the sofa, as if that were quite normal, then put the jug on the floor. "There," he said—and off he went.

It all seemed ghastlier than ever.

My enormous shadow flickered on the walls. The table, the lamp's orange glow and my own face were all reflected in the black window. But could I be sure it was me? Why was my face so pale and narrow?

I screamed. It was him—the Shapeshifter, looking at me from behind his fur collar! I jumped to my feet—and it was me again, my own reflection. But I was still terrified. I ran and hid in a corner where I could no longer see the window, and quietly began to cry.

The man in the sheepskin came in again and said that the horses were now ready.

Once more: dancing shadows, ghosts swooping and swerving along the walls, chasing one another as they tried to hide from the feeble lamplight.

In the courtyard stood an open country sleigh, and two horses in tandem. A skinny young man was sitting up on the box.

"I ordered a covered sleigh," said the Shapeshifter. Morose as ever, he wrapped me up again in his blanket.

"Aye, but summ'n else has took it," the young man replied. "P'lice officer."

We set off. The horses plodded along pitifully. We went through a little forest, down a small hill and out into a dismal, empty steppe.

"Doesn't your master ever feed the horses at all?" asked the Shapeshifter.

The driver gave a start, turned to look at us and said, "Oh aye, he gives 'em a bit nah 'n then."

His face looked strange, his mouth twisted yet gaping open, as if he were guffawing madly.

"Idiot! What do you keep twitching about for?"

"Nothin… I weren't doin owt," the driver mumbled—and turned forward again.

Never-ending bare steppe, with only a thin strip of forest far away to the left. The wind blew and blew, reaching under the doctor's vile blanket, creeping up the sleeves of my coat.

"Why've you taken us so far out?" shouted the Shapeshifter. "You should have stayed close to the shore."

Once again, the driver started and turned to face us. "Fancy a swim, does tha?"

"What!"

"Can't ye see?" said the driver, pointing his whip towards some long patches of black in the snow near the edge of the forest.

"Patches of thaw," muttered Oglanov. "But why did your master send you out today? Wasn't there anyone else?"

"Well, Igor's with t' policeman, in't he?" the driver replied, with a twitch of the shoulders.

"Stop twitching, you scoundrel!" the Shapeshifter cried wildly.

I couldn't bear it any longer.

"Doctor," I began, "why do you keep shouting at him? It's horrible!"

"Keep out of it," Oglanov answered under his breath. "It's the only way to restrain him."

I had no idea what he meant and I was afraid to say any more. I just asked about the patches of thaw.

"We're driving over a lake. Our route takes us across four lakes, one after another."

Up another hill, through another forest—and then back down again. Snow and wind—and more snow and wind. There was no end to it all. The sleigh plunged and swerved. I shivered and began to feel sick, as if I were out at sea, in a nasty swell.

"Thiere! Yonder!" said the driver. He turned towards us and pointed his whip somewhere off to the right. I could see three dark spots moving along the snow, one after the other.

"What are they?" I asked.

"Word 'as it, they're at yer beck an' call!" the driver yelled at Oglanov. Then he turned forward again, towards the horses. He was mumbling, but I heard one word clearly: Shapeshifter.

Or did I imagine it?

"Wolves?" I whispered.

"Don't worry," said the doctor. "It's all right. They won't dare come close."

Then the driver let out a cry. It wasn't even so very loud, but there was something so terrible about it—some note I'd never heard before—that I too screamed and jumped up from my seat, almost tumbling out of the sleigh. As for the driver, his head drooped forward and he began to fall to one side, with strange jerks and spasms.

The Shapeshifter grabbed him by the shoulders, leaned right forward, seized the reins and halted the horses.

"Just as I feared," he said crossly.

Very gently, he laid the young man down in the snow. He twitched about for a while, then went still. The Shapeshifter lifted him up, placed him on his own seat in the back of the sleigh and wrapped him in a fur blanket.

"Is he dead?" I asked timidly.

"Epilepsy," Oglanov answered abruptly. He got up onto the box and took hold of the reins.

And it was back to more wind and snow, all the while with that lifeless body beside me. By then, I was in a bad way. My legs were frozen, and I felt dizzy and nauseous. I began to sob.

"Not much further!" said the Shapeshifter. "Soon we'll be at the warden's."

More snow. More wind. The sleigh dipped and dived, its runners creaking under the strain.

I'm dragged up some steps. Then I'm lying on the floor, on a straw-filled mattress. "Quick," says an old woman in a peasant headdress. "Get 'er some vodka!" Then someone's rubbing my feet, my teeth knock against the thick rim of a glass and something's burning my throat.

"It's all right, it's all right," someone is whispering.

The face of the Shapeshifter—now sorrowful, tender and attentive.

"You poor girl," I hear. "You'll have a hard time with that fool of yours. You took offence… I know… But he'll make life hell for you, you silly, silly thing. I feel for you."

I cry and cry. I don't want to stop.

Gentle hands stroke my face, then wrap me in something warm. If the hands go away for a moment, I cry more loudly, to bring them back again.

Protect me! I want to say, but I can't get the words out. My head spins. I'm falling asleep.

And then—morning. Bright day peeks in through a tiny, ice-covered window. Last night's old woman is grating something into a basin.

"You've woke up, then?" she asks. "Well, let's get thi up an' make thi a brew. Only, we drink willow-herb tea round 'ere. Or St John's wort. Me ol' man's gone into t' village, to fetch thi some 'orses."

"Is it far to The Lakes?" I ask.

"No, luv. Not far at all. Fifteen *versts* or so."

In a corner behind the stove I catch sight of the Shapeshifter's blanket.

"What's that?" I ask. "Under the blanket?"

Why had I got into such a state? What was it had frightened me?

"It's Fedka, the driver. He's took a turn, but he'll soon be reight. It's t' fallin sickness, in't it."

The doctor had even given the driver his sheepskin blanket—his pride and joy.

I remember the outlandish pan and the iron fork. I feel racked by shame. If only out of politeness, I should have at least tried those eggs. I had behaved badly.

The old man comes back, with fresh horses.

As I leave, I quietly stroke the blanket, as if apologizing for the disgust I'd felt earlier.

Later that day, in a grand drawing room full of furniture upholstered in red corduroy, I had to listen to Alexey Nikolaevich. Tall, stupid, utterly alien to me and idiotically jealous at my having travelled with Dr Oglanov—he made quite a scene. And when I told this stupid and evil man that I didn't love him and had no intention of marrying him, his eyes bulged.

"I don't believe it!" he said—and he did indeed sound incredulous.

I never saw Dr Oglanov again. But now and then, if I happen to recall our encounter, I find myself wondering... Did that sly Shapeshifter take on the guise of a perfect gentleman, someone uniquely kind and affectionate, just so that he could ruin my chance of happiness with a splendid husband by the name of Alexey Nikolaevich?

1931

TRANSLATED BY ROBERT AND ELIZABETH CHANDLER WITH SIÂN VALVIS

SOLOVKI

for Ivan Bunin

THE SEAGULLS from the shore accompanied the steamer for a long time. After a while they grew tired and began coming down more often onto the water, barely grazing it with their breasts, spinning round as if on the point of a screw—and then wearily gliding off again, leading first with one wing and then with the other, as if taking long strides.

From the stern, pilgrims threw them bread. Many of them came from far inland. It was their first encounter with the sea and they were astonished by the gulls.

"What strong birds!"

"What great big birds!"

"But people say you can't eat them."

When the boat reached open sea and the shore it had left behind was no more than a low, narrow strip of pale blue, the gulls dispersed. Three last greedy birds took a few more strides, begged again for bread, veered off somewhere to the left, called to one another and disappeared.

The sea was now empty and free. In the sky shone two diffuse bands of crimson: one not yet extinguished, still red-hot from the departed sun, and one now catching fire from the rising sun.

The steamer, lit by the silvery-pink light that cast no shadow, was cutting aslant through the waves; from the deck it appeared to be sailing sideways, skimming weightlessly over the water. And high in the air, fastened to the mast, swaying gently against the pink clouds, a golden cross marked out the boat's path.

The Archangel Michael, a holy boat, was taking pilgrims from Arkhangelsk to the Solovetsky Monastery.[1]

There were a lot of passengers. They sat about on benches, on steps and on the deck itself, conversing quietly and respectfully, and looking with awe at the golden cross in the sky, at the boat's steward—a monk in a faded, now greenish cassock—and at the gulls. They sighed, yawned and made the sign of the cross over their open mouths.

Up on the bridge a monk in a sheepskin coat and a black skull-cap kept coughing hoarsely. Now and then he would call out to the helmsman—his commands as abrupt as the gulls' cries—and then start coughing again.

Waves were beating rhythmically against the hull; the crimson glow had faded; the birds had flown away. The drama of setting sail was now over and the passengers began to settle down for the night.

Peasant women hitched up the calico skirts they had starched for the holiday and this unusual journey, and then lay down on the floor, tucking in their legs and their heavy, awkward feet. The menfolk were talking quietly in separate groups.

Red-haired, thickset Semyon Rubaev came down the ladder and joined the men. His wife remained alone, sitting on one of the steps. She didn't move or even turn her head. She merely gave him a sideways look, full of mistrust and resentment.

Semyon listened for a while to the other men. A tall curly-haired old man from White Lake was talking about the smelt they now caught there. "We've a damage now. A damage. Engineers built it. They needed earth for this damage. They took earth of mine."

"What damage? You're not making sense."

"For the damage… The da… For the dam." The old man fell silent for a moment, then added, "I'm in my nineties, you know. Yes, that's how it is now."

Semyon didn't care in the least about the old man's age, nor about the smelt in the lake. He wanted to talk about his own concerns, but he didn't know how to bring them into the conversation; it was hard to find the right moment. He looked around at his wife. She was sitting sideways to him, looking away. He could barely see her broad face and the pale, taut line of her mouth.

And then nothing could hold him back. "Well, we come from near Novgorod. From the Borovichy district. Penance, a church penance—that's why I've brought 'er along with me."

He stopped. But since no one asked him anything, he eventually began again: "Penance, confession an' penance.[2] Varvara, ma wife. No light matter, I 'ad to take it to the district officer."

Varvara got up from the step. Baring her white teeth like a vicious cat, she moved a little further away, then stood beside the rail, resting both elbows on it.

There was nowhere further to go. The pilgrims sitting on the deck were densely packed. She could hardly use their heads as stepping stones.

Now at least she could no longer hear all that Semyon was saying. The odd word, however, still reached her.

"The whole village were complainin… There weren't one lass that Vanya Tsyganov… The officer… Ma wife Varvara…"

Varvara hunched her shoulders. She was still baring her teeth. Semyon was still talking, talking, talking:

"Varvara, aye, Varvara… 'We just kissed,' she said… A court sentence weren't possible. But a penance, a church penance…"

For ten months Semyon had been telling this story, over and over. And now, like clockwork, all through this journey. On the iron road, at every station where they'd stopped, in the pilgrims' hostel at Arkhangelsk, wherever there were ears to be filled, he had told it once more. Since the day all this began, since their neighbour Yerokhina had run back from the fields, pulled off her kerchief and wailed out that Tsyganov had wronged her—and then old Mitrofanikha had rushed out and yelled that her granddaughter Feklushka was being pestered by Tsyganov too, that Tsyganov wasn't giving the girl a moment's peace. Other women of all ages appeared, all white with fury, kerchiefs slipping off their heads, all cursing Tsyganov and threatening to lodge official complaints and have him driven out of the village. And then Lukina had caught sight of Varvara at her window and shouted out that Varvara had been with Tsyganov too. She'd seen them out in the rye:

"Them two, walking side by side! Arms around each other!"

And from then on, work had been forgotten. Semyon had done nothing but tell this story.

He went along as a witness for Yerokhina. He told the officer about Varvara and demanded that she be brought to trial and punished. He dragged Varvara around with him and wherever they went—on the road, in country inns and town lodgings—he had gone on telling this story. At first he had spoken gently, calling her "Varenka", the same as ever. "So, Varenka, tell me how all this came to happen. All o' the circumstances."

"How wot happened? Nowt happened."

Then he would go purple all over, his red beard seeming to fill with blood. Choking with fury, he would say, "Bitch! Snake! How dare you? How dare you speak so to yer wedded husband!"

And all day long Varvara had busied herself around the house, not exactly working, more just fussing about in one corner after another—anything to get out of earshot, anything not to hear.

As for Tsyganov, he was nowhere to be seen. He had gone off to the city to work as a cab driver. The women began to calm down. Only down by the river in the evening, as they beat the damp linen with their bats, the young girls sometimes sang a jokey song from St Petersburg:

> Vanka, Vanka, wot you done wi yer conscience?
> Where be yer heart of hearts?
> —Wasted 'em both in the taverns
> for love o' billiards an' cards.

Their voices sounded thin, almost mosquito-like.

As for Semyon, he went on and on questioning Varvara and repeating his story. And Varvara fell more and more silent. When the officer asked her about Yerokhina, her only reply, delivered in a tone of true Novgorod obstinacy, was, "Nowt to do wiv me."

And so life went on. In the daytime Varvara hardly spoke. At night she kept thinking things over, reliving that day again and again. She had heard screaming women; she had seen their white-hot, vicious fury. The devil had got into them. And what a lot of them there had been. Even pockmarked Mavrushka had shouted out, as if bragging, "D'ye think he didn't touch me? No, he touched me all right. Only I hold my tongue. But if you all speak, then I'm speakin too!"

Her pockmarks, it seems, had not counted against her. The lads had jeered, "Oh, Mavrushka, Mavrushka! And her wi t' body of a bear!"

Yerokhina, for her part, had lamented, "Eight year, believe me, I've kept a hold o' me honour—and then… Along come this fiend—an' he snatches it from me!"

All shaking in jealous rage. All shouting, as if bragging, "Me too. Aye, me too!"

A sly fellow with the nickname "Tomcat" had smirked mischievously and said, "You lassies be in a right state. What's eatin you, then? Eh?"

He seemed to have hit on something.

They reached Solovki as the bells were ringing for matins.

On the shore to meet them were monks and seagulls.

The monks were thin, with severe faces. The gulls were large and plump, almost as big as geese. They waddled about proprietorially, exchanging preoccupied remarks.

Unloading and disembarkation took a long time. Some of the pilgrims were still packing their knapsacks when the wife of the elderly fisherman returned from the Holy Lake, after bathing in its icy waters. She had put on a clean linen shift and was smiling beatifically, her lips purple with cold.

The hosteller, a tall monk with a neatly combed beard, was dealing with the new arrivals, arranging who should sleep where. Since there were crowds of pilgrims and little space, the Rubaevs were put in part of what had once been a room for gentlefolk. This had whitewashed walls and two windows, but it was now divided into three by partitions. One part had been given to a teacher and his wife, and the biggest part—with three beds and a sofa—to a party of four.

The head of this party was an Oriental-looking abbot. Handsome and well turned out, he had chosen, for convenience while travelling, to abandon his monastic dress for that of an ordinary priest: "People, I understand, have little love for monks, and they criticize them for everything: Why's he smoking? Why's he eating fish? Why's there sugar in his tea? But how can a man observe the rules when he's on the road? Dress as a priest—and you don't tempt people to judge."

Together with the abbot were a merchant, a lanky young *gymnasium* student—and a hypocritical old bigot of a public official. All three were family.

The remaining little cubicle, with no window, was allocated to the Rubaevs.

The pilgrims spent the rest of the day either attending church services, looking around the monastery, wandering about the forest or along the seashore, walking down the long, musty hostel corridor—with its damp and grimy, finger-marked doors, weighted to slam heavily shut—or visiting the little monastery shop and haggling over the price of icons, small cypresswood crosses and prayer-belts for the deceased.[3]

There was one very tall young man whom it was hard not to notice. He was smartly dressed, with a new peaked cap and patent leather boots, and he had come for healing; he suffered from spasms that repeatedly wrenched at his mouth, forcing it open. It was as if his jaw were in the grip of a vast, insuperable yawn; he would involuntarily stick his tongue out and slobber all down his chin and neck. Then the fit would come to an end and his mouth would close, his teeth snapping together like those of a dog that has caught a fly.

Accompanying him was a short little fellow who could have passed for the impresario of an exotic theatre troupe. He wore a silver chain that hung down over his round belly and he bustled about excitedly, taking evident pride in the young man's illness and proffering explanations: "Keeps on yawning, he does. Several years now, yes, indeed. He's the son of rich people. Make way, make way now, if you please!"

The monastery courtyard was full of gulls. They were round and placid, like household geese. They sat between gravestones and on the path leading to the church. They weren't afraid of people and didn't get out of your way—it was for you to walk around them. And on the back of almost every one of them was a chick—like a fluffy, spotted egg propped on two thin little twigs.

The gulls called out to one another in quick, curt barks. They always began loudly, then gradually quietened, as if losing hope. They sat crowded together about the monastery and did not fly anywhere. It was very cold. The small rectangular Holy Lake was swollen with grey-blue water. One gull went down to the lake and gazed for a long time, with a suspicious eye, at its violet ripples. Some way off, a chick was cheeping importantly, as if imparting advice. The gull stretched out one foot, touched the water, quickly withdrew the foot and twitched its head a little.

"Too cold, old girl?" asked a young monk.

Against the grey sky swayed lopsided trees; their branches, reaching towards the sun like arms stretched towards a distant dream, grew only from their southern side. The northern side, gnawed by cold breaths from the throat of the Arctic Ocean, remained naked and sickly all summer, as in winter.

Down by the harbour some young lads, with faded skullcaps over thick strands of fair, curly hair, were throwing pebbles in the water and scuffling with one another. They were like puny young bear cubs, fighting clumsily and without anger. Pomors,[4] from villages along the mainland coast, they had been brought to the monastery to labour for a year or two in fulfilment of vows made by their mothers. "Aye, 'e'll serve t' Lord—and 'e'll earn 'is keep too."[5]

And there were solitary monks wandering along the shore. Now and again they would stop and look at the water, as if waiting for something.

One after another the grey-blue waves uncoiled, splashing against the brown rocks, filling hearts with a leaden sadness.

Along with the other pilgrims, the Rubaevs went to the church and then on into the forest. Monks in faded cassocks emerged from the little chapels. They seemed to struggle to understand even the simplest questions. If someone asked, "Which church is this?", they would reply, "How?", then smile affably and withdraw to gaze at the water.[6]

Outside the chapel of Saint Philaret, the pilgrims took it in turn to lift the long stone that had once served Philaret as a pillow. They laid it on their heads and walked three times clockwise around the chapel—a cure for headaches.[7]

In the furthest of the little chapels, ten *versts* or so from the monastery, the pilgrims were met by the very oldest elders of all. They were barely able to put one foot in front of the other, barely still breathing.

"But how, good fathers, do you walk to the church?"

"We go, good people, but once a year. On Easter Sunday, yes, to Holy Matins. That day we all meet together—from cliffs, from woods, from bogs, from t' open fields. Every one of us goes—and they count us up. As for food, we get by. They bring us our bread."

The hostel was no place to sit in for long. The Rubaevs' cubicle was dark and damp. Semyon would come in, sit down on the bed and start to drone on once again:

"Mind you tell it all. As God is your witness. Each and every circumstance. Tell everything, or woe betide you!"

Varvara did not reply.

Behind the partition the merchant and the *gymnasium* student kept demanding more hot water for their tea. The official was sighing piously.

Behind the other partition the teacher's wife was criticizing the ways of the monastery: "They just stand there and stare at the water. Will that save their souls? And at table they defile themselves with mustard.[8] Will that save their souls?"

And then the pilgrims would all wander up and down the shore again, or along the monastery corridors.

They looked at the paintings of the Last Judgement and the Parables of Our Lord. A huge beam planted in the eye of the sinner who so clearly beheld the mote in his brother's eye. The temptation of beauty, illustrated by a devil—with a rather appealing canine muzzle, shaggy webbed paws, a curly tail and a modest brown apron tied around his belly[9]—and a fragrant legend: as the brothers were praying in church, this devil had slipped unseen between them, distributing the scented pink flowers known as house lime.[10] Whoever received a flower found himself unable to go on praying; tempted by the spring sun and grasses, he would steal out to freedom[11]—until in the end the devil was caught by the Holy Elder. And portrayals of every kind of ordeal and hardship, of sins and torments, sins and torments…

Towards evening they were called to the refectory. The women sat in a separate room.

To one side of Varvara was a woman all covered in scabs. Sitting opposite her was an old woman with a nose like a duck's beak. Before dipping her spoon into the communal bowl, she would lick it all over with her long, flaccid, rag-like tongue. They ate salt-cod soup and drank bland monastery kvas[12] with a faint taste of mint. A monk read aloud to them in a dismal monotone: "Lechery, lechery, the devil."

There was no night. The partitions did not reach the ceiling and the Rubaevs' windowless stall was lit by a wan light that cast no shadow.

The hypocrite official got up at cockcrow and—in reproach to his companions—began bowing and crossing himself before the icon. With loud sighs—part whistle and part whisper—he repeated, "Woe is me, O Lord, O Lord—for my loins are filled with mockings."[13]

The abbot awoke, shamefacedly put on his clothes and left the room. The merchant held out for a long time but couldn't get back to sleep. In a loud, clear voice, as if to the student, he said, "You get some more sleep! Yes. It's too early for church. Not even the monks have got up yet." He then repeated all this—really, of course, for the benefit of the hypocrite official, who was by then creating more of a disturbance than ever.

The official finished praying, looked around censoriously, sighed and turned away. There are sights best not seen, he appeared to be saying.

Varvara had had a bad night. There was no peace anywhere and the seagulls kept calling to one another with their dismal barks. Towards morning she dozed off. She saw a field of rye and a cart. There on the cart was Vanya Tsyganov, laughing:

"'Ere again, are ye? Well, there'll be no getting away this time."

He got down from the cart, took her by the shoulders and looked into her eyes.

"Ashamed? As if yer a maiden!"

Not a good dream, and it left her with a sense of dread.

Once again everyone went off to the church or out into the forest. After the service, Semyon sat down beside the teacher, on a bench outside the hostel, and was soon telling his same old story.

Varvara went back to the room. The student was alone there, sitting at the table and eating curd cheese from a large clay bowl. On his face was a look of sly embarrassment.

"Want some?" he said to Varvara. "I got it from the dairy. I'm famished. All we get in the refectory is cabbage soup seasoned with holy relics." He giggled.

"No, thank you."

The student stopped eating and looked at Varvara intently. With an awkward smile, blushing and more giggling, he said, "You're quite a woman, you know. As for that husband of yours… And your eyes—your eyes are gorgeous. But sit yourself down, for the love of God."

Varvara looked straight into his bashful but laughing eyes and felt a sense of horror. It seemed as if she was looking not at a young student, but at Vanya Tsyganov—and was unable to get away from him.

"O Lord, O Lord! What is all this?"

She wanted to tear her hair, to weep and wail.

Slowly, still looking the student straight in the eye, Varvara backed towards her door.

"Is th-that where you s-sleep?" the student stammered, still blushing.

Varvara heard footsteps out in the corridor. She locked her door, sat down on the bed and listened to her heart trembling. The merchant and the hypocrite official came back, caught sight of the curd cheese and were incensed with rage.

"Huh! Like that, is it? Can't even last three days?[14] Well then, what's stopping you? Eat! You bought that cheese—so you eat it!"

"I've had all I want."

"Eat that cheese!"

Both men felt the same craving. And the stronger their craving, the fiercer their rage.

"Eat, I say!" hissed the official. "You bought it—so you eat it!"

"What's wrong with you?" the merchant chimed in. "If you know no shame, then eat all you want!"

The two men swallowed down their saliva, unable to take their eyes off the cheese.

During the afternoon a large-winged boat flew in, bringing Pomor women from the mainland coast. So high were the waves that no one even saw the boat draw in to the pier.

The women spilled out onto the shore. They were a bright, loquacious flock, in pink, green, lilac and pale-blue dresses, with pearl rings on their headbands. They had fair eyebrows and the eyes of seagulls or mermaids—round yellow eyes with black rims and black dots for pupils.

The women chattered away and laughed. The pilgrims watched from a distance, the men twisting their beards between their fingers.

"Them Pomors are a rich lot. They catch fish, they shoot animals for their pelts, they gather down from eider ducks. No wonder they go around in pearls."[15]

A woman in a rose-lilac dress, with a yellow-eyed child on her back, was teasing a gull, holding out a piece of bread, then withdrawing it, repeating, "Bread for t' gull-bird? Bread for t' gully-bird?"

The gull, who also had a child on her back, stretched out her neck crossly.

The seagull and the woman—two of a kind and with the same yellow-eyed children—both understood that this was a game.

"Mock away, mock away!" people called out. "But wait till she's up above yer head! See what she does to you then! Them gulls can get mighty cross."

Towards evening a gale blew up. As if through a funnel, it blew straight down the icy throat of the Arctic Ocean, shaking the trees, twisting skirts and cassocks around legs, stopping people in their tracks or knocking them to the ground, flinging sea foam against the hostel's windows. Flocking swiftly together, the Pomor women got back on board and hoisted sail. Pink, lilac and pale-blue dresses swirled in the wind. The boat had no thwarts and no gunnels—the women simply stood on the planking. Someone cast off. Two young lads got out their squeeze-boxes and began to play; pink, lilac and pale-blue skirts swirled and danced near the edge of the boat. The following wind filled out the sails, driving the boat on so fiercely that, for a moment, the entire stern rose high above the waves. The wind snatched the song away, brought it back, carried it off again—and then blew everything into the sea, burying both boat and song under a huge, turbid wave that smelled of fish scales. A few minutes later the pilgrims were pointing to a tiny craft now rounding a distant headland:

"Look—already there! They're a desperate lot, them Pomors."[16]

That evening in the refectory the old woman with the flaccid tongue was once again licking her spoon. The monk with the nasal voice read the same words about lechery, sin and the Devil. The yawning youth was once again led through the yard. A new group of pilgrims appeared—old women in black, smelling of cod and incense.

The gulls in the yard seemed cross, and something was frightening them. The gale was making their feathers stand up on end, and they were squealing shrill complaints.

Semyon took Varvara to confession. And, just as when she'd been questioned by that officer in Novgorod, her soul closed up in blank, obstinate misery. Back then, she had said, "Nowt to do wiv me." Now, in the church, she fastened her eyes on the bronze clasp of the Gospels, repeated to the priest, "I have sinned, I have sinned"—and said no more.

No one in the room slept long that night—thanks to the hypocrite official, who chose to prolong his devotions until the second cockcrow. He groaned, prostrated himself and intoned his prayers in a noisy whisper: "Lord, Lord, who art present even in the uttermost depths of the sea. Even there Thou art present." Seven beds, from seven corners, creaked angrily back.

But the official inadvertently overslept. Eventually, he got up along with everyone else and sat down by the window, trying not to catch anyone's eye. And then, still not looking at anyone, he sidled off to church.

The church was thronged with people. There was a smell of cod, sheepskin, something sour and melted wax. Candle flames swayed before the flat, dark faces on the ancient icons; where the saints' hands emerged from their gilt covering, the paint had long ago wrinkled and blistered from the touch of thousands upon thousands of lips. As they went past the holy relics, the pilgrims gazed with awe and horror at a deceased *skhimnik*, a monk who had followed the most extreme of the monastic rules: all that could be seen of him, poking out from a black shroud embroidered with bones, was the tip of a waxen nose, along with some wisps of grey beard and two bony hands.

High above everyone rose the head of the yawning youth, mouth suddenly gaping open with a groan and then snapping shut. The wind knocked at doors and windows, bursting into the church, then howling as it withdrew. Now and again white wings swept past the windows—and a mermaid's round yellow eye would peep in.

In the alcoves the monks' silent, shadowy figures were barely stirring, as if their prayer beads had gone stiff in their fingers. A ripple passed through the congregation as people stepped back to let the communicants through. The choir was already singing the Cherubic Hymn,[17] the boys' high voices soaring up to the cupola, when a woman began shrieking frenziedly, "Kuda-a-a! Ku-u-da-a-a! Ku-da-a-a!"[18]

Her shrieks grew ever more piercing, ever more violent.

"Possessed," whispered the peasant women. "Possessed good 'n proper!"[19]

Then someone else let out a scream and a wail—and began to bark like a dog, not letting up.

Varvara clenched her hands tight. The chandelier swayed, slid to one side—and she felt her legs and shoulders begin to shudder, swiftly, violently, while her whole face stretched as if clinging tight to her cheekbones, and her stomach swelled, climbing right up to her throat, and a wild scream flew out from somewhere deep and dark, twisting her whole body, tearing her body apart, smashing red lights against the crown of her head: "A-a-i-i! Da-a-a! Da-a-a!"[20]

A fleeting thought: *Should I stop?*

But something made her tense herself more and more powerfully, forcing her to cry out more and more loudly, to clench her whole body, to will on the convulsions. The words didn't matter. The first sounds to burst out had been "A-a-i-i!" and "Da-a-a!"—and so she had gone on. What mattered was not to stop, to expend more and more of herself in the cry, to give herself to it more intensely, yes, more and more of herself: *Oh, if only they didn't get in her way. Oh, if only they let her keep going…* But it was so hard. Would she have the strength?

"A-a-i-i! A-a-i-i!" If only… If only… *How sweet… How sweet that would be…*

Someone's feet, next to her cheek. A strip of rug, a flax rug.

Am I lying down now? Oh, who cares? I can't keep going now. But another time. Another time, somehow…

And suddenly she was being lifted up. She was being hoisted up, by hands under her shoulders—and there before her eyes was a vast golden chalice, vast as the world.

"Varvara," someone was saying beside her.

"Varvara," she heard someone else repeat.

And a sharp golden spoon, also vast, was parting her lips and knocking against her clenched teeth.[21] Her teeth unclenched of their own accord, a gentle quiver passed through her arms and legs and her head fell forward; she could no longer hold it up. Small beads of sweat were cooling her forehead.

How sweet! Oh, how sweet!

And her whole body became empty. As if everything heavy, swollen and black had left with the scream.

They seated Varvara on a bench outside the hostel. She had turned suddenly thinner. She had thrown back her head, her hair uncovered, and she was smiling with a look of exhausted bliss.

Not daring to go at all close, the other pilgrim women were looking at her in fear and awe, just as they had looked at the deceased *skhimnik*. Semyon was also looking at her in speechless fear and awe. And Varvara was saying in a delirious voice, her words coming out in fits and starts, "Oh, my darlings! All of you! What sweetness! Lord God! My dearest Semyon! And now—a long, long way, on foot, to Saint Tikhon of Zadonsk.[22] How dear the sky is. Sweet sky, bright sky. And the gulls... the dear gulls..."

1921

TRANSLATED BY ROBERT AND ELIZABETH CHANDLER

PART THREE

Revolution and Civil War

Teffi first became famous for the witty satirical sketches she published in the early 1900s in the popular journal *Satirikon*. From the outbreak of the First World War, however, her work took on a darker tone; she was one of a surprisingly small number of Russian writers to write about the war as experienced by civilians.

A liberal socialist, she welcomed the 1905 Revolution and the overthrow of the tsarist regime in March 1917, but she did not support the Bolshevik coup in November 1917. Appalled by the Bolsheviks' brutality and aware of the precariousness of her own position, she set off from Moscow in autumn 1918, beginning the long journey through Russia and Ukraine that she recounts in *Memories*. Her initial plan was simply to travel via Kyiv to Odessa to earn money by giving public readings. Eventually, however, she left Russia on a boat bound for Istanbul. Her professed hope was to return to Russia, but the depth of emotion imbuing the last pages of *Memories* suggests that she may have sensed that she was leaving Russia forever.

Teffi wrote an unusual memoir of Rasputin, too long to include here. She also wrote a substantial article, *New Life*, about the six weeks in late 1905 when she worked for the first legal Bolshevik newspaper in Russia. The incisive portrait of Lenin ends:

> A man was good only insofar as he was necessary to the cause. And if he wasn't necessary—to hell with him. Anyone harmful or even just inconvenient could be done away with—and this would be carried out calmly and sensibly, without malice. Even amicably. Lenin didn't even seem to look on himself as a human being—he was merely a servant of a political idea. Possessed maniacs of this kind are truly terrifying.

What follows, along with extracts from *Memories*, are several of the articles Teffi published in Kyiv and Odessa newspapers in late 1918 and early 1919. Teffi drew on some of them for *Memories*, as did Bulgakov for his novel *The White Guard*.

PETROGRAD MONOLOGUE

No! No more! I've promised myself not to say another word about the question of food. Enough is enough! It's become downright unbearable! No matter what one is talking about, one always ends up on the subject of food. As if there's nothing else in the world of any interest.

What about beauty? What about art? What, for goodness' sake, about love?

I ran into Michel recently. People always used to go on about him being such an aesthete; they used to say his soul was a sugared violet. Some violet! I was talking to him about *Parsifal*, but all *he* wanted to talk about was horse meat! Meat, meat, meat—a fine *meeting* of minds I call it! It was dreadful. And I adore *Parsifal*! Have you seen the new production? It's wonderful! I seem to have forgotten the name of the fellow with the big belly who sang Parsifal himself... But he was wonderful. Ah, how I love art! Not long ago I was at a World of Art[1] exhibition. Have you ever seen Boris Grigoriev? Ah, what an artist! Subtle, piquant, delicious! Aesthetic erotica and erotic aesthetica! You know, whenever I look at his paintings, I feel he's moving his brush not over the canvas, but over my body and soul. Honest to God. So there I was at the exhibition, standing in front of his painting. I closed my eyes so I could take it in better. Suddenly someone was grabbing hold of my arm. Madam Bunova! "Hurry!" she said, "Let's go to the next room. An artist has painted these enormous apples. We must get his address and find out which cooperative he belongs to. There's no way he could have conjured up something this wonderful just from his imagination!"

And do you know? They really were remarkable apples. I haven't seen apples like that for a long time. Great big red apples. I wonder how much they would cost. I saw an apple a little like them at Yeliseyev's, but it wasn't the same—nothing like as big. But the way they pamper that apple you'd think it was Lina Cavalieri[2]—they bathe it and tart it up, and every morning the shop assistants give it a manicure. Although, would you believe it, apparently that apple isn't even for sale! The proprietors are waiting for the value of the rouble to go up.

And yesterday the Bolonkins' cooperative was distributing rice… Oh, don't say I've got back onto the subject of food! Well, I won't do it again, I really won't. I swear I won't. One must take spiritual respite in beauty, in art.

Speaking of which, being beautiful these days is so difficult it's just dreadful.

Can you imagine, even good face powder is impossible to get your hands on. It's dreadful! Madam Bolonkina says you can use face powder to make flatbread. You just mix it with either cold cream or lipstick. And it's very tasty, only you feel sick for a long time afterwards. These days, we can take it that people are making flatbread from anything and everything. Madam Bunova's brother says he's made flatbread from window putty, and the recipe is ever so simple: you just pick it out of the window frame and eat it… Ah, goodness gracious, I'm going on about food again! Pardon, it's just a nervous tic—it will pass. And I haven't forgotten my promise. One must take spiritual respite. These are such trying times. Yesterday I ran into a certain composer—such talent, such beauty! And can you imagine, *he* doesn't have any money either. "I'm selling my entire collection of Persian rugs one by one," he said. "That's how I'm feeding myself. I'm like a moth, feeding on rugs." Well, if you ask me, better rugs than horse meat. I'm so sick and tired of this horse meat that I can't even bear to hear about it. But Madam Bolonkina eats it. She may pretend she doesn't, but she certainly does. She recently invited us all over for roast beef. "I've got some wonderful roast beef," she said. But when the maid was bringing it out to the table, instead of saying, "Your first course is ready," she said, "Your horses are ready." So much for her roast beef! Oh dear, have I done it again? Good heavens, forgive me—I know I gave you my word. We shall talk about love, about art.

Now what was I going to say? Oh yes, Merkin the dentist makes flatbread from fillings and cardamom. He sings its praises. It's got a lot going for it, he says. If it gets stuck in your teeth, it'll do you nothing but good. Oh, but what am I saying? Not again! Oh, goodness gracious! But I do love art, I really do!

KYIV, 11 NOVEMBER 1918

TRANSLATED BY ANNE MARIE JACKSON

THE GUILLOTINE

I dedicate these memoirs to Trotsky, with heartfelt gratitude.

As I would not be able to write these memoirs after being guillotined, I am forced to write them now.

Still, it really doesn't matter: I noticed some time ago that my actual future usually turns out to be almost identical to my dreams of the future. So I write these memoirs of the future safe in the knowledge that this is just how it will be.

IN THE EVENING, just as we were about to have supper, Vera Valeryanovna called in.

"I can only stay a minute," she said. "I'm in a dreadful hurry."

"What's the rush?" we said. "Stay awhile!"

"No, I can't. I'm in a hurry. I only popped in to say goodbye. I'm due to be guillotined tomorrow."

"But Vera, darling!" we exclaimed. "What a wonderful coincidence! We're all scheduled for tomorrow!"

"Spend the night at my place," I said. "We can all go together. You don't want to go all the way from Galernaya Street to Palace Square. It's a lot closer from here. And tonight we can eat the last of the strawberry jam."

She wasn't to be persuaded easily.

"You know how it is; there's always so much to do at the last minute..."

But I was delighted. We'd have a grand time together. After all, it's not much fun waiting for three hours for your turn to come round.

The day before, apparently, the chopping personnel had gone on strike for better wages and left people standing about in the freezing cold until five o'clock.

A delegation from the choppers had appealed to the condemned for support. Naturally, the condemned were sympathetic: they promised that, if worst came to worst, they too would go on strike, refusing to be executed until the government had conceded to the choppers' demands. And by five o'clock the whole incident had been dealt with decisively.

But these queues are really quite outrageous! You have a line on one side stretching almost as far as Nevsky Prospekt, a line on the other up to Palace Bridge and a third winding right round the back of the Hermitage. Despite the latest technology and the electric motor, the guillotine works slowly. What's the point of being able to lop off five hundred heads at once if you still have to lay all those five hundred people into position first? People pushing and shoving—utter chaos! The wait is never less than two hours, and in the freezing cold. The crowd starts complaining, muttering.

"They squeeze us for taxes, but they can't organize anything properly. So much for all this talk of strong government. Put a fool in charge and you'll be the first to suffer."

They do have a point. Would it really be so difficult to issue people with cards? Or to put up district guillotines?

We sat around talking till midnight, swapping all sorts of funny stories. Apparently, certain fashionable Russian ladies have devised a special wig "à la Marie Antoinette" for the guillotine.

The wigs cost a fortune. But is it really worth it? The wigs lose their curl in the damp air, and in any case, the whole thing just looks daft—imagine, some Marie Antoinette standing in a queue.

It was different during the French Revolution. Back then, a woman went up on the scaffold as if it were a stage. The crowd would be watching—she would be seen by everyone.

In those days, ordinary people were fascinated by the guillotine: it frightened and attracted them. The man who invented it seemed to them a mysterious and marvellous creature.

Boys on the street would sing songs about him:

Guillotin,
Médecin,
Politique…[1]

The executioner was also a notable person, an object of universal interest.

"Monsieur de Paris."[2]

But things are different now. The guillotine is set up like a factory machine, operated by workers. It's all so clear and simple.

And all these bourgeois pretensions, seeking to lend the affair an air of beauty and solemnity, are just plain silly. When, oh when, will we finally grow up and adopt the correct attitude towards the everyday details of modern life?

The Russian people got used to the guillotine so quickly, feel so much at ease with it, that it's hard to believe there was ever a time when we didn't have it.

They treat the guillotine with that affectionate warmth so unique to the Russian people, calling it "Gallotina Ivanovna":

The street songs have now acquired a new verse:

> If you don't get up this morning
> Bake me up a birthday pie
> Off I go to Gallotina
> You can wave my head goodbye!

We got up early the next morning.

Vera Valeryanovna was right. There is always a great deal to do at the last minute.

At nine o'clock, Michel, a family friend, knocked on the door. He had managed to swap places with a colleague—now he could be guillotined with us.

By the time we had had a cup of tea and something to eat, the clock had struck ten and it was time to get ready.

Michel is an absolute treasure: he had made sandwiches for the journey.

"We may have to wait three hours in the queue," he said. "We'll get hungry."

Off we went. Not a cab to be found, of course. And all the trams were full to bursting. So we set off on foot along Sadovaya Street.

"Awful!" grumbled Vera Valeryanovna. "Bad luck at the start. That doesn't bode well."

She's rather superstitious, you see.

At last, near Sennaya Square, we came across a cab driver.

"How much?" we asked.

"Thirty roubles."

"Are you mad?" we protested. "We're not off on some jaunt, you know. We're going on important business. To be guillotined."

"It's all the same to me," whined a beard from under a hat. "It's all one to me, wherever I take yous. Some might look on it different, and pay extra, seeing as it's the last time they take a cab."

"And just why should we pay you extra?"

"It's all right for some," muttered the beard. "Yous are all getting your heads chopped off and that's the end of it. Some of us have to work. Some of us have horses to feed. Oats don't come cheap these days, you know..."

"Take twenty roubles." Michel tried to beat him down. "And if you drive well, you'll get something extra."

"I know your sort," said the cab driver, now in a nasty mood. "I'm the one who loses out, giving rides to yous condemned. Had one in my cab the other day. Kept talking about the nice tip he'd give me. So I took him to the guillotine, and he goes, 'Wait here, I must get some change. All I have is a million rouble note,'[3] and then he dives into the crowd. So I wait and I wait till I get sick of waiting, and I get down and go off to look for him. I'm asking around, 'Hey, citizens, anyone seen a dark fellow in a brown cap?' And everyone starts laughing. 'It's not him, by any chance, is it?' I look and there he is—already got himself executed, his head lying there in the snow!"

The cab driver's funny story put us in a happier mood. The next minute another cab turned up, and we set off.

There were masses of people on Palace Square. Carriages, motor cars, pedestrians. But there wasn't much in the way of pushing and shoving. This was probably thanks to Trotsky's proclamations, plastered all over the walls, stating that those to be guillotined were themselves responsible for maintaining order.

We paid the cab driver and gave him a tip. He told us to "break a leg".[4]

There were so many people we knew! In one queue we saw Olga Nikolaevna and Natalia Mikhailovna, both in wigs "à la Marie Antoinette", though for some reason the wigs weren't powdered, but ginger. Their faces were blue with cold, and it's fair to say that the overall effect was not a pretty sight.

A clean-shaven man was putting on quite a show for the crowd. People said he was a compère from some minor theatre.

Newspaper boys were nipping about among the queues, together with vendors of *sbiten*[5] and fried pies. Michel wanted to try one, but I talked him out of it—such filthy things, smelling of tallow candles.

There was a bit of a scene in one of the queues. A nimble young man with dark hair had managed to jump the queue and get himself executed before those around him even knew what was happening.

There was no end of fuss! People were shouting that bribes had changed hands, and wasn't that just typical of the Jews, always sneaking to the front of the queue?

It was getting cold. We were bored.

Michel asked us to save his place in the queue and went up to have a closer look at the guillotine. He was concerned that the opening for the heads wasn't big enough.

"I've got a big head. All in all, I'm a big chap!" he said. "I'm afraid I'll scrape my ears."

Nearby, two ladies were having a tiff.

"How can you douse yourself in perfume like that before the guillotine? It's absolutely not on, I tell you! Now I have a migraine coming on."

"Well, well, aren't we sensitive?" snorted the other. "Don't worry, my dear, your migraine won't have time to come on."

She was right.

The doors of the enclosure around the guillotine were thrown open and our queue began to stream forward.

"Now, now—no pushing!"

"Show a bit of manners!"

"Honestly, this crowd."

"Such inconsiderate types. We condemned ought to take things into our own hands. We should form a union. Why should it only be other people who enjoy the perks of being guillotine operators?"

"It's too late now."

"What were we thinking of earlier?"

"Keep moving, now, keep moving. Don't hold everybody up."

"We're coming. We're coming."

1918

TRANSLATED BY ROSE FRANCE

EXTRACTS FROM *MEMORIES*

Walking Across the Ice

THOSE LAST DAYS WERE STRANGE INDEED.

At night we hurried past the dark houses, down streets where people were strangled and robbed. We hurried to listen to *Silva*[1] or else to sit in down-at-heel cafés packed with people in shabby coats that stank of wet dog. There we listened to young poets reading—or rather howling—their own and one another's work; they sounded like hungry wolves. There was quite a vogue for these poets, and even the haughty Briusov would sometimes deign to introduce one of their "Evenings of Eros".[2]

Everyone wanted company, to be in the presence of other people.

To be alone and at home was frightening.

We had to know what was going on; we needed to keep hearing news of one another. Sometimes someone would disappear and then it would be almost impossible to find out what had happened to them. Had they gone to Kyiv? Or to the place whence there was no return?

It was as if we were living in the tale about Zmey Gorynych, the dragon that required a yearly tribute of twelve fair maidens and twelve young men.[3] One might well wonder how the people in this tale could have carried on, how they could have lived with the knowledge that a dragon would soon be devouring the finest of their children. During those last days in Moscow, however, we realized that they too had probably been rushing from one little theatre to another or hurrying to buy themselves something from which to make a coat or a dress. There is nowhere a human being cannot live. With my own eyes I have seen sailors taking a man out onto the ice in order to shoot him—and I have seen the condemned man hopping over puddles to keep his feet dry and turning up his collar to shield his chest from the wind. Those few steps were the last steps he would ever take, and instinctively he wanted to make them as comfortable as possible.

We were no different. We bought ourselves some "last scraps" of fabric. We listened for the last time to the last operetta and the last exquisitely erotic verses. What did it matter whether the verses were good or terrible? All that mattered was not to know, not to be aware—we had to forget that we were being led onto the ice.

News came from Petersburg that the Cheka[4] had arrested a well-known actress for reading my short stories in public. She was ordered to read one of the stories again, before three dread judges. You can imagine what fun it was for her to stand between guards with bayonets and declaim my comic monologue. And then—miracle of miracles!—after her first few trembling sentences, the face of one of the judges dissolved into a smile.

"I heard this story one evening at comrade Lenin's. It's entirely apolitical."

Reassured by this, the judges asked the suspect—who was, of course, also greatly reassured—to continue her reading, "by way of revolutionary entertainment".

Still, all in all, it probably wasn't such a bad idea to be going away, even if only for a month. For a change of climate.

Scrubbing the Deck

That morning Smolyaninov came to see me. He was in charge of various administrative tasks on our ship. In his previous life he may have worked for *The New Age*,[5] though I don't know for sure.

"I have to tell you," he said, "that some of the passengers are unhappy that you didn't join in yesterday when they were gutting fish. They're saying you're work-shy and that you're being granted unfair privileges. You must find a way to show that you are willing to work."

"All right, I'm quite willing to show my willingness."

"But I really don't know what to suggest. I can hardly make you scrub the deck."

Ah! Scrubbing the deck! My childhood dream! As a child I had once seen a sailor hosing the deck with a large hose while another sailor scrubbed away with a stiff, long-handled brush with bristles cut at an angle. I had thought at the time that nothing in the world could be jollier. Since then, I've learned about many things that are jollier, but that stiff, oddly shaped brush, those rapid, powerful splashes as the water hit the white planks, and the sailors' brisk efficiency (the one doing the scrubbing kept repeating "Hup! Hup!") had all stayed in my memory—a wonderful, joyous picture.

There I had stood, a little girl with blue eyes and blonde pigtails, watching this sailors' game with reverence and envy, upset that fate would never allow me this joy.

But kind fate had taken pity on that poor little girl. It had tormented her for a long time, but it never forgot her wish. It staged a war and a revolution. It turned the whole world upside down, and now, at last, it had found an opportunity to thrust a long-handled brush into the girl's hands and send her up on deck.

At last! Thank you, dear fate!

"Tell me," I said to Smolyaninov. "Do they have a brush with angled bristles? And will they be using a hose?"

"What!" said Smolyaninov. "Do you mean it? You're really willing to scrub the deck?"

"Of course I mean it! Only don't, for heaven's sake, change your mind. Come on, let's go…"

"You must at least change your clothes!"

But I had nothing to change into.

For the main part, the *Shilka*'s passengers wore whatever they could most easily do without. We all knew that it would be impossible to buy anything when we next went ashore, so we were saving our everyday clothes for later. We were wearing only items for which we foresaw no immediate need: colourful shawls, ball gowns, satin slippers…

I was wearing a pair of silver shoes. Certainly not the kind of shoes I'd be wearing next time I had to wander about searching for a room.

We went up on deck.

Smolyaninov went off for a moment. A cadet came over with a brush and a hose. Jolly streams of water splashed onto my silver shoes.

"Just for a few minutes," whispered Smolyaninov. "For appearances' sake."

"Hup! Hup!" I exclaimed.

The cadet looked at me with fear and compassion.

"Please allow me to relieve you!"

"Hup-hup!" I replied. "We must all do our share. I imagine you've been humping coal; now I must scrub the deck. Yes, sir. We must all do our share, young man. I'm working and I'm proud of the contribution I'm making."

"But you'll wear yourself out!" said somebody else. "Please, allow me!"

"They're jealous, the sly devils!" I thought, remembering my childhood dream. "They want to have a go too! Well, why wouldn't they?"

"Nadezhda Alexandrovna! You truly have worn yourself out," said Smolyaninov. "The next shift will now take over."

He then added, under his breath, "Your scrubbing is abominable."

Abominable? And there I was, thinking I was just like that sailor from my distant childhood.

"And also, you look far too happy," Smolyaninov went on. "People might think this is some kind of game."

I had no choice but to relinquish my brush.

Offended, I set off down below. As I passed three ladies I didn't know, I heard one of them say my name.

"Yes, I've heard she's here on our boat."

"You don't say!"

"I'm telling you, she's here on this boat. Not like the rest of us, of course. She's got a cabin to herself, a separate table, and she doesn't want to do any work."

I shook my head sadly.

"You're being terribly unfair!" I said reproachfully. "She's just been scrubbing the deck. I saw her with my own eyes."

"They got her to scrub the deck!" exclaimed one of the ladies. "That's going too far!"

"And you saw her?"

"Yes, I did."

"Well? What's she like?"

"Long and lanky. A bit like a gypsy. In red boots."

"Goodness me!"

"And nobody's breathed a word to us!"

"That must be very hard work, mustn't it?"

"Yes," I said. "A lot harder than just stroking a fish with a knife."

"So why's she doing it?"

"She wants to set an example."

"And to think that nobody's breathed a word to us!"

"Do you know when she'll be scrubbing next? We'd like to watch."

"I'm not sure. I've heard she's put her name down to work in the boiler room tomorrow, but that may just be a rumour."

"Now that really is going too far!" said one lady, with concern.

"It's all right," came the reassuring reply. "A writer needs to experience many things. It's not for nothing that Maxim Gorky worked as a baker when he was young."

"But that was before he became a writer."

"Well, he must have known he'd become a writer. Why else would he have gone to work in a bakery?"

Holy Saturday

Another night. A dark, still night.

Far off, in a half circle, the lights of the shore.

A very still night indeed.

I stand there a long time, listening into the silence. I keep thinking I can hear the sound of a church bell from the dark shore. Maybe I really can... I don't know how far we are from the shore. All I can see are the lights.

"Yes," says someone nearby, "it's a church bell. The sound carries well over water."

"That's right," says someone else. "It's the night before Easter."

Holy Saturday.

We have all lost our sense of time. We have no idea where we are either in time or in space.

Holy Saturday.

This distant ringing that has come to us over the waves of the sea is solemn, dense and hushed to the point of mystery. As if it has been searching for us, lost as we are in the sea and the night, and has found us, and has united us with this church on the earth, now bathed in light, in singing, in praise of the resurrection.

This sound I have known all my life, this solemn sound of the Holy Eve, takes hold of my soul and leads it far away, past the screams and the bloodshed, to the simple, sweet days of my childhood.

My little sister Lena... She was always by my side—we grew up together. A round rosy cheek, and a round grey eye, were always there at my shoulder.

When we argued, she would hit me with her tiny fist, soft as a rubber ball. Then, horrified by her own wild violence, she would weep, as she repeated again and again: "I could kill you!"

She was a crybaby. When I wanted to draw her portrait (when I was five, art was something for which I felt a real love—a love that my elders eventually managed to kill), I always began by drawing a round open mouth and filling it in with black. Only after that would I add her eyes, nose and cheeks. These, as I saw it, were mere extras, of no significance—what mattered was this open mouth that so perfectly captured the very essence of my model's physical and spiritual being.

Lena liked to draw too. She always did what I did. When I was sick and had to take medicine, she too had to have a few drops in a glass of water.

"Well, Lenushka, feeling better now?"

"Yes, thank God, I seem to be a little better," she would say with a sigh.

Lena, like me, liked to draw, but she set about it very differently. She often drew Nyanya, and she always began, very carefully, by drawing four parallel lines.

"What's that?"

"It's the wrinkles on Nyanya's forehead."

Two or three more quick strokes—and there was Nyanya, now complete. But getting those first wrinkles right was difficult and Lena would huff and puff and spoil sheet after sheet of paper.

Lena was indeed a crybaby.

I remember one terrible, shameful incident.

I had already been going to the *gymnasium* for a whole year when Lena started there too. She was in the junior preparatory class.[6]

And then one day our whole class was lined up on the stairs waiting to go down into the entrance hall. The little ones from the preparatory class had gone down already.

And then I saw a small figure with a clipped tuft of hair on its forehead, dragging a heavy bag of books, fearfully trying to edge its way along beside the wall but not daring to go past us.

Lena!

Our class mistress went up to her:

"What is your surname? Which class are you in?"

Lena looked up at her with an expression of animal terror, and her lower lip began to tremble. Without answering, she hunched her shoulders, snatched up her bag, and, her tuft of hair shaking as she burst into loud sobs, rushed down the stairs—a small bundle of misery.

"What a funny little girl!" said our mistress, and began to laugh.

This was more than I could bear. I closed my eyes and hid behind a friend's back. The shame of it! What if the class mistress found out that she was my sister? A sister who, instead of saying straightforwardly and with dignity, "I'm from the junior preparatory class" and then bobbing a curtsy, simply began to howl. The shame of it!

...The sound of Easter. Now I can hear the bell quite clearly...

I remember how, in our old house—in the half-dark of the hall, where the chandeliers' crystal drops used to tremble and tinkle of their own accord—Lena and I would stand side by side, looking out into the night and listening to the bells. We were a little scared—because we were alone, because the bells sounded unusually solemn and because Christ would soon be risen.

"But why," asked Lena, "why isn't it angels ringing the bells?"

In the half-dark I could see a little grey eye—shining and frightened.

"Angels only come," I replied, "when it's your last hour." And I felt scared by my own words…

Why now? Why, on this Easter Eve, has my sister come thousands of miles, to this dark sea? Why does she stand beside me as a little girl—the little girl she was when I loved her most of all.

I don't know.

Only three years later will I find out that on this very night, thousands of miles away in Arkhangelsk, my Lena was dying.[7]

1930

TRANSLATED BY ROBERT AND ELIZABETH CHANDLER
WITH ANNE MARIE JACKSON AND IRINA STEINBERG

STAGING POSTS

I.

ON THAT MORNING IT WAS ALWAYS SUNNY.

The weather was always bright and cheerful. So, at least, both Liza and Katya remembered it for the rest of their lives.[1]

On that morning, Nyanya would always dress them in new, light-coloured dresses. Then she would go to the "big" dining room, where the adults were drinking tea, and come back up again with half a hard-boiled egg, a piece of *kulich* and a piece of *paskha* for each of them.[2]

Nyanya herself always broke her Lenten fast early in the morning when she came back from the Liturgy. She would have cream with her coffee, and the children knew that she would grumble all day and start to feel out of sorts by evening.

The hard-boiled egg would always get stuck somewhere in Liza's chest and they would have to pummel her hard on the back to dislodge it.

The housekeeper, who on that day always smelled of vanilla, would come to wish them a happy Easter.

And she would tell them the story of how, twenty years ago, the mistress of a certain house had made a *baba*[3] using beaten egg white, and how the *baba* had "fallen in the oven". And the mistress had strung herself up from the shame of it.

Liza knew this story, but she could never work out which of the two women had strung herself up and which had fallen into the oven: the *baba* or the mistress? She imagined a huge blazing oven, like the "fiery furnace" in holy pictures into which the three youths were thrown.[4] And she imagined a great fat *baba*—the mistress—falling into the oven. In short, she couldn't make head or tail of it, but it was clearly something horrid, even though the housekeeper told the story cheerfully, with relish.

The housekeeper would also always reminisce about a certain August Ivanovich, a gentleman she had once worked for.

"Would you believe it—a German and all, but such a religious man he was! All through Holy Week he wouldn't take a bite of meat. 'It will taste all the better when I break my fast on Easter morning,' he used to say. A German and all, but he would never sit down to Easter breakfast without ham on the table—not for all the world. That's how religious he was!"

In the evening Liza remembered something very important, went along to her elder sister and said, "Last year, you told me you were already a growing girl, and I was still a child. But this year I fasted for Lent, so that means I'm a growing girl now too."

Her sister turned away, annoyed, and muttered, "You may be a growing girl, but I'm a young lady. Anyway, you should be in the nursery. Go away, or I'll tell Mademoiselle."

Liza pondered these words bitterly. She would never catch up with Masha. In four years' time she herself might be a young lady, but by then, Masha would already be an old maid. She would never catch up with her.[5]

2.

The church is crowded and stuffy. Candles splutter quietly in the hands of the worshippers. A pale-blue blanket of incense-smoke is spread out high in the dome. Down below—the gold of the icons, black figures and the flames of the candles. All around—black, candlelight and gold.

Liza is tired. She breaks off pieces of melted wax, rolls them into pellets and sticks them back onto the candle, noting how much of the Gospel the priest has read. He is reading well, clearly enough for Liza to hear him even though she is standing a long way back.

Liza listens to the familiar phrases but cannot concentrate. She is distracted by the old woman in front of her, who keeps turning round malevolently and piercing Liza with a cold stare, with a yellow-ringed eye like the eye of a fish. The old woman is afraid that Liza will singe her fox-fur collar.

Liza is also distracted by all kinds of other thoughts. She is thinking of her friend, fair, curly-headed Zina. Zina is like a bee—all honey and gold. Her bronze hair grows in tight curls. One summer, at the dacha, Zina had been sitting holding a little lapdog, and a woman coming past had said, "Humph, just look at that… poodle!" And in all seriousness Zina had asked, "Was she talking about *me*, or Kadochka?" Zina is silly, and so like a bee that Liza calls her Zuzu.

What is the priest reading about now? "And the second time the cock crew."[6] How had it all happened? Night. A fire in the courtyard of the high priest. It must have been cold. People were keeping warm next to the fire. And Peter was sitting with them. Liza loved Peter; for her he always had a special place among the apostles. She loved him because he was the most passionate of them. She didn't like to think that Peter had denied Christ. When they asked him if he had been with Jesus of Nazareth, and he didn't admit it, it was only because he didn't want to be thrown out. After all, he had followed Christ into the high priest's courtyard—he had not been afraid then.

Liza thinks of how Peter wept and of how he walked away "the second time the cock crew", and her heart aches, and, in her soul, she walks side by side with Peter, past the guards, past the terrible, cruel soldiers, past the high priest's servants, who look on with malevolent suspicion, and out through the gate and into the black, grief-stricken night.

And so the night goes on. From the square outside Pontius Pilate's house comes the hubbub of the crowd. And just then a voice, loud and forceful as fate itself, cries out, "Crucify Him! Crucify Him!" And it seems as if the flames of the candles shiver, and an evil, black breath spreads through the church: "Crucify Him! Crucify Him!" And from age to age it has been passed down, that evil cry. What can we do, how can we make amends, how can we silence that cry, so that we no longer need hear it?

Liza feels her hands grow cold; she feels her whole body transfixed in a sort of ecstasy of sadness, with tears running down her cheeks. "What is it? Why am I crying? What's the matter with me?"

"Perhaps I should tell Zuzu?" she thinks. "But how can I make Zuzu understand? Will Zuzu be able to understand how the whole church fell silent, how the flames of the candles shivered and how that loud, terrible voice called out, 'Crucify Him! Crucify Him!'? I won't be able to tell her all that. If I don't tell it well, Zuzu won't understand anything. But if she does understand, if she feels what I feel, how wonderful, how glorious that would be. It would be something quite new. I think somehow we would start to live our whole lives differently. Dear Lord, help me be able to tell it!"

*

Easter Sunday was always jolly. A great many visitors would come to wish them a happy Easter. Liza had put on a spring dress made to a pattern of her own choosing. And she had chosen it because the caption beneath it in the fashion magazine read: "A dress for the young lady of thirteen." Not for a little girl, or for a growing girl, but for a young lady.

Zuzu came round for breakfast. She was looking pleased, as if she were full of secrets. "Let's go to your room. Quick. I have so much to tell you," she whispered.

The news really was extraordinary: a cadet! A divine cadet! And not a young boy, he was sixteen already. He could sing "*Tell her that my fiery soul…*"[7] Zuzu hadn't heard him, but Vera Yaroslavtseva had told her he sang very well. And he was in love with Zuzu. He had seen her at the skating rink and on Palm Sunday at Vera Yaroslavtseva's. He had seen Liza, too.

"Yes, he's seen you. I don't know where. But he said you were a magnificent woman."

"Did he really?" Liza gasped. "Did he really say that? And what does he look like?"

"I don't know for sure. When we went for a walk on Palm Sunday, there were two cadets walking behind us, and I don't know which of the two he was. But I think he was the darker one, because the other one was ever so fair and round, not the sort to have strong feelings."

"And you think he's in love with *me*, too?"

"Probably. Anyway, what of it? It's even more fun if he's in love with both of us!"

"Don't you think that's immoral? It feels a little strange to me."

The bee-like Zuzu, all curls and honey, pursed her rosy lips mockingly.

"Well, I'm amazed at you, truly I am. The Queen of Sheba had all the peoples of the world in love with her—and here you are, afraid of just one cadet. That's plain silly."

"And it's really true, what he said about me? That I'm..."

Liza was embarrassed to repeat those extraordinary words ("a mag-ni-fi-cent wo-man").

"Of course it's true," said Zuzu, in a matter-of-fact way. "It's what Vera Yaroslavtseva told me. Do you think she'd make up something like that just for fun? She's probably bursting with envy."

"But all the same, don't you think it might be a sin?" Liza fretted. And then: "Wait, there's something I wanted to tell you. And now I've forgotten. Something important."

"Well, it'll come back to you. We're being called to breakfast."

In the evening, when she was going to bed, Liza went up to the mirror, looked at her fair hair, at her sharp little face with its freckled nose, smiled and whispered, "A magnificent woman."

3.

The night was black.

Over to starboard, the sea flowed into the sky and it seemed that there, quite close, only a few metres from the ship, lay the end of the world. A black void, space, eternity.

Over to port, one or two little lights glimmered in the distance. They were alive, flickering, moving. Or were we just imagining this, since we all knew there was a town there? Living people, movement. Life.

After two terrible, boring weeks on board, with nobody sure where they were going and when they would arrive, or whether they would ever feel the earth beneath their feet again, or whether that earth would be kind to them, or whether it would lead them to sorrow, torment and death; after that, how frustrating it was to see those living lights and not dare to sail towards them.

In the morning the captain promised to contact the shore, find out the situation there and then decide what to do.

Who was in the town? Who had control of it? Friend or foe? Whites or Reds? And if it was in enemy hands, where could we go? Further east? But we wouldn't get far on this little coaster. We'd be drowned.[8]

Tired people wandered about on deck, looking towards the lights.

"I don't want to look at those lights," said Liza. "It makes me feel even more hopeless. I'd rather look at the black, terrible night. It feels closer to me. But isn't the sea making a strange booming sound? What is it?"

A sailor passed by.

"Can you hear?" asked Liza. "Can you hear the sea booming?"

"Yes," said the sailor, "it's church bells from the shore. That's a good sign. It means the Whites are there. Today is Holy Thursday. The Feast of the Twelve Gospels."

The Twelve Gospels. A memory comes back, from long ago. Black, gold, candlelight. The pale-blue smoke of incense. A little girl with blonde braids clasps her hands around a wax candle that drips and flickers. She clasps her hands and weeps, "What can we do, how can we make amends, how can we silence that cry, so that we need no longer hear it: 'Crucify Him! Crucify Him!'"

How strangely and clearly it all came back to her! So much time had passed, such a vast life, and then suddenly that moment—which, at the time, she had forgotten almost immediately—had suddenly come right up to her, in the form of church bells booming over the water, in the form of lights glowing on the shore like wax candles. It had caught up with her and now it was standing there beside her. It would never go away again. Never again?

And Zuzu? Would Zuzu come running up again too, to buzz, to dance, to fly around her? The Zuzus of this world run fast, after all. They always catch up…

"And the second time the cock crew…"

1940

TRANSLATED BY ROSE FRANCE

THE GADARENE SWINE

THERE ARE NOT MANY OF THEM, of these refugees from Sovietdom. A small group of people with nothing in common; a small motley herd huddled by the cliff's edge before the final leap. Creatures of different breeds and with coats of different colours, entirely alien to one another, with natures that have perhaps always been mutually antagonistic, they have wandered off together and collectively refer to themselves as "we". They have wandered off for no purpose, for no reason. Why?

The legend of the country of the Gadarenes comes to mind. Men possessed by demons came out from among the tombs, and Christ healed them by driving the demons into a herd of swine, and the swine plunged from a cliff and drowned.

Herds of a single animal are rare in the East. More often they are mixed. And in the herd of Gadarene swine, there were evidently some meek, frightened sheep. Seeing the crazed swine hurtling along, these sheep took to their heels too.

"Is that our lot?"

"Yes, they're running for it!"

And the meek sheep plunged down after the swine and they all perished together.

Had dialogue been possible during this mad dash, it might have resembled what we've been hearing so often in recent days:

"Why are we running?" ask the meek.

"Everyone's running."

"Where are we running to?"

"Wherever everyone else is running."

"What are we doing with *them*? They're not our kind of people. We shouldn't be here with *them*. Maybe we ought to have stayed where we were. Where the men possessed by demons were coming out from the tombs. What are we doing? We've lost our way, we don't know what we're…"

But the swine running alongside them know very well what they're doing. They egg the meek on, grunting, "Culture! We're running towards culture! We've got money sewn into the soles of our shoes. We've got diamonds stuck up our noses. Culture! Culture! Yes, we must save our culture!"

They hurtle on. Still on the run, they speculate. They buy up, they buy back, they sell on. They peddle rumours. And the fleshy disc at the end of a pig's snout—it may look like it's only a five-kopek coin, but the swine are selling them now for a hundred roubles.

"Culture! We're saving culture! For the sake of culture!"

"How very strange!" say the meek. "'Culture' is our kind of word. It's a word we use ourselves. But now it sounds all wrong. Who is it you're running away from?"

"The Bolsheviks."

"How very strange!" the meek say sadly. "Because we're running away from the Bolsheviks, too."

If the swine are fleeing the Bolsheviks, then it seems that the meek should have stayed behind.

But they're in headlong flight. There's no time to think anything through.

They are indeed all running away from the Bolsheviks. But the crazed swine are escaping from Bolshevik truth, from socialist principles, from equality and justice, while the meek and frightened are escaping from untruth, from Bolshevism's black reality, from terror, injustice and violence.

"What was there for me to do back there?" asks one of the meek. "I'm a professor of international law. I could only have died of hunger."

Indeed, what is there for a professor of international law to do—a man whose professional concern is the inviolability of principles that no longer exist? What use is he now? All he can do is give off an aura of international law. And now he's on the run. During the brief stops he hurries about, trying to find someone in need of his international law. Sometimes he even finds a bit of work and manages to give a few lectures. But then the crazed swine break loose and sweep him along behind them.

"We must run. Everyone is running."

Out-of-work lawyers, journalists, artists, actors and public figures—they're all on the run.

"Maybe we should have stayed behind and fought?"

Fought? But how? Make wonderful speeches when there's no one to hear them? Write powerful articles that there's nowhere to publish?

"And who should we have fought against?"

Should an impassioned knight enter into combat with a windmill, then—and please remember this—the windmill will always win. Even though this certainly does not mean—and please remember this too—that the windmill is right.

They're running. They're in torment, full of doubt, and they're on the run.

Alongside them, grunting and snorting and not doubting anything, are the speculators, former gendarmes, former Black Hundreds[1] and a variety of other former scoundrels. Former though they may be, these groups retain their particularities.

There are heroic natures who stride joyfully and passionately, through blood and fire, towards—ta-rum-pum-pum!—a new life!

And there are tender natures who are willing, with no less joy and no less passion, to sacrifice their lives for what is most wonderful and unique, but without the ta-rum-pum-pum. With a prayer rather than a drum roll.

Wild screams and bloodshed extinguish all light and colour from the souls of these tender natures. Their energy fades and their resources vanish. The rivulet of blood glimpsed in the morning at the gates of the commissariat, a rivulet creeping slowly across the pavement, cuts the road of life in two. Once and for all—it's impossible to step over this rivulet.

It's impossible to go further. Impossible to do anything but turn and run.

And so these tender natures run.

This rivulet of blood has cut them off forever, and that's the end of it.

Then there are the more everyday people, those who are neither good nor bad but entirely average, the all-too-real people who make up the bulk of what we call humanity. The ones for whom science and art, comfort and culture, religion and laws were created. Neither heroes nor scoundrels—in a word, just plain ordinary people.

To exist without the everyday, to hang in the air without any familiar footing—with no sure, firm earthly footing—is something only heroes and madmen can do.

A "normal person" needs the trappings of life, life's earthly flesh—that is, the everyday.

Where there's no religion, no law, no conventions, no settled routine (even if only the routine of a prison or a penal camp), an ordinary, everyday person cannot exist.

At first he'll try to adapt. Deprived of his breakfast roll, he'll eat plain bread; deprived of bread, he'll settle for husks full of grit; deprived of husks, he'll eat rotten herring—but he'll eat all of this with the same look on his face and the same attitude as if he were eating his usual breakfast roll.

But when there's nothing to eat at all? Then he loses his way, his light fades and the colours of life turn pale for him.

Now and then there's a brief flicker from some tremulous beam of light.

"Apparently they take bribes too! Did you know? Have you heard?"

The happy news takes wing, travelling by word of mouth—a promise of life, like "Christ is Risen!"

Bribery! The everyday, the routine, a way of life we know as our own! Something earthly and solid!

But bribery alone does not allow you to settle down and thrive.

You must run. In pursuit of your daily bread in the biblical sense of the word: food, clothing, shelter and labour that provides these things and law that protects them.

Children must acquire the knowledge needed for work, and people of mature years must apply this knowledge to the business of everyday life.

So it has always been, and it cannot of course be otherwise.

There are heady days in the history of nations—days that have to be lived through, but that one can't go on living in forever.

"Enough carousing—time to get down to work."

Does this mean, then, that we have to do things in some new way? What time should we go to work? What time should we have lunch? Which school should we prepare the children for? We're ordinary people, the levers, belts, screws, wheels and drives of a vast machine; we're the core, the very thick of humanity—what do you want us to do?

"We want you to do all manner of foolish things. Instead of screws we'll have belts; we'll use belts to screw in nuts. And levers instead of wheels. And a wheel will do the job of a belt. Impossible? Outdated prejudice! At the sharp end of a bayonet, nothing is impossible. A theology professor can bake gingerbread and a porter give lectures on aesthetics. A surgeon can sweep the street and a laundress preside over the courtroom."

"We're afraid! We can't do it, we don't know how. A porter lecturing on aesthetics may believe in the value of what he is doing, but a professor baking gingerbread knows only too well that his gingerbread may be anything under the sun—but it certainly isn't gingerbread."

Take to your heels! Run!

Somewhere over there… in Kyiv… in Yekaterinburg… in Odessa… some place where children are studying and people are working, it'll still be possible to live a little… For the time being.

And so on they run.

But they are few and they are becoming fewer still. They're growing weak, falling by the wayside. They're running after a way of life that is itself on the run.

And now that the motley herd has wandered onto the Gadarene cliff for its final leap, we can see how very small it is. It could be gathered up into some little ark and sent out to sea. But there the seven unclean pairs would devour the seven clean pairs and then die of gluttony.[2]

And the souls of the clean would weep over the dead ark: "It grieves us to have suffered the same fate as the unclean, to have died together with them on the ark."

Yes, my dears. There's not much you can do about it. You'll all die together. Some from eating, some from being eaten. But "impartial history" will make no distinction. You will all be numbered together.

"And the entire herd plunged from the cliff and drowned."

ODESSA, MARCH 1919

TRANSLATED BY ANNE MARIE JACKSON

THE LAST BREAKFAST[1]

In times gone by, when Europe was peaceful and life settled, a condemned man would be offered breakfast on the morning of his execution. His last breakfast.

Le dernier déjeuner!

Witnesses to this last breakfast always noted with surprise the heartiness of the man's appetite.

Strange indeed.

If, in normal circumstances, someone is woken at four in the morning and offered breakfast, it is unlikely he'll respond with much interest. But a condemned man, knowing he has no more than two or three hours left to live, will gladly devote half an hour to a plate of roast beef.

Those whose last hours have been counted out and who have been handed the bill may, perhaps, slip into some peculiar state—a state of psychological coma. The soul has died away, died off, but the body's complex and cunning laboratory continues to function of its own accord. The smell of food makes nostrils flare; saliva fills the mouth, digestive juices start to flow and what we call an appetite arises. The body lives. Surprising though it may seem, the body continues to live. It lives and breakfasts with relish. Nobody, of course, believes that the Bolsheviks might be coming. To believe such a thing would be improper, impolite, a sign of ill breeding and ingratitude. There is no escaping the patriotism of the moment.

Nobody believes such a thing.

Yet every epoch, even every little turning point in an epoch, has a phrase or word—a leitmotif—that captures the general mood. You will hear this word everywhere: in theatres, in cafés, in restaurants, at business meetings, at the card table and out on the street. Wherever people are talking, whatever they are talking about, you cannot get away from this word.

The word of the moment is "visa".

Remember the day, take note of the day, when you don't hear this word.

In the month of March, 1919, life in Odessa is ruled by the sign of "visa".

"I am getting a visa."

"You will get a visa."

"He has got his visa already."

"We…" etc.

"The Bolsheviks aren't coming, but I'm trying to get hold of a visa."

"For where?"

"Anywhere—it's all the same to me."

This could be accurately translated as: "I, of course, have not been condemned to death, but just to be on the safe side I am petitioning for a pardon anyway."

Or to put it more simply: One fine morning people come and assure you, in the most impassioned of tones, that you have absolutely nothing to worry about, your life is really not in any danger. And your previous sense of peace and calm is lost forever.

"I believe you. I know full well that I'm not in any danger. But why do you have to keep telling me that? Hmm?"

"The Bolsheviks aren't coming. It won't be allowed. Have you got a visa?"

Perhaps this is true—the Bolsheviks won't come, and their coming is simply not possible. But in that corner of your consciousness, in that region of your brain that deals with the intricacies of obtaining foreign passports, the Bolsheviks have already taken over. They have been allowed into the city, they are making themselves at home here and they are doing as they please with you. And fate offers you a last breakfast. *Le dernier déjeuner*. Clubs and restaurants are packed to bursting. People are guzzling chicken feet at eighty roubles each. People are blowing their "last odd million" in games of chemin de fer. Bellies bulging, lifeless eyes, and a one-way visa to the island of Krakatakata (wherever that may be). And you're not allowed to stop anywhere en route.

Cold dreary days. Apocalyptic evenings.

In the evening people gather together, wearing hats and fur coats. With pale lips, their breath coming in clouds, they repeat, "The Bolsheviks, of course, aren't coming. A visa—must get hold of some kind of visa."

And they throw the last chair into the stove, after taking turns to sit on it for a minute by way of farewell.

This too is a kind of *dernier déjeuner*.

Cold days.

But if one morning the sun happens to leap up into the faded sky—a sky that is exhausted from waiting for spring—what absurd pictures we will see. These pictures are gloomy and sinister; they are not pictures fit for the sun.

The owner of a sugar refinery has walked out of a gaming house. He has been playing cards with abandon—and by morning he has lost two and a half million. By any standards that is quite a sum. But he has promised that by tomorrow he'll come up with some more money, to win back his losses.

The sun hurts the man's eyes, which are weary from his sleepless night. He squints, unable for a moment to take in a curious little scene being acted out right there in front of him.

On the pavement a man is poking about in a hole dug for a tree. Evidently a former actor—you can tell from the stubble on a face that has now gone some time without a shave. The skin hangs from his cheeks in deep folds, pulling down the corners of his mouth. The actor is wearing only a light summer coat, and over it—like a beggar king—a brownish-black threadbare blanket.

The actor is engaged in a serious task. He is picking through discarded nut shells. Searching for a mistakenly spat-out kernel. Ah! He seems to have found something. He lifts this something up to his face and, slightly squinting, with a quick monkey-like movement of both hands, picks out a fragment of nut. The owner of the sugar refinery, screwing up his tired eyes, watches all this for a few seconds, calmly and without embarrassment, as one might observe a monkey unwrapping a sweet. The actor looks up, also only for an instant. Then he returns to his task. Equally calmly and without embarrassment, like a monkey being watched by some other species of wild animal.

He carries on with his *dernier déjeuner.*

"Hey, sun! Put those beams of yours away. Nothing worth gawping at here!"

And what's all this about "psychological comas"? It's nothing of the kind.

People are just carrying on with their lives, living the way they have always lived, as is their human nature.

ODESSA, 2 APRIL 1919

TRANSLATED BY BEE BENTALL AND ROBERT AND ELIZABETH CHANDLER

EXTRACT FROM *MEMORIES*

Leaving Novorossiisk

SUMMER IN YEKATERINODAR...

Heat. Dust. Through a murky veil of dust, turmoil and all the years that have passed, I glimpse faces and images.

Professor Novgorodtsev. The pale-blue, very Slavic eyes of Venedikt Miakotin. The ever-sentimental Fiodor Volkenstein's thick mane of hair. The faraway, intent gaze of Piotr Ouspensky, the mystic...[1] And others, "slain servants of the Lord" whom we were already remembering in our prayers.

And there was Prince Y, one of my many Petersburg acquaintances. Always cheerful, feverishly animated—still more so after being shot through the arm.

"The soldiers adore me," he would say. "I know how to treat them. I bash them in the face—just like you bash a tambourine."

What they really loved him for, I think, was his reckless daring and his extraordinary cheerful bravado. They liked to tell the story of how he had once galloped through a village held by the Bolsheviks, whistling loudly, his epaulettes clearly visible on his shoulders.

"But why didn't they shoot at you?"

"They were flabbergasted. They couldn't believe their eyes: a White officer—suddenly riding through their village! They all rushed out to look, eyes popping out of their heads. It was ever so funny!"

I've heard the most astonishing accounts of Prince Y's subsequent adventures. In due course, in some other town in the south, he fell into enemy hands. He was tried—and sentenced to hard labour. Since the Bolsheviks didn't have any proper labour camps at that time, they simply put him in prison. But then they turned out to need a public prosecutor; it was only a small town and everyone with any education had either fled or gone into hiding. And they knew that the prince had completed a degree in law. So they thought for a bit, then appointed him public prosecutor. Prince Y would be escorted to the court to prosecute and to pass sentence, and he would then return for the night to his "hard labour". Many people felt envious: They too would have been glad of free bed and board.

Yekaterinodar, Rostov, Novorossiisk, Kislovodsk, …

Yekaterinodar, city of the elite. And in every government establishment—the picturesque beret, cloak and curls of Maximilian Voloshin, declaiming his poems about Russia and petitioning on behalf of the innocent and endangered.[2]

Rostov, city of traders and profiteers, its restaurant gardens the scene for hysterical drinking bouts that culminated in suicides.

Novorossiisk, city of many colours, ready to spring into Europe. Young men and chic ladies, motoring about in English cars and bathing in the sea. Novorossiisk-les-Bains…

Kislovodsk, which greeted approaching trains with an idyllic picture of green hills, peacefully grazing flocks and—against the backdrop of a scarlet evening sky—a finely etched black swing with a stub of rope.

A gallows.

I remember how haunted I was by that singular picture. I remember leaving the hotel first thing in the morning and setting off towards those green hills, seeking the evil mountain.

Towards it I went, climbing a steep, well-trodden path. Seen from close to, the swing was no longer black. It was grey, like any other piece of ordinary unpainted wood.

I stood right in the centre, beneath its strong crossbeam.

What, in their last moments, had these people seen? Hangings were, as a rule, carried out early in the morning. From this spot, they would have seen their last sun. And this line of hills and mountains.

Down below to the left, the market was already getting underway. Brightly dressed peasant women were taking earthenware from their carts and laying it out on straw, the morning sun glistening wetly on the glazed jugs and bowls. Then, too, there would probably have been this same market. And to the right, further off among the hills, were flocks of sheep. In tight waves (like the curls of the Shulamite),[3] these flocks were now rolling slowly down the green slope, and shepherds in furs were leaning on long crooks straight out of the Bible. A blessed silence. They, too, would have heard this silence.

It would all have been utterly simple and routine. People would have led someone up here, then stood them exactly where I was now standing myself. One of the shepherds might have looked this way, shielding his eyes with the palm of his hand, and wondered what was going on up above him.

One of those hanged here had been Ksenya G, the famous anarchist.[4] Bold, merry, young, beautiful—always chic, and the companion of Mamont Dalsky.[5] Back in the days of revolutionary fever, many of my friends had gone out carousing in the company of these two and their lively, entertaining fellow-anarchists. And they all, without exception, had struck us as fakes and braggarts.

Not one of us had taken them seriously. We had known Mamont's colourful persona too well and too long to believe in the sincerity of his political convictions. It was posturing, hot air, a hired costume, the greasepaint of a tragic villain. Intriguing and irresponsible. Onstage Mamont had, throughout his career, played Edmund Kean in the play by Alexandre Dumas; off stage he had played not only Kean but also the "genius" and the "libertine" of the play's title. But Mamont had died (oh, the little ironies of fate!) because of an act of old-fashioned courtesy. Standing on the running board of a tram, he had stepped back to make room for a lady. He lost his footing and fell beneath the wheels. And several months later his companion, merry, chic Ksenya G, had stood here, in this very spot, smoking her last cigarette and screwing her eyes up as she looked at her last sun. Then she had flicked away the cigarette butt—and calmly thrown the stiff noose around her neck.

Sunlight playing on the glazed earthenware in the bazaar. Brightly dressed women, milling about by the carts. Further away—shepherds moving slowly down the steep green slopes, leaning on their staffs. And probably, a faint ringing, as there always is in the mountain silence. And the silence was blessed.

People often complain that a writer has botched the last pages of a novel, that the ending is somehow crumpled, too abrupt.

I understand now that a writer involuntarily creates in the image and likeness of fate itself. All endings are hurried, compressed, broken off.

When a man has died, we all like to think that there was a great deal he could still have done.

When a chapter of life has died, we all think that it could have somehow developed and unfolded further, that its conclusion is unnaturally compressed and broken off. The events that conclude such chapters of life seem tangled and skewed, senseless and without definition.

In its own writings, life keeps to the formulae of old-fashioned novels. We learn from the epilogue that "Irina got married and I have heard tell she is happy. Sergey Nikolaevich was able to forget his troubles through service to society."

All too quick and hurried, all somehow beside the point.

Those last days in Novorossiisk before our contrived, unexpectedly far-fetched departure were equally hurried and uninteresting.

"It'll be difficult to return to Petersburg right now," I was told. "Go abroad for a while. Come spring you'll be back in the motherland."

"Spring", "motherland"—what wonderful words…

Spring is the resurrection of life. Come spring I'd be back again.

Our last hours on the quayside, beside the steamer *The Grand Duke Alexander Mikhailovich*.[6]

Hustle, bustle, much whispering. The strange whispering that, along with a constant looking back over the shoulder, had accompanied all our arrivals and departures as we slid down the map, down the huge green map across which, slantwise, was written: "The Russian Empire".

Yes, everyone is whispering; everyone is looking back over their shoulder. Everyone is frightened, constantly frightened, and not until their dying day will they find peace, will they come to their senses. Amen.

The steamer shudders, whipping up white foam with its propeller, spreading black smoke over the shoreline.

And slowly, softly, the land slips away from us.

Don't look at it. You must look ahead, into the wide, free expanse of blue.

But somehow the head turns back. Eyes are opening wide and they keep looking, looking…

And everyone is silent. Except for one woman. From the lower deck comes the sound of long, obstinate wails, interspersed with words of lament.

Where have I heard such wails before? Yes. I remember. During the first year of the war. A grey-haired old woman was being taken down the street in a horse-drawn cab. Her hat had slipped back onto the nape of her neck. Her yellow cheeks were thin and drawn. Her toothless, black mouth was hanging open, crying out in a long tearless wail: "A-a-a-a-a!" Probably embarrassed by the disgraceful behaviour of his passenger, the driver was urging his poor horse forward, whipping her on.

Yes, my good man, you didn't think enough about whom you were picking up in your cab. And now you're stuck with this old woman. A terrible, black, tearless wail. A last wail. Over all of Russia, the whole of Russia… No stopping now…

The steamer shudders, spreading black smoke.

With my eyes now open so wide that the cold penetrates deep into them, I keep on looking. And I shall not move away. I've broken my vow, I've looked back. And, like Lot's wife, I am frozen. I have turned into a pillar of salt forever, and I shall forever go on looking, seeing my own land slip softly, slowly away from me.

1930

TRANSLATED BY ROBERT AND ELIZABETH CHANDLER
WITH ANNE MARIE JACKSON AND IRINA STEINBERG

BEFORE A MAP OF RUSSIA

In a strange house, in a faraway land,
her portrait hangs on the wall;
she herself is dying like a beggar woman,
lying on straw, in pain that can't be told.

But here she looks as she always did look—
she is young, rich, and draped
in the luxurious green cloak
in which she was always portrayed.

I gaze at your countenance as if at an icon…
"Blessed be your name, slaughtered Rus!"
I quietly touch your cloak with one hand;
and with that same hand make the sign of the cross.

FIRST PUBLISHED, IN A LONGER VERSION, IN
1925; THIS VERSION PUBLISHED IN 1953
TRANSLATED BY ROBERT AND ELIZABETH CHANDLER

ISTANBUL (*from* "ISTANBUL AND SUN")

THEN CROSS THE BRIDGE into the oldest part of the city, called Istanbul.

Here it is untouched: no Europeans, no moneychangers.

Turn to the right and go deeper into the old bazaar to the street of the *kitapçı*—religious booksellers.

Their small wooden shops are strewn with scraps of mouldy pages from the Koran. The grimy walls of their little shacks are decorated with sayings of Muhammad written on time-yellowed paper and placed in chipped frames. A low table or nothing more than an overturned wooden crate, a cracked porcelain cup with a brush, and a mortar and pestle for grinding powder dyes—that's the entire shop.

The bookseller is almost always old, bearded, wearing a turban and glasses.

He sits on a very low bench—so low he is almost squatting—and copies the Koran.

You can enter the shack and stand silently for a long time—you could stand there for two hours—and the old man won't interrupt his work and won't say a word to you. But if you speak to him and turn out to be knowledgeable about the Eastern art of calligraphy, he will come to life. He will show you a curlicue on a yellowed scrap of an old Koran, clicking his tongue and wagging his head with excitement.

In the East the manuscript plays the role of a painting. A simple page with a short saying lightly touched by gilding and paint might have far greater value than an entire handwritten Koran. I once saw a page like that sell for several hundred lira.

Experts in Eastern calligraphy can recognize a seemingly endless number of handwriting and styles. There is the Persian style, the Arabic style, the new style and simply individual styles.

A copier works on his text for years. He writes with a fine wooden pen that he sharpens every five to ten handwritten lines. In a fine manuscript the place where the copier stops to sharpen his pen must not be noticeable. The pressure, the width of each line, the size of each tail of a letter and every full stop—everything must be identical.

The copier then passes the work on to an artist, who decorates it with gold, paints every full stop—each one unique—and divides one chapter from another with colourful ornamentation: colours, arabesques, stars, fine, lacy cross-hatching. The borders are decorated by tulips that are unique in colour, style and form on each page.

But no matter how marvellous and artistic the drawings are, at the end the Koran is signed only by the copier, because he is considered the main artist. A work signed by one of these legendary artists is considered a great treasure, a precious object of pride to be preserved and admired.

Almost all the bookstalls are next to one another by the old bazaar, where in the labyrinth of the first galleries you can find vendors of Eastern perfumes. There aren't many of them, and they don't have much, since Arabia is cut off from the world right now and they are unable to obtain ambergris, myrrh and musk.

A scent seller will reluctantly give you a few drops of ambergris—dark, thick, heavy ambergris from Mecca, a scent that is nearly sacred. They also have jasmine and mimosa, which are also thick, mixed with olive oil. These are not perfumes but scented oils of the sort that in biblical times were used to massage the skin of the beauteous Judith, the gentle Tamar and the proud Jezebel and all the others who were leading and being led astray, captivating and being captivated.

Ambergris is used to make incense to be used in cassolettes and medicinal pellets for old sultans.

Sultan Abdul Hamid had a unique Arab specialist who "presided over the making of marvellous scents". He alone knew how to make ambergris to be burnt like incense or to be slathered on skin like oil—or to give other pleasures to the client.

"Ambergris! Ambergris!" the trader says, lowering his voice as he pronounces the name of this most valuable of fragrances. His hand trembles as he drips—carefully and precisely—each heavy, dark droplet from his bottle into the buyer's small, faceted flacon.

"Ambergris from Mecca!"

Swarthy hands gather the ambergris as someone sings shimmering vocals. Slow-moving camels rock it gently on their humped backs as they walk under the desert sun. A hot wind snatches up puffs of scent, wafting them away, imbuing the silver crystal sand with the aroma of ambergris as a sleepy lion catches the scent, lazily stretches his front paws, silently rises from under his rock and watches the caravan pass, his narrow slits of eyes glinting.

"Ambergris from Mecca!"

"Two drams."

Now it's yours, that ambergris.

Thirty thick, heavy drops. The blood of the Kaaba, the stone of Muhammad.

*

Sellers of prayer beads always have many customers. Foreigners like to buy them as souvenirs.

A strand has either 33 or 99 beads. They are made of fragrant sandalwood, amber that is sweetly slippery between the fingers—crystal beads for fops, or brightly coloured beads for those who don't understand a thing about them.

A true person of the East must have prayer beads. They give idle hands something to do and prevent superfluous gesturing.

The beads vary in size, from very large—almost the size of a pigeon egg—to very small, the size of a grape seed.

For obscure reasons of court politics, Sultan Selim murdered all his infant children one by one. He now rests in a magnificent mosque, surrounded like a true patriarch by all his progeny in 40 little caskets. This sultan had prayer beads that weighed nearly 36 pounds, each bead the size of an orange.

Cigarette holders are also sold here—refined work with inlays for those who understand their worth and Austrian fakes for foreigners.

Here in the East a smoker chooses a cigarette holder not only for its style and the quality of the work, but primarily for the sensation when he places it to his lips. Silky, caressing amber is the finest material and highly valued. Amber cigarette holders are made with large, rounded facets. A smoker does not put it in his mouth—he pulls out the smoke with quick, delicate kisses.

After wandering through the bazaar, shoppers go for tea to the *çaycı*—tea-seller—Old Mersin. Everyone calls him mad because he is obsessively fastidious.

In Mersin's small stall everything shines, from the freshly painted walls and newly varnished tables and chairs to two enormous samovars that are clean as a whistle and spoons scrubbed until they gleam.

Mersin pours the tea and serves it himself, first holding up each glass of tea in the light and carefully examining it. If he sees a tea leaf or a bit of dust in a glass, he dumps it all out and pours fresh tea.

If one of his guests spills or drips tea on the table, Mersin stares severely at the guilty party. He has been known to scold.

Mersin's stall—between two other tea houses that have dirty glasses, leftover scraps of food on wet tables, smoky samovars green with patina and broken stools—does indeed make an odd impression, and you do begin to wonder if Mersin is mad.

In the evenings Istanbul poets gather in the tea-seller's stall. They drink tea, make fun of mad Mersin and recite their poems.

Then you walk on along narrow little streets with braziers roasting pistachios, shashlik,[1] *leblebi*—chickpeas—and sheep heads. The sheep heads with torn skin and bared teeth are specially loved by the local gourmands. There are shops windows filled with pyramids of these skulls—a horrible image reminiscent of the famous painting by Vereshchagin, *The Apotheosis of War*.[2] Roasted chickpeas are the favourite treat, and amusing little songs are written about the *leblebi* sellers.

"For one of your kisses," a *leblebi* vendor sings, "I'd toss all my chickpeas onto the street."

"Why would you do that?" the beautiful girl replies. "I'd rather eat them and not give you a kiss."

And so she did.

In little taverns where all the food is set right out on the street to tempt passers-by, dignified bearded mullahs eat with their hands—everything, even soup. They dunk bread into the soup, first tearing it with a ceremonial biblical gesture, fingers spread wide, and then circle it up to their lips. The tavern keeper puts everything on the plates with his hands, too, and in his haste to serve he doesn't wipe them clean, one moment thrusting them into sheep heads and the next into boiled fish. By the end of the day the flavours of all these dishes blend together into a unique and queer delicacy.

The mullahs and other esteemed diners chew their meals slowly and wordlessly, staring at the place where the wall meets the ceiling. They don't eat, they partake of a repast. They have a ritual feast. Like Abraham at table with the three angels under the Oak of Mamre.[3]

Then onward, deeper into these narrow little streets... streets that meander, circle around and perhaps never lead you back to the place you came from.

This real Istanbul is too spicy, too vibrant, too loud and too sweet. But once you've had a taste of it, all that is not Istanbul will seem too insipid, too dull, too quiet...

Someone who had lived here for many years once told me, "I went home and was happy. But in my happiness, every evening when I was by myself, I would turn my face to the East and look off to where Istanbul was. I could not forget."

Istanbul is the first door to the East—dreary and cheerful, black and vibrant—the true East. The door is covered with European mildew and water stains, and you struggle to slowly wrench it open. But once you open it, you'll never shut it again.

BERLIN, 1921

TRANSLATED BY MICHELE A. BERDY

PART FOUR
Russian Paris

"*Ke fer?*" (Que Faire?)—a virtuoso evocation of the Russians' sense of alienation in Paris—was published in April 1920, in the first issue of *The Latest News*. The swiftness with which Teffi distilled the essential features of the topsy-turvy émigré world is remarkable. *The Latest News* proved to be the most important and long-lived of the émigré newspapers and Teffi contributed regularly to it until its closure in 1940.

The first lines of "*Que Faire?*" are dense with reversals of many kinds. *What Is to Be Done?* (1863) is the title of a famous revolutionary novel by Nikolay Chernyshevsky—a novel that inspired Lenin; Teffi not only puts this slogan into the mouth of a tsarist general but also reverses its meaning. Exiled thanks to the revolution Chernyshevsky helped bring about, this general—unlike both Chernyshevsky and Lenin—has no idea *what is to be done*. He cannot even make up his mind what language to speak; he begins with two words of French, then tries feebly to russify them, reversing the word order and inserting the syllable "*to*", a colloquial particle that emphasizes the preceding word: "*Ke fer? Fer-to ke?*" According to Teffi's fellow satirist Don-Aminado, these five syllables became "a proverb, a constant refrain of émigré life…"[1]

In "Nostalgia", published a month after "Que faire?", Teffi wrote, "We don't believe in anything. We don't expect anything. We don't want anything. We've died. We were afraid of a Bolshevik death—and we've met our death here." Teffi does not pull her punches. Characteristically, though, she then encourages her readers to make the best of things, writing only a few lines later, "But there is so much to be done. We must save ourselves and save others. Though there is so little will and so little strength left to us."[2]

"A Little Fairy Tale" is a mini-encyclopedia of Russian folklore, filtered through two lenses: first, through experience of the early Soviet Union, then that of a bewildered émigré. Though little known, it is one of her wittiest and most unusual stories.

From March 1922 until August 1923, Teffi lived in Germany; and for a year following the German invasion in 1940, in the south of France. Teffi spent the rest of her life in Paris. During most of those thirty years—except when ill and during the war—she published articles or stories at weekly intervals. Making a living was a constant struggle and there were times, especially towards the end of her life, when she depended on gifts from admirers and handouts from émigré cultural organizations.

Teffi played a central role in the émigré world—in its concerts, theatrical productions, charity and benefit evenings, literary-philosophical discussion groups, and in the lively and creative Russian Orthodox community. She seems always to have been a voice of good sense and tolerance. Nevertheless, her most precious gift to this world—the weapon with which she tried to "save ourselves and save others"—was her life-giving humour. Her humour is all the more liberating because, rather than denying the ubiquity of cruelty and tragedy, it springs from a penetrating understanding of them. It is a supreme embodiment of quiet courage—of grace under pressure.

QUE FAIRE?

I HEARD TELL OF A RUSSIAN GENERAL, a refugee, who went out onto the Place de la Concorde and looked around. He looked up at the sky and round at the square, the houses, the shops and the colourful, chattering crowd. He scratched the bridge of his nose and said, with feeling:

"All this, ladies and gentlemen, is well and good. Even very well and good, all this. But, well… *que faire?* What is to be done? Fair's fair, but *que* bloody *faire* with it all?"

The general was by way of an appetizer. The meat of the story is still to come…

We—*les russes*, as they call us—live the strangest of lives here, nothing like other people's. We stick together, for example, not like planets by mutual attraction, but by a force quite contrary to the laws of physics—mutual repulsion. Every *lesrusse* hates all the others—hates them just as fervently as the others hate him.

This general antipathy has given rise to several neologisms. Hence, for example, a new grammatical particle, "that-crook", placed before the name of every *lesrusse* anyone mentions: "that-crook Akimenko", "that-crook Petrov", "that-crook Savelyev".

This particle lost its original meaning long ago and now equates to something between the French "le", indicating the gender of the person named, and the Spanish honorific "don": "don Diego", "don José".

You'll hear conversations like this, "Some of us got together at that-crook Velsky's yesterday for a game of bridge. There was that-crook Ivanov, that-crook Gusin, that-crook Popov. Nice crowd." A chat between businessmen might go like this:

"I'd advise you to get that-crook Parchenko in on this deal. Very useful chap."

"But isn't he, er… Can he be trusted?"

"Good Lord, yes! That-crook Parchenko? Pure as the driven snow. Trust him with my life!"

"Wouldn't we be better off with that-crook Kusachenko?"

"Oh no. He's a great deal crookeder."

New arrivals are startled to begin with, even alarmed, by this prefix. "Why a crook? Who said so? Have they got proof? What did he do? Where?"

And they're even more alarmed by the nonchalant reply, "What… Where… Who knows? They call him a crook and that's fine by me."

"But what if he isn't?"

"Get away with you! Why ever wouldn't he be?" And that's right—why wouldn't he?

The *lesrusses* sticking together here by mutual repulsion fall into two distinct categories: those selling Russia and those saving Russia.

The sellers lead a merry life. They frequent theatres, dance the foxtrot, have Russian cooks and invite the saviours of Russia over to share their Russian borsch. Amid all this frivolity, they don't neglect their main occupation, but if you should ask how much they're selling Russia for these days, and with what conditions attached, you're unlikely to get a straight answer.

The saviours are a very different kettle of fish. They're hard at it day and night—constantly on the move, always ensnared in political intrigues and forever denouncing one another.

They rub along quite happily with the sellers and get money from them to save Russia. But they loathe one another with a white-hot passion.

"Did you hear about that-crook Ovechkin? What a snake he's turned out to be! He's selling Tambov."

"Well, I never! Who to?"

"What do you mean 'who to'? To the Chileans."

"What?"

"To the Chileans—that's what!"

"What do the Chileans want with Tambov?"

"What a question! They want a Russian base!"

"But Tambov doesn't belong to Ovechkin. How can he be selling it?"

"I told you, he's a snake. He and that-crook Gavkin played a vile trick on us: Can you imagine, they took—they lured—our young lady over to them with her typewriter, at the very moment when we should have been supporting the government of Ust-Sysolsk."

"Does Ust-Sysolsk have a government?"

"Did have. But not for long, it seems. There was a lieutenant colonel—can't remember his name—who proclaimed himself its government. He managed to hold out for a day and a half. If we'd come to his aid in time, we could have saved the situation. But how can you get anywhere without a typewriter? That's how we let the whole of Russia slip through our fingers. And all because of him—because of that-crook Ovechkin. And what about that-crook Korobkin—have you heard? That's pretty rich, too. He accredited himself as ambassador to Japan."

"Who appointed him?"

"No one knows. He claims it was some kind of government of Tiraspol Junction station. That existed for all of fifteen or twenty minutes… through some misunderstanding. Then it got embarrassed and dissolved itself. But that Korobkin, he didn't waste a moment—in those fifteen minutes he managed to wangle the whole thing."

"But does anyone recognize him?"

"Oh, he doesn't mind about that. All he wanted out of it was a visa—that's why he accredited himself. It's a disgrace!"

"But did you hear the latest news? They say Bakhmach has been taken!"

"Who by?"

"No one knows."

"Who from?"

"We don't know that either. It's a disgrace!"

"Where on earth did you find all this out?"

"On the radio. We get the Ukraine Telegraft and listen to Bullshevik Broadcasting from Moscow—and now we've got our own pan-European station, Eurogarble News!"

"What does Paris make of it?"

"Paris? We all know Paris won't lift a finger. Like dogs in their cosy French manger! Makes no difference to them."

"Now tell me—does anyone understand any of this?"

"Not really. You must know what Tiutchev said all those years ago: 'You cannot understand Russia with your mind.'[1] And since the human body has no other organ of understanding, all we can do is throw up our hands in despair. They say one of our public figures was starting to understand with his stomach. So they sent him packing."

"Hmm…"

"Hmm…"

So anyway… this general looked around and said, with feeling, "All this, ladies and gentlemen, is well and good. Even very well and good. But *que faire?* Fair's fair, but *que* bloody *faire?*"

Que indeed.

PARIS, 1920
TRANSLATED BY CLARE KITSON

SUBTLY WORDED

LETTERS BEGAN TO APPEAR from the Soviet Union. More and more often. Strange letters.

The kind of letter that lends strength and credence to the rumour that everyone in the Soviet Union has gone crazy. Journalists and public figures trying to draw conclusions from these letters about the economic and political situation in Russia—or even just everyday life there—got caught in such dense thickets of nonsense as to arouse scepticism even among those whose faith in the infinite nature of Russia's potential was usually unshakeable.

Several such letters have come my way.

One of them, addressed to a lawyer by his doctor brother, began with the words: *Dear Daughter!*

"Ivan Andreyevich, how come you've ended up as the daughter of your own brother?"

"I've no idea. I'm scared to think."

The letter contained the following news: *Everything's splendid here. Anyuta has died from a strong appetite…*

"He must mean appendicitis," I guessed.

And the whole Vankov family have also died from appetite.

"Hmm, something's not right."

Pyotr Ivanovich has been leading a secluded life for four months now. Koromyslov began leading a secluded life eleven months ago. His fate is unknown.

Misha Petrov led a secluded life for only two days, then there was a careless incident with a firearm he happened to be standing in front of. Everyone feels awfully delighted.

"Dear God! What is all this? They're not people but beasts. A man perishes in an unfortunate accident and they feel delighted!"

We went round to your apartment. There's a lot of air there now…

"What on earth! What's that meant to mean?"

"I'm scared to think. I don't want to know."

The letter finished with the words: *I write little because I want to continue to mix with society and not to lead a secluded life.*

This letter weighed on me for a long time.

"What a tragedy," I said to people I knew. "The brother of our Ivan Andreyevich has lost his mind. He calls Ivan Andreyevich his daughter, and he writes such nonsense I'd be embarrassed to repeat it."

I felt very sorry for the poor fellow. He was a good man.

Then I heard there was some Frenchman offering to take a letter right into Petrograd.

Ivan Andreyevich was delighted. I decided to add a few words too. Maybe the man wasn't yet quite off his rocker; maybe he'd understand a few simple words.

Ivan Andreyevich and I agreed to compose the letter together. So it would be clear and simple and not too much for a mind whose powers were failing.

We wrote:

Dear Volodya!

We received your letter. What a pity everything is so terrible for you. Is it true that people have now begun eating human flesh? How horrific! What's got into you? They say your death rate is terribly high. All this worries us like crazy. Life's going well for me. If only you were here, too, everything would be quite wonderful. I've married a Frenchwoman and I'm awfully happy.

Your brother Ivan.

At the end of the letter I added:

My warmest greetings to all of you,

Teffi.

The letter was ready when a mutual friend dropped in, a worldly-wise and experienced barrister.

Learning what we had been doing, he looked very thoughtful and said in a serious tone, "But did you write the letter correctly?"

"Er, what do you mean, 'correctly'?"

"I'm asking if you can guarantee that your correspondent will not be arrested and shot because of this letter of yours."

"Heavens! What do you mean? It just says the simplest things, nothing dangerous."

"May I have a quick look?"

"Please do. There's nothing secret."

He took the letter. Read it. Sighed.

"Just as I thought. A firing squad within twenty-four hours. That's what happens."

"For the love of God! What's wrong with the letter?"

"Everything. Every sentence. First, you should have written as a woman. Otherwise, your brother will be arrested as the brother of a man who has evaded military conscription. Second, you shouldn't mention having received a letter, since correspondence is forbidden. And then you shouldn't let on that you understand how awful things are there."

"But then what should I do? What should I write?"

"Allow me. I'll reword your letter in the appropriate style. Don't worry—they'll understand."

"All right then. Reword it."

The barrister did a little writing, a little crossing out, then read out the following:

Dear Volodya!

I didn't receive your letter. How good that everything is going so well for you. Is it true that now people have stopped eating human flesh? How truly delightful! What's got into you? They say your birth rate is terribly high. All this calms us like crazy. Life's going badly for me. If only you were here, too, everything would be quite terrible. I've married a Frenchman and I'm awfully unhappy.

Your sister Ivan.

The postscript:

To hell with the lot of you.

Teffi.

"There," said the barrister, grimly admiring his composition and adding commas in appropriate places. "Now the letter can be sent with no risk at all. You're safe and sound, and the recipient will remain alive. And the letter will reach him. Everything in order and subtly worded."

"I'm just worried about the postscript," I remarked timidly. "It does somehow seem a bit rude."

"That's as it should be. We don't want people getting themselves shot because of you and your endearments."

"All this is quite brilliant," Ivan Andreyevich said with a sigh. "The letter and everything. But then what are people there going to think of us? After all, the letter is, if you don't mind my saying so, idiotic."

"It's not idiotic, it's subtle. And even if they do think we've become idiots, who cares? At least they'll still be alive. Not everyone today can boast of having living relatives."

"But what if it frightens them?"

"Well, if you're scared of wolves, don't go into the forest. It's no good being frightened if you want to receive letters."

The letter was sent.

Lord, have mercy on us. Lord, save and preserve us.

PARIS, 3 MAY 1920

TRANSLATED BY ROBERT AND ELIZABETH CHANDLER

A LITTLE FAIRY TALE

Everyone was busy at home and Grisha was allowed to go out for a walk on his own. But only on one condition: that he didn't go too far into the forest. He didn't speak French well and he had been at this French dacha for only three days. How would he be able to ask anyone the way if he got lost? It was best to be careful.

And so, on this condition, he was allowed out.

But Grisha was not a particularly obedient boy, and he always thought he knew better than anyone else what he should and shouldn't do.

And so, when he came to the first trees, he calmly turned off the path and went straight into the densest part of the forest.

The trees grew close together. And between them, twining around the trunks, were thick brambles. There were moments when Grisha found it hard to fight his way through.

He had eaten his fill of blackberries, and he had ripped his stockings and torn all his clothes very badly. He was beginning to wonder how to get back to the path when he realized that, to his right, the forest seemed to be thinning out a little. Yes, he could see more light over there. It must be the way back to the path.

He struggled through the undergrowth and came out into the open.

But instead of getting back to the path, he found himself in a small glade.

In the middle of this glade was an old moss-covered tree stump. Beside it flowed a small gurgling brook, half-hidden by forget-me-nots.

Grisha felt tired. He sat down on the grass, leaned back against a little mound and even closed his eyes.

"First I'll have a proper rest," he said to himself. "Then I'll find my way back to the path. What's the hurry? When I get back, I'll just get a caning because of my stockings and the state of my clothes and because why did you have to go into the forest when we told you not to?"

Grisha closed his eyes.

A cricket in the grass sang, "Grrrree-eesh! Grrrree-eesh!"

A bee buzzed by. It was as if someone had twanged a string: "Dzzz-oon."

From somewhere in the bushes, a bird asked, "Soo-oon? Soo-oon?"

And then, as if imitating its own song, it repeated, "Oo-oon? Oo-oon?"

And then, articulating the words with absolute clarity, some kind of pipe or flute sang out:

Deep, deep in the forest,
Between blue forget-me-nots,
I'll catch you on my hook,
Hook you on my line.
And soon, stranger, soon
You'll be dancing to my pipe,
Dancing to my tune.

This surprised Grisha, but by then he was feeling too drowsy even to open his eyes.

Then there seemed to be someone laughing. And then a loud click as something landed smack in the middle of Grisha's forehead.

A hazelnut!

A fresh, green hazelnut, still wrapped in its outer leaves.

Grisha looked round—but no one was there.

This was getting stranger and stranger. Where had the hazelnut come from? There was nothing near him except a tree stump, forget-me-nots and dense brambles.

He stretched, then closed his eyes again.

Bang!

Another hazelnut, also smack in the middle of his forehead. This time it really hurt.

Grisha leaped to his feet. He turned round. Looking at him out of the tree stump were two quick, bright eyes. They were gleaming; it was as if they were laughing. Grisha looked more closely. There, hiding inside the tree stump, was a very small man.

He was a strange little man—entirely naked. He looked sunburnt, brown all over. His legs were shaggy, as if he were wearing thick woollen stockings and had pulled them up above his knees. He had thick lips and two tufts of hair sticking up over his forehead. He was looking straight at Grisha, and it seemed as if he might burst into laughter any moment. He seemed to be shaking all inside him. And it was almost impossible to look at this little man without laughing oneself. Grisha could feel a tickling in his throat, and his legs were starting to twitch.

Not taking his eyes off Grisha, the little man suddenly put a small green pipe to his lips. And the pipe began to sing. It sang the following words:

The bear, the goat and her kids,
The vixen and her cubs
The wolf and the blind mole—
Caught now on my hook,
Hooked now on my line.
And soon, stranger, soon
You'll be dancing too,
Pirouetting to my pipe,
Dancing to my tune.

Grisha was astonished. "Are you Russian?" he asked.

The little man laughed.

"You'll be dancing too!"

"So you're Russian, are you?"

The little man removed the pipe from his lips.

"I'm not Russian," he said. "I'm internashional."

This annoyed Grisha. "You're making fun of me. We've been taught every nation in the world—and there isn't any nation called internashional!"

But the little man didn't take offence. He didn't seem in the least bothered by Grisha's reply. He just narrowed his eyes and thought for a moment. "So you're Russian, are you?" he said. "Excellent. You can do me a great service, and in return I'll show you the way out of the forest."

"All right," said Grisha. "What you want me to do?"

The little man thought, scratched one of his feet against the other and said, "A relative of mine's come on a visit. From Russia. She's a refugee. Heaven knows what she's after, I can't make head or tail of anything she says. It's a nightmare. You come along and have a word with her! Maybe the two of you will be able to understand each other."

The little man led Grisha through the forest. Anyone would have thought he was walking through his own apartment. He knew every twist and turn of the way. He knew which bough to slip underneath, which tree stump to walk round, which bush marked a fork to the left or the right.

After maybe a long time—or maybe a short time—the little man led Grisha into a dense hazel thicket. He parted the branches. Grisha saw an ant hill. And sitting on top of this ant hill was an old woman. Her hair was dishevelled and she was dressed in rags. Her fingers ended in claws, like the claws of a crow, and her face was all hidden behind a great mat of hair.

Grisha looked at the woman, and somehow he felt scared.

He did not move. He did not speak.

The old woman shook her hair. All of a sudden, like the wind in a chimney, she boomed out: "Seems I can smell the smell of a Russian!"

She parted her great mat of hair. Now he could see her big, green eyes, her hooked nose and the yellow fang jutting out of her mouth.

Grisha shook from head to toe and howled, "Baba Yaga!"[1]

He wanted to run away, but terror rooted him to the spot.

But Yaga was smiling, her yellow fang wobbling about.

"Good day," she said, "my fine warrior! You're lucky I've lost my appetite or I'd have you for supper. Why are you gawking at me like that? I'm in an extremely difficult position here, and there isn't even anyone I can have a moan to. This here shyster doesn't understand a thing I say." Yaga pointed one thumb over her shoulder, towards the little man who had brought Grisha there, and spat on the ground. "And everything I owned has gone to the winds. The government even requisitioned my copper mortar. If it weren't for my broomstick, I'd never have got away at all.

I'm just grateful for old Leshy! He serves at that Enlightenment Commissariat of theirs and he managed to sort me out a visa."[2]

Yaga hunched up in despair, resting her cheek on her bony leg.

"Our whole clan's been liquidated. Kaput! Done away with! They've taken Koshchey the Deathless off to London—Europe needed living proof that even under the new regime not everybody kicks the bucket! Tom Thumb, the little slyboots, has wormed his way into counterespionage. Little Humpbacked Horse got eaten in Moscow by people who were fed up with fasting.[3] And Sleeping Beauty's on the staff of the Council of People's Commissars;[4] she's manning the telephone. As for the bog devils, they've joined a choir, they sing in the new-style churches. Yes, nowadays bride and groom carouse and say their marriage vows beneath a New Year tree. And the bogles sing for them—well, everyone has to make a living somehow. And as for Zmey Gorynych[5]—tough as they come, but not even he could resist temptation. He signed up with the Cheka[6] to supervise the disposal of dead bones. Kikimora's working in the field of State aesthetics.[7] As for the poor werewolf—he's snuffed it. He'd become a quick-change artist—he was turning his coat twenty times a minute—and the public still wasn't satisfied. He said he couldn't keep up—and then he just keeled over."

Baba Yaga began to cry.

"I'm unhappy; I'm in a bad way. What am I going to do? There isn't even going to be any proper snow here. How am I going to whirl up a whirlwind? How can I sweep over my tracks with a broom? All this is going to be the end of me, it's clear as daylight."

Baba Yaga was weeping, sobbing and sobbing. Grisha was still frightened, but he felt sorry for Baba Yaga; he could even feel his nose starting to prickle.

Yaga wiped away her tears with a burdock leaf and said to Grisha, "You go home, my fine warrior. Go your own way. I haven't even got anything here I could roast you in. There are no proper stoves anywhere. They seem to have installed some kind of central heating in this forest of theirs—damn them!"

Grisha turned round. The strange little man was nodding to him from behind a bush.

"All right? Could you understand what she said?"

"Yes."

"Hmm. I couldn't understand a word myself."

The little man grabbed Grisha by the hand and whirled him back through the forest. Together they ran and span through the trees—through bushes, over stumps and jagged roots. The little man was singing and laughing:

> I caught you on my hook,
> By a forest brook,
> And you were dancing too,
> Dancing to my tune.

He span Grisha round like a top, gave him a shove in the back and was gone. And then, somewhere far away in the forest there was a hoot and the sound of something rolling over.

Grisha looked round. He could see familiar bushes—and, beyond them, the path back to the dachas.

He plodded back.

At home he got it in the neck—for his ripped stockings, for his filthy clothes, and because why did he have to go into the forest at all?

And above all—for telling such a pack of lies.

There is, evidently, no justice in the world.

PARIS, 1923

TRANSLATED BY ROBERT AND ELIZABETH CHANDLER

A SMALL TOWN

It wasn't a big town—about 40,000 people, one church and a disproportionate number of taverns.

A river flowed through the centre of the town. In ancient times, it was called the Sequanne. Later—the Seine. And when the small town was founded, its inhabitants began to call it our "little Neva".[1] But they still half-remembered the old name and would sometimes grumble, "Neva much joy on the Seine."

Everyone lived close together—either in Passy or on the Reevgosh.[2] Their occupations were varied. Most of the young worked in transport—as cab drivers. People of mature years kept taverns or worked in these taverns: the blondes dressed as Ukrainians, the brunettes as gypsies, Georgians or Armenians.

The women made hats and ran up dresses for one another. The men ran up debts.

As well as men and women, there were ministers and generals. Only a few of these worked as cab drivers; their occupation was mostly debts and memoirs.

These memoirs were written to glorify the name of the writer and to heap shame on his comrades-in-arms. The memoirs differed insofar as some were typed and others written by hand.

Life was very monotonous.

Now and again, some little theatre would open. There would be dancing clocks and plates that came to life. The citizens demanded free tickets but showed little enthusiasm for the performances. The management handed out free tickets, then quietly passed away to the accompaniment of the public's triumphant abuse.

The town also had its own newspaper. Everyone expected to receive this for free too, but the newspaper stood up for itself. Unbowed, it lived on.

People took little interest in public affairs. They were more ready to gather together in the name of Russian borsch—but only in small groups, because they all hated one another so fiercely that there was no getting twenty people together without ten of them being sworn enemies of the other ten. Or immediately turning into their sworn enemies.

The small town was oddly situated. It was surrounded not by fields, forests or valleys but by the streets of the world's most dazzling capital, with wonderful theatres, museums and art galleries. But the town's inhabitants did not mix with those of the capital nor did they take the opportunity to enjoy the fruits of a foreign culture. They had their own little shops. And they seldom visited the museums and galleries. They didn't have time—and anyway, why bother? "No, not for the likes of us..."

At first, the inhabitants of the capital looked at the town dwellers with interest. They studied their customs, their art and their way of life, just as they had once studied the cultural world of the Aztecs.

A dying tribe... Descendants of those great and glorious people whom... to whom... in whom humanity takes such pride.

Then this interest faded.

The town dwellers made fairly good cab drivers and embroiderers. Their dances were amusing and their music quite entertaining...

They spoke a strange patois, though philologists found it easy enough to detect Slavic roots.

The town dwellers loved it when one of their tribe turned out to be a thief, a con man or a traitor. They also loved curd cheese and long telephone conversations.

They never laughed and were full of bitterness.

PARIS, 1923

TRANSLATED BY ROBERT AND ELIZABETH CHANDLER

HOW I LIVE AND WORK

MANY PEOPLE find it surprising that I live somewhere so busy, right opposite Montparnasse station. But I like it. I adore Paris. I like to hear it here beside me—knocking, honking, ringing and breathing. Sometimes, at dawn, a lorry rumbles past beneath my window so loud and so close that it seems to be coming straight through my room, and I draw up my legs in my sleep so they won't be run over. And then what wakes me an hour or two later is Paris itself—dear, elegant, beautiful Paris. Far better than being woken by some bewhiskered old crone of a concierge, with eyes like cockroaches.

Many people ask if it's possible for a small *pension* to provide one with complete comfort. To which I modestly reply, "Well, I wouldn't say quite complete."

Is it this little table you're looking at? Yes, I know it's very small, but there's nothing it doesn't do. It's a writing table, a dining table, a dressing table and a sewing table. It's only three and a half feet across, but on it I have an inkwell, some writing paper, my face powder, some envelopes, my sewing box, a cup of milk, some flowers, a Bible, sweets, manuscripts and some bottles of scent. In layers, like geological strata. The Augean table. Remember how Hercules had to clean the Augean stables?[1] Well, if Augeas's stables were in such a state, what do you think his writing table would have been like? Probably just like mine. So, how do I write? I put the cup of milk, the Bible and the bottles of scent on the bed, while the sewing box falls of its own accord onto the floor. I need to keep everything essential close at hand—and anyway there's nowhere else to put anything. Though I suppose the flowers could go into the cupboard.

The Bible takes up a quarter of the table, but I need it because Professor Vysheslavtsev, whose outstanding lectures I attend on Mondays (and I recommend everyone else to do the same), often refers to the Epistles of Paul.[2]

So I need to consult the Bible.

Sometimes there are landslides on my table. Everything slips sideways and hangs over the edge. And then it takes only the slightest disturbance of the air (mountaineers will know what I mean); it takes only the opening of a window or the postman knocking at the door—and an entire avalanche roars and crashes to the floor. Sometimes I then discover long-lost items—things I've replaced long ago: gloves, a volume of Proust, a theatre ticket from last summer, an unsent letter (and there I was, impatiently waiting for an answer!), a flower from a ball gown… Sometimes this excites a kind of scientific interest in me, as if I were a palaeontologist who has happened upon the bone of a mammoth. To which era should I assign this glove or page of manuscript?

Worst of all are flowers; if there's a landslide, they create a flood. If someone gives me flowers, they are always taken aback by my look of sudden anxiety.

As for domestic animals, I have only a bead snake and a small monster—a varnished cedar cone standing on little paws. It brings me luck.

While we're on the theme of domesticity and creature comforts, I did also once have a venetian blind. But there wasn't room for it; if I'd hung on to it, it could have created mayhem.

I'm not planning to write anything at all big. I think you'll understand why.

We must wait for a big table. And if we wait in vain—*tant pis.*[3]

PARIS, 1926

TRANSLATED BY ROBERT AND ELIZABETH CHANDLER

from "THE VIOLET NOTEBOOK"

One wonders about our refugee children, with no memories of the old Russia. What kind of image do they have of her?

First, some kind of perpetual borsch. Borsch with kasha, borsch with fatback, borsch with cheese pastries, borsch with ham. With whatever was to hand in that province.

In these provinces there were also towns and landscapes. The towns were the homes of provincial governors. The landscapes were the homes of peasants.

The provincial governors were most gracious and they smiled welcomingly.

The peasants were the talented Russian people. They sang the songs of the Russian people and ate the dishes of the Russian people.

As well as governors and peasants, there were various regiments, in which there were officers. The wives of these officers, around 80,000 of them, surged out during the Revolution into Europe and America.

The fourth estate in Russia was composed of Dostoevsky's demons in two volumes. There were only two volumes of them, but they were still able to corrupt minds and deprave morals.[1]

Then came an explosion. The governors were flung out. Strange though it may seem, half of Dostoevsky's demons were flung out too. Into Europe.

"So where have your intrigues got you, unclean spirits?"

The governors were flung out backwards; they are now writing memoirs.

Dostoevsky's demons were flung out looking forwards; they landed in journals and newspapers.

In foreign lands both governors and demons have forgotten their former squabbles. They address one another in the manner of old chums and drink to their new intimacy. Together they enjoy the borsch of every province.

"So I gave orders for you to be arrested back then, did I?"

"Yes, that's right. We were preparing a bomb for you."

"Must note that in my memoirs. Waiter, *encore de kasha*!"

PARIS, 1927

TRANSLATED BY ROBERT AND ELIZABETH CHANDLER

PART FIVE
Last Years

On 10 June 1940, after the German invasion, Teffi moved first to Angers and then to Biarritz. Initially, she had been reluctant to leave Paris: "I myself didn't want to go […] War and revolution had chased us so much all around the world. But before, it was new and interesting and it stimulated the nerves. Now it was all so familiar and so boring."[1]

In late summer 1941, Teffi returned to Paris, where she remained until her death in October 1952. Her elder daughter Valeria spent most of the war years in London, working for the Polish government in exile; from autumn 1944, she was able to send her mother gifts of food, money and clothing. In her first letter to Valeria after the liberation of Paris, Teffi wrote, "My health, to be honest, is pretty awful. My heart spasms began back in Biarritz. My heart can't cope with exhaustion or agitation. The stupid thing (my heart) needs life to be easy and pleasant. Air raids don't affect it—it is brave—but it can't cope with the troubles and burdens of everyday life. It is old and noble. I'm still young, but it's in its seventies. After almost every spasm I feel terribly weak and need to lie down. Sorry to be depressing, but we need to know the truth about each other."[2]

The post-war years were a bleak time for Teffi and her fellow writers. The Red Army's victory and the left-wing sympathies of the French intelligentsia made the dwindling émigré community seem more of an anomaly than ever. Even Teffi herself and her close friend Ivan Bunin appear to have at least toyed with the possibility of returning to Russia. One of Teffi's reasons for staying in France was a fear that, if she left, she might never be able to see Valeria again. Another was her awareness that, after a brief lull during the four years of the war, the Soviet authorities were once again intensifying their persecution of writers. During an interview in November 1946, she recalled entering the spa town of Piatigorsk during her last days in Russia:

> I saw an enormous placard across the road: "Welcome to the first Soviet Health Resort." The sign was held up by two posts, from which two hanged men were swinging. Now I'm afraid that when I enter the USSR I'll see a placard with the inscription: "Welcome, Comrade Teffi," and Zoshchenko and Akhmatova will be hanging from the supporting poles.[3]

A heart attack in November 1947 led to a long, nearly fatal illness and Teffi's already desperate financial situation was aggravated by her inability—even as she began to recover—to work at her more routine journalism. Her physical weakness, however, did not prevent her from writing some of her most ambitious stories. "And Time Was No More"—a stream-of-consciousness evocation of her thoughts and dreams during her recent illness—is one of several late works in which she addresses such unanswerable questions as the nature of the divine and the origins of evil and of human suffering. In a letter to Bunin, she explained that she couldn't help but write this story—"it sat inside me and gnawed at me".[4]

The story's narrator talks eloquently about a world soul. Her words recall a passage from "On the Unity of Love", a lecture Teffi gave in 1929 to a literary-philosophical discussion group called The Green Lamp. In it she summarized the understandings of one of the sixth-century desert fathers, Abba Dorotheos:

> The universe is a circle. The centre of the circle is God. The radii from this centre to the circumference are the paths of the soul. The closer souls are to one another, the closer to God.
>
> And on that penultimate ascent along the radii of love, along which the souls of the righteous soar in blissful ecstasy—on this ascent, every love is close to every other love. And so the righteous see the soul of a wolf, of a bear, of a flower, and of a grasshopper. They see every soul where there is love. And they are in touch with that soul. There, in that sphere, all dividing walls collapse. All beings reach out along the radii of love. An ecstatic nun with stigmata on her hands, a sinful Sodomite who has washed his clothes clean with his own tears of anguish, an old woman with a wretched geranium, Saint Francis's little brother the hare, God's servants the dandelion and the violet—beings of every kind ascend along the radii of love. There are many ways to the One, to the centre, to God.

In 1951 Teffi sent the manuscript of *My Chronicle*, her collection of memoirs of writers and other public figures, to a Russian-language publishing house in New York. *My Chronicle* was not published as a whole, but the individual memoirs had either already been published or were published separately after Teffi's death. "Ilya Repin" was probably meant to be the book's last chapter; Teffi's words about the sadness of wandering about "the graveyard of my tired memory" would have made a fitting conclusion.

The relationship between comedy and tragedy is a subject Teffi returned to many times. In response to a request from a well-meaning editor for "a few funny little stories" to tell at a benefit he was arranging for her in New York, she wrote in October 1951, "You want a few jolly stories from the life of someone now worn out and mindless. But I'm sure you know that an anecdote is amusing when recounted—but not when it is lived through. A joke you live through is a tragedy. My life has been a joke through and through—i.e., a tragedy through and through." [5]

The letters Teffi wrote during her last years to Bunin and a few other close friends include frequent witticisms about her poverty and ill health. On 19 May 1952, she wrote, "All my contemporaries are dying, but I somehow carry on living. It's as if I'm sitting in the waiting room at the dentist's while he summons his patients in what is obviously the wrong order. It feels awkward to say anything and I just keep sitting there, tired and bad-tempered."[6]

Shortly before Teffi's death, her friend Tamara Panteleimonova brought her some morphine, which allowed her a brief period of freedom from pain. By then, Teffi was finding it difficult to speak. She thanked Tamara in writing, and with her still unfailing wit. On a page of paper torn from a notebook, she wrote, "There is no higher love than that of someone who gives to his brother his own morphine."[7]

Teffi died of heart failure on 6 October 1952.

THE OTHER WORLD

In the summer of 1945, it was rumoured that Teffi had died; one New York journal even published her obituary. Teffi responded with her characteristic wit, publishing the following in the Paris daily newspaper Russian News.

PERHAPS ONE SHOULD BEGIN WITH SOMETHING LIKE THIS:

"Dear Sir, Esteemed Editor,

Allow me, by means of your respected newspaper, to thank all who have had prayers sung for my departed soul, and to offer to all my relatives my condolences with regard to my untimely end. I also thank the authors of my obituaries."

No—too dry. It needs, somehow, to sound more heartfelt. People have, after all, expressed feelings and not begrudged candles. Moreover, I am truly moved. But I'm out of my depth. There is no accepted etiquette in relation to such an unprecedented event—no guidance as to how the genteel deceased should behave.

An appropriate etiquette is sure to evolve soon, since nowadays we all too often meet people whose obituaries we have read and for whose departed souls we have wept and prayed. It's not simply a matter of idle gossip, of someone making up stories for the fun of it. What lies behind this phenomenon is an entirely correct understanding: that for many of us today dying is more natural than living. Can someone weak, elderly and in poor health really be expected to live happily through the winter in an unheated building, on an empty stomach, to the wail of air-raid sirens and the roar of bombs, and in a state of grief and despair for those close to them, for those far away, for humanity and for the world as a whole?

A great poet once wrote:

> Whatever threatens us with doom
> Brings to a mortal heart
> A thrill of ineffable delight. [1]

I do believe the great poet. But then the impending winter without heating is certain to be the death of me—and this brings me no thrill of ineffable delight. Absolutely not—not the least hint of ineffable delight.

What brings ineffable delight, I suppose, is a historical death, a beautiful, inspired death in the name of some ideal, with words on one's lips that will go down in history. But such a death, a death consciously chosen by someone strong in spirit, is a far cry from our own aimless, spineless, abject and impotent whining. And how and why, anyway, are we still alive at all—in this pre-Promethean world, with neither light nor warmth?[2]

"Apparently, so and so has died."

"Yes, we've heard words to that effect. We must offer our condolences. And have prayers sung for his soul."

"Where has this news come from?"

"From London."

"From America."

"From Paris. But is it true?"

"Of course. There have been obituaries. Prayers for the repose of his soul. It must be true."

And then the deceased reads his own obituary. He shakes his head and doesn't know how he's supposed to feel. Should he be grateful—or take offence? After all, being struck off the list of the living is generally seen as offensive and is certainly inconvenient. If the deceased is a person of means, this obituary may give rise to unpleasant family squabbles. His heirs may make awkward demands:

"My dearest uncle, we gave up our apartment, expecting—in view of your death—to move into yours. How can we recover the expenses we have incurred? Might you be able to take it upon yourself…"

It is being rumoured in Russia—and these rumours have been reliably confirmed—that Ivan Bunin has died. Bunin is a member of the Russian Academy of Sciences and a Nobel laureate—our pre-eminent man of letters. A state publishing house has decided to bring out a posthumous edition of his collected works. Posthumous—yet Bunin is alive.[3] A living writer prepares his works for publication himself, perhaps omitting some adolescent verses he now considers rather weak. The position of an author of a posthumous edition is exceedingly awkward. It doesn't matter to a dead author, but a living author—especially one so celebrated, one who will take his place among the classics—finds it most vexing to see his works presented in what to him seems the wrong way. And the publisher, for his part, might well value the author's opinion. How this matter will be resolved, there's no knowing.

Our life today is very strange. Everything about it is strange. People, events, politics, phenomena of every kind. People suddenly go missing; the deceased visit one another. Maybe some of these deceased believe that they really have died and that everything they now see before them, everything they find so astonishing, is indeed the other world, a life beyond the grave, a non-human, everyday life outside the bounds of human logic. And maybe, they really have died. After all, according to the testimony of such experts in mortal matters as Maurice Maeterlinck,[4] people lose consciousness at the moment of death and do not sense the transition to another life. So how can we know that we have not already made that transition?

In some respects, this new other-worldly life is reminiscent of our old life. Yet, when you look more closely, it appears to have lost its axis, lost its logic. But then logic is entirely a matter of human reason—and what does human reason count for in the other world? Everything here is inexplicable. It would, of course, be easier if this new life had no similarities at all to our old life. But we have no say in the matter.

Everyday life in the other world has little to recommend it. In our earthly lives we knew that we all have bodies and—in spite of many attempts of all kinds to prove that animal life, i.e. the life of our bodies, does not deserve our respect—we all understood that we need to show some concern for this animal life. Even the church said, "For no man ever yet hated his own flesh; but nourisheth and cherisheth it."[5] And so we nourished and cherished it. We recognized the human body's right to existence. We thought up special institutions to improve food distribution. States entered into trade agreements. Ministers flew in planes to foreign countries; menus of their breakfasts and dinners were printed in newspapers; and, to a musical accompaniment, their concerned, slightly smiling faces were shown on cinema screens. All this was done in order to support the animal life of the nations to which the breakfasting ministers belonged. Flesh had the right to exist and it demanded our respect and concern.

But here, in this other world, there is no concern for the flesh.

"Coal? You want coal? What eccentrics you are! How can you expect coal when nothing has been resolved yet and we may require coal for a future war?"

"Ah, now we understand. It's needed to finish us off—and we idiots were simply hoping to warm ourselves. Thank God, there are clever people to explain things!"

And we must, finally, understand, that if we *are* in the other world, then our bodies are not our former bodies but astral bodies. All right, let's make that assumption. But in that case, the authorities should be offering us astral coal and astral sugar. An astral body evidently has its own requirements, and these merit consideration. But they are being given no consideration at all, and inhabitants of the other world are having to look after themselves. But how can they? Money doesn't enable one to obtain anything at all, since our money is now worthless. Astral money. Money of no use to anyone but a medieval devil bargaining for the soul of some profligate who has squandered his father's inheritance.

Here in the other world there are attempts to organize entertainment. Even here, people can't do without it. And we do indeed have the cinema. Posters urge us to see newsreels about the former concentration camps. Images, apparently, that will stay with us throughout the whole of our life hereafter.

And so we go to the cinema.

There we are shown corpses. Corpses that have kept their human shape, with bared teeth, with eyes that have rolled back into the skull, with arms and legs twisted in death agony. Corpses of the drowned and corpses of those who have been burned; corpses of those who have been hanged, of those who have been shot, of those buried alive. We are shown skulls, bones, entire skeletons, and fragments and slivers. Then we are shown Majdanek.[6]

An aerial view. A flat plateau. Small rectangular buildings evenly spaced. All correct and orderly. Only in the middle, protruding from a somewhat larger building—a tall factory chimney.

"What is this place? A factory settlement? God, how bleak and dismal it looks. How could anyone live here?"

"They didn't. That's a crematorium chimney. People died here."

This clear, orderly little picture embodies such despair, such infinite anguish that the heaps of bones we have just seen begin to seem straightforward and unremarkable. A man dies, and his skeleton remains. Earth to earth, dust to dust. But what we have here—this crystallized despair, invented by man, created by human will—is ghastlier than any heap of skeletons. Heaped-up skeletons, a chaos of human bones—that is something we can imagine. On battlefields, in countries passed over by the whirlwind of revolution, we could have seen such pictures. But we could never have imagined this neat, well-ordered settlement of despair, its streets laid out in a grid and with a chimney of death standing over it.

Murders and vicious cruelty are inconceivable to us in the absence of chaos. Chaos tells us, loud and clear, that we have transgressed all boundaries, that we have passed beyond the limit of order, of all that is normal and human. And so even here, in the other world, these clean, orderly little buildings are impossible for us to comprehend.

By way of conclusion we are shown a dead city, the skeleton of a murdered Hamburg. We have seen many ruins, but never have we seen such a white, transparent skeleton—as if fashioned from fragile bisque porcelain. The city has not fallen to the ground, but it is wholly transparent, door-less, roof-less and window-less. On the water are skeleton ships, as if frozen. They too are white and transparent. And there are no sounds. No human beings and no animals. No birds flying over this spectre.

Did we ever, in our earthly life, see anything of the kind—the Book of Ecclesiastes, stiff and frozen, as if engraved with the finest of needles?

Über alles?

Satan was the best of God's angels, but he grew proud and fell lower than all.

PARIS, 3 AUGUST 1945

TRANSLATED BY ROBERT AND ELIZABETH CHANDLER

VOLYA

O to live free, freer than free;
O to live free as the wind.

NOVGOROD FOLK SONG

"SEE, SUMMER'S HERE!"

"Spring's come. It's May. Spring."

How can you tell? Spring? Summer? A few days of stifling heat—and then: rain, a little May snow, and it's back to lighting the stove. And then—it's stifling hot again.

It wasn't like that for us. Our northern spring was a real event.

The sky changed—and so did the air, the earth, the trees.

Secret powers—all the secret saps and juices accumulated during the winter—would suddenly burst free.

Animals roar; wild beasts snarl. The air fills with the sound of wings. High up, just beneath the clouds, like a heart soaring over the Earth—a triangle of cranes. The river—all crashing ice floes. Streams babble and gurgle along ravines. The whole earth trembles with light, with ringing, with rustles, whispers and loud cries.

And the nights did not bring calm, did not cover our eyes in peaceful darkness. Day would fade; it would turn a pale pink, but never depart.

People would wander about, pale, languid, listening intently—like poets in search of a rhyme for an image already clear in their minds.

It grew difficult to live an ordinary life.

What could one do? Fall in love? Write poems about love and death?

Not enough, not nearly enough. Our northern spring is too powerful. With all its light, with all its whispers, rustles and ringing, it lures us away—towards the open horizon, towards free *Volya.*

Volya is not at all the same as freedom.

Freedom—*liberté*—is the rightful state of a citizen who has not infringed the laws governing his or her country.

"Freedom" can be translated into all languages and is understood by all peoples.

Volya is untranslatable.

When you hear the words "a free man", what do you see? You see this: A gentleman walking along the street, cap tilted slightly back, cigarette between his teeth, hands in his pockets. Passing a watchmaker's, he glances at the clock, nods—yes, he still has time—and goes off into the park, along the embankment. He strolls about for a while, spits out his cigarette, whistles a few notes and enters a little café.

What do you see when you hear the word *Volya*?

An unbroken horizon. Someone striding along, sure-footed but not thinking about tracks or paths, not going anywhere in particular. Bareheaded. The wind ruffles his hair and blows it over his eyes—since for his kind, every wind is a tail wind. A bird flies by, spreading its wings wide, and this man waves both arms high in the air, calls out to the bird in a wild voice, then bursts into laughter.

Freedom is a matter of law.

Volya takes no account of anything.

Freedom is an individual's civil status.
Volya is a feeling.

We Russians, the children of Old Russia, were born with this feeling of *Volya*.

Peasant children, children of the rich bourgeoisie, children of the intelligentsia—regardless of background and upbringing, all sensed and understood the call of *Volya*.

Thousands of vagrants, such as you'd never see in any another country, answered this call. And if there were fewer vagrants in other countries, this was not because their better living conditions and stricter laws meant that there was neither need nor opportunity to leave the home nest. We too treated vagrants strictly. We arrested them, sentenced them and tried to force them to settle. Anyway, it's not as if every Russian who left their home had a hard life there. No, there must be some other explanation.

Was it simply a love of journeying?

But if you buy one of these vagrants a ticket, send them with money, in luxury, to some wonderful destination, to the Caucasus or the Crimea, they will jump out somewhere near Kursk, drink away the money and head off north to Arkhangelsk on foot. Why?

"Wood tar's cheap up there."

"And why do you need wood tar?"

"Well, you never know."

The point isn't the tar, it's the need for movement. To follow your nose, to go where your eyes look.

There we have it—the eternal aim of the Russian soul.

To go where your eyes look.

Like in the old fairy tales—to go thither, I know not whither.

Old and young walk and walk. They walk the length and breadth of Russia—this way and that way, along her roads, along her paths, across her virgin soil.

Catch one of these wanderers, take them back to their birthplace—and they're off again at once. In the North we used to call them Spiridon-Turnabouts.[1]

A Spiridon-Turnabout strides along the road, wearing heaven knows what kind of hat—a Jewish kippah, a monk's skullcap, a crush hat, a Panama hat without a brim or even a Panama without a top. You name it—even a woman's kerchief. Shoes falling apart and no footcloths;[2] a knapsack or cloth bundle on his back. A tin kettle hanging at his side.

He strides along as if that were his be-all and end-all in life, but he has no idea where he's heading, or why.

Among these Spiridon-Turnabouts are representatives of every class—from runaway monks to the sons of village priests or rich merchants.

In Novgorod province—as I remember—there lived an old district police superintendent. As in a fairy tale, he had three sons. Except that it was not only the two older ones who were normal and sensible. All three were regular, sensible boys, and all three went to military school. The eldest, who was in good health and good spirits, graduated from the school and received his commission. Then he went back home for a few days. He seemed lost in thought. But not for long. One morning they found his boots and uniform in his room, but no sign of the boy himself. Where he'd gone and what he was now wearing, no one knew.

A few months later, he returned. Though that's hardly the word—he made a brief appearance, and in such a state that it would have been better if he hadn't shown up at all. He was drunk, dressed in rags—yet full of joy, even ecstatic.

His father was in despair. He did all he could. He revoked his paternal blessing. He cursed and wept. He offered his son money. He took to drink himself. Nothing helped.

The only response to his arguments and entreaties was a load of balderdash about the importance of understanding the fern flower,[3] and about the birds in heaven—how they pray to God every dawn.

And with that the boy went on his way.

And two years later, the second son left home in exactly the same fashion.

When the third son turned sixteen, the father decided not to wait for him to get lost in thought. He summoned three policemen and ordered the boy to be flogged. Strangely enough, this had a positive effect. The boy graduated successfully and even got started on his military career. Maybe he'd have been all right anyway; maybe he wouldn't have got lost in thought and his father's heroic measures were neither here nor there. But we didn't keep in touch, and I've no idea what became of him.

Until recently there were always pilgrims in Russia. They went from monastery to monastery and were not always led by religious feeling. What mattered was simply to be on the move. They felt the same pull as migratory birds. A mysteriously strong pull. We Russians are not so cut off from nature as Europeans. We have only a thin overlay of culture; nature can quickly and easily pierce through it. In spring, when the earth awakes and her voices grow louder, summoning us to *Volya*, we have no choice but to follow her resonant call. We are like mice in thrall to a medieval sorcerer playing a pipe.

I remember how my first cousin, a fifteen-year-old cadet, a quiet, obedient boy and a good student, twice ran away from his military school and made his way deep into the northern forest. When he was tracked down and returned to his home, he was quite unable to explain himself. Both these occasions were in early spring.

"What were you thinking of?" we asked.

He smiled shyly. "I don't know. Something was pulling me."

Later, as an adult, he would look back on this chapter of his life with a kind of tender astonishment. He was unable to understand or explain what it was that had so pulled him.

He had been able to imagine his mother's anguish and had felt desperately sorry for her. And he'd known very well what a hullabaloo there'd be at his military school. But all that had been a mere blur. His ordinary life had seemed like a dream. And his wonderful forest life had felt real. He even found it hard to understand how he could have lived such a tedious, difficult and unnatural life for so long—for fifteen whole years.

But he hadn't done very much thinking. For the main part, it had been a time of feeling. He had felt *Volya*: "Dense forest. You wander along without a path. Only pine trees and sky—no one else in the world. And suddenly, with all your might, you let yourself go. At the top of your voice, you let out a cry of such wild, primal joy that for hours afterwards all you can do is laugh and shake."

Later, he said more: "Once I was lucky enough to see a bear enjoying music. He was lying on his back beside a giant tree felled by a storm. It was a very old tree. The trunk had split apart and the wood was all splintered. And there was the bear, stretching out a front paw and plucking the wood. The slivers hummed and buzzed, creaked and cracked. And all the time, the bear was letting out quiet growls of pleasure. He certainly liked this music… Then he seized some more slivers and played with them too. I'll never forget the sight. A white night, a northern white night. In the far North, by the way, a white night isn't as pale as, say, in Petersburg. In the far North it's pinker, because there's always a glow in the sky. Dawn starts to brighten before the evening light fades. There's a rosy haze in the forest and, in this haze—a remarkable picture: a bear making music and a boy watching him from the bushes and almost crying—maybe he really does cry—out of love and delight. Who could ever forget this?"

This boy, incidentally, had been hard to track down. Information about him had been sent to police all over northern Russia, but it was only by chance that he was caught—in the north of Olonets province. On his way through a village, he stopped at an inn. He'd spent the night in the woods. It was a cold day and it was raining. He was chilled to the bone and he wanted a hot meal. He asked for some cabbage soup.

"What kind?"

"With meat," he replied.

The innkeeper was shocked. "What do you mean? It's Friday. What kind of person eats meat on a Friday?" And he sent for the constable.

The constable came and asked for his passport. The boy, needless to say, didn't have a passport. He was arrested and questioned. He burst into tears and confessed all. And so ended his days of *Volya*.

Nowadays, you often hear talk like this:

"Oh to be in Russia. Even for just one day. I'd go to the forest—*that* can't have changed. I'd go for a good wander. I'd get a lungful of sweet *Volya*."

I too have my memories. There, it's always spring. A white night. The small hours, perhaps two o'clock. It's light, there's pink in the sky.

VOLYA

I'm standing on a terrace. Below me, beyond the flower garden—a river. The muffled sound of a bell, and the cries of a young boy goading his oxen along the towpath. A barge is being towed towards the distant Volga.

My heart misses a beat, and my tired, sleepless eyes half close in the pink light.

Across the river, someone overwhelmed by joy belts out a wild, senseless, ecstatic song:

> The boy lived free, freer than free;
> The boy lived free as the wind.
> If a bird flew by, high in the sky,
> He shot—not once did he miss.
> If a maiden came by,
> Brightening his way,
> He swiftly gave her a kiss.

And then the refrain—heart-rending, piercingly joyful, like a sudden yelp, coming from somewhere too deep in the soul:

> O to live free, free as the wind!
> Sing *Volya, Volya, Volya*!

And somehow, not knowing what I'm doing, I raise my hand and wave at the dawn and this wild song. And I laugh, and cry out, "*Vo-o-o-lya-a-a!*"

1936

TRANSLATED BY ROBERT AND ELIZABETH CHANDLER AND MARIA EVANS

AND TIME WAS NO MORE

"JUST ONE LEFT TILL MORNING."

What does this mean? I keep repeating the words in my head. They've got stuck there. I'm fed up with them. But this often happens to me. A sentence or part of a tune will get stuck in my head and won't leave me alone.

I open my eyes.

An old woman is kneeling on the floor, lighting the little stove. The kindling crackles.

> And my stove is crackling away.
> It lights up my bed in the corner
> Behind the bright-coloured curtain.

How often I'd sung those lines.

The bright-coloured bed curtain is gathered into pleats; light is shining through its scarlet roses.

The old woman, who is wearing a brown shawl and a dark headscarf, is hunched into a little ball. She's blowing onto the kindling, clanging the iron poker against the stove. I look at the small window. Sunlight is playing on the glass, which has frosted over.

> No sooner has the light of dawn
> Begun to play with the clear frost
> Than…

Just like in the song. How does it go on? Ah, that's right:

> Than the samovar has begun to boil
> On the oak table…

Yes, there's the samovar, boiling on the table in the corner, a little steam escaping from under its lid. It's boiling and singing.

Along the bench struts the cockerel. He goes up to the window, tilts his little head to one side and looks out, his claws clicking against the wood. Then he moves on.

But where's the cat? I can't live without the cat. Oh, there he is on the table, stout and gingery, purring as he warms himself behind the samovar.

Someone has begun stamping inside the porch, shaking snow from their felt boots. The boots make a soft thudding sound. The old woman has got laboriously to her feet and waddled to the door. I can't see her face, but it doesn't matter. I know who she is…

I ask, "Who's that?"

She replies, "It's that fellow, what's his name…"

I can hear them talking together. The old woman, standing on the threshold, says, "Well, I suppose I could roast it."

There in her arms, upside down, is an enormous bird, black with thick red eyebrows. A wood grouse. It's been given to us by the huntsman.

I must get up.

Next to the bed are my felt boots—my beloved white *valenki*. Long ago in St Petersburg the Khanzhonkov Studio organized a hunting trip for a group of actors and writers and their friends. We were meant to be hunting elk. They drove us out over the firm white snow to Tosno, where we had a long, convivial lunch with champagne. Early the next morning we set out on low, wide sledges to the edge of the forest. How I loved my pointy-toed white-felt skiing *valenki*. I remember my white cap, too. Against the snow neither my head nor my feet would be visible. No beast would recognize me as a human being. It was a hunting ruse all of my own invention.

A steward of some sort showed us all to our correct spots. We were told not to smoke or talk, but we decided it couldn't do any harm if we only talked and smoked a little bit. I was standing with Fiodorov, the writer. We could hear the cries of the beaters. Later we found out that some elk had come, looked at us through the bushes and gone away. They hadn't liked what they'd seen. Instead of the elk, some hares leapt out—one of them right in front of me. Not moving at any great speed, it slipped slyly from bush to bush—neither quite running away nor quite taking cover. Fiodorov quickly raised his gun and took aim. "Don't you dare!" I yelled, jumping up and flinging my arms open right in front of him. He began yelling even louder—something like "You foo—", except that the word got stuck in his throat. And then, "That could have been the end of you!" I didn't mind him yelling at me. What mattered was that we'd saved the hare. My white, slim, nimble *valenki* did a little dance in the snow.

Later my *valenki* went missing. The maid's husband, a drunken layabout, had stolen them and sold them for drink. But now they'd come back again. Here they were by my bed, as if that were the most ordinary thing in the world. I slipped my feet into them and went into the little box room to get dressed.

There's a narrow window in the box room, and a small mirror on the wall. I look at my reflection. How strange I seem. My face could be from a childhood photograph. Anyone would take me for a four-year-old. I have a cheeky smile and dimples. As for my hair, it's short, with a fringe. It's fair and silky and it lies close to my head. Just like it was when I used to walk down Novinsky Boulevard with my *nyanya*. And I know exactly how I used to look then. When we were going down the front staircase, the big mirror on the landing would reflect a little girl in an astrakhan coat, white gaiters and a white bashlyk hood with gold braid. When she raised her leg high you could see her red flannel pantaloons. Back then all of us children wore red flannel pantaloons. And there in the mirror behind this girl would be a second little girl just like her, only smaller and wider. Her little sister.

I remember how we used to play on the boulevard, my sister and I and other little girls like us. Once a lady and a gentleman stopped and watched us for a while, smiling.

"I like that little girl in the bonnet," said the lady, pointing at me.

The thought of her liking me was intriguing. I immediately opened my eyes wide and puckered my lips, as if to say, "Look at me! Aren't I wonderful?" And the gentleman and his lady smiled and smiled.

On this Novinsky Boulevard I so loved, there was also a big, bad boy, about eight years old, who hung around being naughty and picking fights. His name was Arkasha. Once he climbed onto the very top of a bench, tried to look impressive and poked his tongue out at me. But I stood up for myself. Even if he was big, I wasn't afraid of him. I taunted him, saying, "Arkasha eats baby kasha! Arkasha eats baby kasha!"

And he said, "Yah, you're just a little squirt."

But I wasn't afraid of him and I knew I would always be able to make fun of spiteful fools, no matter how high they might climb.

Then there was that proud moment of my first bold triumph, my first triumph of ambition. There on that same boulevard. We were walking past our house when Nyanya pointed to a short, stout figure up on the balcony.

"Look, there's Elvira Karlovna. She's come out for some fresh air."

Elvira Karlovna was our nursery governess. We were little and her name was so hard for us to say that we just called her "Baba". But suddenly I felt bold.

"Irvirkarna!" I called. Not "Baba" but "Irvirkarna"—like a big girl. I said it in a loud ringing voice so that everyone would hear that I could talk like a big girl. "Irvirkarna!"

It seems I had once been bold and ambitious. Over the years I had lost all this, more's the pity. Ambition can be a powerful force. If I had been able to hold onto it, I might have shouted out something for all the world to hear.

But how wonderful everything was on that boulevard. For some reason it's always early spring there. The runnels gurgle as they start to thaw, it's as if someone's pouring water out of a narrow little jug, and the smell of the water's so heady that you just want to laugh and kick up your heels; and the damp sand shimmers, it's like little crystals of sugar and you want to put some of it in your mouth and chew it; and a spring breeze is blowing into my woolly mittens. And off to one side, by a little path, has appeared a slender green stem. It stands there, quivering. And the lambs'-fleece clouds whirling about in the sky look like a picture from my book about Thumbelina. And the sparrows bustle about, the children shout, and you take all this in at the same time, all in one go, and all of it can be expressed in a single whoop of "I don't want to go home!"

This was in the days when my hair was fair and silky. And now, all of a sudden, my hair's like that again. How strange. But is it really so very strange? Here in this little house with the cockerel strutting along the bench, what could be more ordinary?

Now I'll put on my little cap, the one I wore on that hunting trip, and go out on my skis.

I walk out onto the porch. There, propped against the wall, are my skis. No sign of the old woman and the huntsman. Eagerly I slip my feet into the straps. I grab the poles, push off and glide down the slope.

Sun. The odd powdery snowflake. One flake falls onto my sleeve and doesn't melt; it's still crystalline when it blows away. I feel so light! I'm held by the air; happiness is carrying me along. I've always known and I've often said that happiness isn't a matter of success or achievement—happiness is a feeling. It's not founded on anything, it can't be explained by anything.

Yes, I remember one morning. It was very early. I'd been on my knees all night long, massaging the leg of someone very ill. I was numb from cold and trembling from pity and fatigue, as I made my way home. But as I was crossing the bridge, I stopped. The city was just beginning to wake up. The waterside was deserted apart from a longshorewoman the likes of whom you'll see only in Paris. Young and nimble, a red sash around her waist and pink stockings on her legs, she was using a stick to fish for rags in the dustbins. The still sunless sky was just brightening in the east, and a faint haze, like pencil shading on pink blotting paper, showed where the sun's rays were about to burst through. The water below wasn't flowing the way it's supposed to flow; instead, it was whirling around in lots of flat little eddies, as if dancing on the spot. It was waltzing. And trembling gaily in the air was a faint ringing sound—perhaps the sound of my fatigue. I don't know. But suddenly I was pierced by a feeling of inexplicable happiness—a feeling so marvellous it made my breast ache and brought tears to my eyes. And reeling from fatigue, laughing and crying, I began to sing:

Wherever the scent of spring may lead me…

I hear a rustling behind me. The huntsman. Now he's standing beside me. I know his face, his outline, his movements. His earflaps are down; I can see him only in profile. But who is he?

"Wait," I say. "I think I know you."

"Of course you do," he says.

"Only I can't quite remember…"

"There's no need to remember. What use is remembering? Remembering is the last thing you need."

"But wait," I say. "What's that sentence that's been bothering me? Something like, 'Just one left till morning.' What on earth does it mean? Something nasty, I think."

"It's all right," he says. "It's all right."

I've been ill for so long, and my memory is poor. But I do remember—I made a note: I want to hear the *Lohengrin* overture one more time, and I want to talk once more to a certain wonderful person, and to see another sunrise. But *Lohengrin* and the sunrise would be too much for me now. Do you know what I mean? And that wonderful person has left. Ah, I remember that last sunrise, somewhere in France.

Dawn had just begun to glow, its wine-red hue beginning to spread. In a moment the sun would come up. The birds were getting agitated, twittering and squawking. One little bird was loudly and insistently repeating, "*Vite, vite, vite…*" Tired of waiting, it was urging the sun on. I joined in this reproach to the sun, saying (in French, of course, since it was a French bird), "*Il n'est pas pressé.*"[1] And suddenly there was the sun, round and yellow, as if breathless and embarrassed about being late. And it wasn't even where I'd expected it to be, but somewhere far off to the left. Out came the midges, and the birds fell silent and got down to their hunting.

The poetic conceit that birds greet the rising of the sun god with a hymn of rapture is ever so droll. On the whole birds are a restless, garrulous tribe. They make just as much fuss when they're going to bed as when they wake up, but you can hardly make out that they're hymning the sun late in the evening. In Warsaw, I remember, in one of the squares, there was what you could call a sparrow tree. In the evening people would gather to watch the sparrows go to bed. The birds would flock around the tree and make a clamour you could hear all over the square. From the tone of their twittering you could tell that these were squabbles, disputes, brawls and just plain mindless chatter. And then everything would calm down and the sparrows would settle in for the night.

Although I shouldn't reproach the birds for this garrulousness. Nature gives each bird a single motif: "cock-a-doodle-doo" or "chink-chook" or just plain "cuckoo". Do you think you could get your message across with a sound as simple as that? How many times would you have to repeat yourself? Imagine that we human beings were given a single motif according to our breed. Some of us would say, "Isn't the Dnieper wonderful in fine weather?" Others would ask, "What time is it? What time is it?" Still others would go on and on repeating that "The angle of incidence is equal to the angle of reflection." Try using a single sentence like that to rhapsodize about the Sistine Madonna, to expound on the brotherhood of nations or to ask to borrow money. Although, maybe this is exactly what we do do and we just never realize it.

Sunrise! How varied it can be, and how I love it in all its guises. There's one sunrise I remember well. I waited for it a long time; for some reason I was really longing for it. And there in the east was a strip of grey cloud or light mist. I raised my arms like an ancient pagan worshipping the sun and beseeched the heavens:

Sun, our god! Oh, where are you?
We are arrayed in your flowers,
Our arms upraised to your blue,
We are calling, invoking your powers…

And then there it was, an orange coal ringing through the grey mist. Slowly before us rose a bronze sun, swelling, incandescent, malicious. Its face was blazing with rage; it was quivering and full of hate. Sometimes sunrise can be like that…

And I remember another very curious sunrise.

In a patch of grey there suddenly appeared a round hole, like the spyhole in a stage curtain that actors look through to check the size of the audience. Through this little hole in the sky peeped out a hot yellow eye; then this eye disappeared. A moment later, as if deciding—Now!—out jumped the sun. It was very droll.

Sunset, on the other hand, is always sad. It may be voluptuous, and opulent, and as richly sated with life as an Assyrian king, but it is always sad, always solemn. It is the death of the day.

They say there is a reason for everything in nature—the peacock's tail serves to perpetuate the species, the beauty of flowers attracts the bees that will pollinate them. But what purpose does the mournful beauty of sunset serve?

Nature has expended herself in vain.

Here's the huntsman again, standing beside me.

"Where's your gun?" I ask.

"Here."

It's true, I can see his gun behind his back.

"And your dog?"

"There."

Up bounds his dog. Everything's as it should be.

I feel I ought to say something to the huntsman.

"How do you like my little house?" I ask. "When it gets dark, you know, we light a lamp."

"Does Nyanya light it?"

"Nyanya? Oh, yes, yes, the old woman—that's Nyanya," I say, remembering. Nyanya… She had died in an almshouse. She was very old. When I visited her, she would ask, "Just what are these granchilder? Some countryfolk keep coming round and saying, 'But, Grandma, we're your granchilder.'"

"They're your daughter Malasha's children," I explained. Malasha had been our housemaid when I was little.

I remember it all so vividly it's uncanny. Someone has spilt some needles on the window sill and I'm stroking them. I think they're absolutely wonderful. And someone is saying, "Liulia has spilt some needles."

I hear but I don't realize that this Liulia is me. Then someone picks me up. I'm touching a plump shoulder tightly encased in pink cotton. This, I know, is Malasha. And as for the needles—I've loved needles and everything sharp and glittery all my life. Maybe I began to love them back then, before I realized that Liulia was me. We were talking about Nyanya. She was very old. And now she's here in this little house. In the evening she lights the lamp; from outside, the little window shines orange, and out from the forest comes a fox. It comes up to the window and sings. You've probably never heard the way a fox sings? It's extraordinary. Not like Patti or Chaliapin,[2] of course—but far more entertaining. It sings tenderly and off-key, in a way that's utterly bewitching: very soft, yet still audible. And the cockerel's here inside, standing on the bench, its comb like raspberry gold with the light shining through it. It stands there in profile and pretends not to be listening.

And the fox sings:

Cockerel, cockerel,
With your comb of gold,
Your combed little beard,
And your shiny little head,
Come, look out the window.

But the cockerel clicks its claws on the bench and walks away. Yes, at least once in your life you should listen to a fox singing.

"It sings at night," says the huntsman, "but you don't like night, do you?"

"How do you know? Does that mean you've known me a long time? Why's it so hard for me to remember you when I'm quite certain that really I know you very well?"

"Does it matter?" he says. "Just think of me as a composite character from your previous life."

"If you're a composite character, then why are you a huntsman?"

"Because all the girls of your generation were in love with Hamsun's Lieutenant Glahn.[3] And then you spent your entire life seeking this Glahn in everyone you met. You were seeking for courage, honesty, pride, loyalty and a passion that ran deep but was held in check. You were, weren't you? You can't deny it."

"But wait… You said I don't like the night. That's true. Why? What does it matter? Tiutchev said, and he's probably right, that it's because night rips away the veil that prevents us from seeing the abyss.[4] And as for the anguish inspired by the stars—'The stars speak of eternity'—what could be more terrible? If a person in pain gazes up at the stars as they 'speak of eternity', he's supposed to sense his own insignificance and thus find relief. That's the part I really can't understand. Why would someone who's been wronged by life find comfort in his complete and utter humiliation—in the recognition of his own insignificance? On top of all your grief, sorrow and despair—here, enjoy the contempt of eternity, too: You're a louse. Take comfort and be glad that you have a place on earth—even if it's only that of a louse. We look up at the starry sky the way a little mouse looks through a chink in the wall at a magnificent ballroom. Music, lights, sparkling apparitions. Strange rhythmical movements, in circles that move together and then apart, propelled by an unknown cause towards an incomprehensible goal. It's beautiful and frightening—very, very frightening. We can, if we like, count the number of circles traced by this or that sparkling apparition, but it's impossible to understand what the apparition means—and this is frightening. What we cannot understand we always sense as a hostile force, as something cruel and meaningless. Little mouse, it's a good thing that *they* don't see us, that we play no role in their magnificent, terrible and majestic life. Have you ever noticed how people lower their voices when they're looking at the star-filled sky?"

"Nevertheless, the stars speak of eternity," said the huntsman.

"Eternity! Eternity! How terrifying! 'Forever' is a terrifying word. And the word 'never' is no different—it is eternal in the same way. But for some reason 'never' frightens us still more. Maybe this is because 'never' includes a negative element, almost a prohibition, which we find abhorrent. But enough of that—or I'll start feeling wretched. A while ago, a group of us were talking for some reason about how impossible it is to grasp the concept of infinity. But there was a little boy with us who made perfect sense of it just like that. He said, 'It's easy. Imagine there's one room here, and then another, and then another five, ten or twenty rooms, another hundred or million rooms, and so on and so on… Well, after a while it gets boring, you just can't be bothered any more and you say, *To hell with it all!*' That's what it is—that's infinity for you."

"What a muddle you're in," said the huntsman, shaking his head. "Eternity and starry despair, a singing fox and a little boy's prattle."

"But to me it's all quite clear. I simply want to talk without any logic or order, the way things come to me. Like after morphine."

"Precisely," said the huntsman. "After morphine. Because this little house of yours never really existed either. It's just something you used to like drawing."

"Look, I'm tired and ill. Does it really matter? When all's said and done, we invent our entire lives. After all, don't we invent other people? Are they really, truly the way they appear to us, the way we always see them? I can remember a dream I once had. I went to the home of a man I loved. And I was greeted there by his mother and sister. They greeted me very coldly and kept saying he was busy. They wouldn't let me see him. So I decided to leave. And as I was leaving, I caught sight of myself in the mirror and let out a groan. My face was fat and puffy and I had tiny squinting eyes. On my head was a hat with bugle beads, the kind that used to be worn by elderly shopkeepers' wives. On my shoulders was a brown cape, and on my short neck a filthy, coarsely knitted scarf. 'Good God!' I said to myself. 'What's happened to me?' And then I understood. This was how those women saw me. And I know now that you will never find even two people on earth who see a third in the same way."

"You seem to have set great store by dreams," said the huntsman.

"Oh yes. Dreams, too, are life. I've seen and experienced much that is noteworthy, beautiful, even wonderful—and yet I don't remember it and not all of it has become an essential component of my soul in the way that two or three dreams have done. Without those dreams I wouldn't be the person I am. I had an astounding dream when I was eighteen—how could I ever forget it? It seems to have foretold my whole life. I dreamed a series of dark, empty rooms. I kept opening doors, making my way through one room after another, trying to find a way out. Somewhere in the distance a child began to cry and then fell silent. He'd been taken away somewhere. But I walked on, full of anguish—until, finally, I reached the last door. It was massive. With a great effort, pushing with all my strength, I opened this door. At last I was free. Before me lay an endless expanse, despondently lit by a lacklustre moon. It was the kind of pale moon we see only by day. But far away in the murk something was gleaming; I could see it was moving. I was glad. I wasn't alone. Someone was coming towards me. I heard a heavy thudding of horses' hooves. At last. The sound was getting closer. And an enormous, bony, white nag was approaching, its bones clattering. It was pulling a white coffin sparkling with brocade. It pulled the coffin up to me and stopped… And this dream is my entire life. It's possible to forget the most vivid incident, the most remarkable twist of fate, but a dream like this you'll never forget. And I never have done. If my soul were reduced into its chemical components, analysis would reveal the crystals of my dreams to be a part of its very essence. Dreams reveal so very, very much."

"Yours is a very nice little house," he says, interrupting me. "And it's a good thing you've finally come to it."

"You know," I say, "today my hair is just like it was when I was four. And so is the snow. I used to love resting my head on the window sill and looking up to watch the falling snow. Nothing on earth creates a sense of peace and calm like falling snow. Maybe because when something falls it's usually accompanied by some noise, by a knock or a crash. But snow—this pure and almost unbroken white mass—is the only thing that falls without any sound. And this brings a sense of peace. Often now when my soul feels restless, I think of falling snow, of silently falling snow.

And always there's one snowflake that seems to recollect itself and does its best, zigzagging its way through the crowd of obediently falling snowflakes, to fly back up into the sky."

The huntsman didn't speak for a long time. Then he said, "Once, you made out that there are five doors through which one can escape the terror that is life: religion, science, art, love and death."

"Yes, I think I did. But do you realize that there is a dreadful force that only saints and crazed fanatics can defeat? This force closes all those doors. It makes man revolt against God; it makes him scorn science for its impotence, turn a cold shoulder to art and forget how to love... It makes death, that eternal bogeyman, come to seem welcome and blessed. This force is pain. Torturers the world over have always known this. The fear of death can be overcome by reason and by faith. But only saints and fanatics have been able to conquer the fear of pain."

"And how have you overcome your fear of death?" he asked with a strangely mocking smile. "By reason or by faith?"

"Me? Through my theory of a world soul—a single soul, common to all people and animals, to every living creature. It is only the ability to be aware of this soul, and above all to give it expression, that varies according to the physical make-up of the creature in question. A dog can distinguish between good and evil every bit as well as a human being can, but a dog of course can't put any of this into words. Anyone who has carefully observed the life of animals knows that the moral law is inherent in them, just as in human beings. Which reminds me of a certain little hare, a silly little woodland creature. Someone caught this hare and it soon grew tame. It liked to stay close to its owners, and if they quarrelled it always got terribly upset. It would run back and forth between the two of them and it wouldn't calm down until they made up. The hare loved its friends and wished them to have a peaceful life. This was for their sake, not for the hare's, because their quarrels did not affect it directly. What upset the little wild beast was the suffering of others. The hare was a bearer of the world soul. This is how I feel about the world soul, and this, therefore, is how I feel about death. Death is a return to the whole, a return to the oneness. This is how I see things myself; this has been my important illumination. There's nothing mathematical about it; certainly nothing that can be proved. For some people the concept of the transmigration of souls has been an important illumination. For others, the illumination that matters has been that of life after death, and redemption through the eternal torment of remorse. For others still, like my old *nyanya*, what mattered most was devils with pitchforks. But I'm telling you what has been important for me. And there's one more thing I can say. Yes, let me tell you a story. Listen. There once was a woman who had a vision in her sleep. She seemed to be kneeling and reaching out with both her hand and her soul to someone whom she had loved and who was no longer among the living. She was staying in Florence at the time and the air in her dream—probably influenced by Simone Martini's Annunciation—was translucent gold, shimmering as though shot through with rays of gold. And within this extraordinary golden light and blessed intensity of love was that ecstasy no one can endure for more than a moment. But time did not exist, and this moment felt like eternity. And it was eternity, because time was no more. As it says in the Book of Revelation, 'And the Angel lifted up his hand to Heaven and swore by Him that liveth forever and ever that there should be time no more.'[5] And then the woman realized that this was death, that this is all there is to death: it is something tiny, indivisible, a mere point, the moment when the heart stops beating and breathing ceases and someone's voice says,

'He's dead now.' That's eternity for you. And all the elaborations of a life beyond the grave, with its agonies of conscience, repentance and other torments—all these are simply what we experience while we're alive. There is no place for such trivial nonsense in eternity. Listen, Huntsman, when I'm dying, I'll say to God, 'Oh Lord! Send your finest angels for my soul that was born of Your Spirit, for my dark, sinful soul, which has rebelled against You, in its sorrow always seeking but never finding…'"

"Never till now," corrected the huntsman.

"Never till now," I repeated. "And bless my body, created by Your Will, bless my eyes that have looked without seeing, my lips that have grown pale from song and laughter, and bless my womb that has accepted the fruit of love, all according to Your Will, and my legs…"

"… that have been kissed so many, many times," interrupted the huntsman.

"No, I won't say that. I'll simply say, 'Oh Lord, bless this body and release me into the immortality of your world. Amen.' That's what I'll say."

"But you've said it!" exclaimed the huntsman. "You've said it now!"

"I may have said it, but I'm not dying yet."

My skis came to a stop. I looked down at my feet. The white-felt *valenki* were gone. In their place were tall, yellow-leather boots laced right up to the knee. I knew them well. I had worn them when I went to the front during the war.[6] I began to feel strangely apprehensive.

"I don't understand," I said.

The huntsman was silent. Suddenly, with a slight bend of his knees and a single coordinated movement of his entire body, he pushed off and quickly glided ahead and down a slope. Then he flew up over a hillock and disappeared from view. Far ahead he appeared fleetingly at the top of another rise.

"Hello-o-o!" I cried out. "Come back! I don't want to be alone!"

What is his name? How can I call out to him? I don't know. But I can't bear to be left all alone.

"Hello-o-o-o! I'm frightened…"

But no, this isn't quite true: I'm not frightened. I'm just used to thinking that I'm frightened of being alone. I'll go back to my little house. Yes, I still have something on which I can build life. I've still got the little house I once drew… But I'm cold. So cold.

"Come back! Hello-o-o-o-o!"

"It's all right, I'm right here," says a voice beside me. "There's no need to shout. I'm here."

I turn this way and that way. No one is there. Just the whitest white all around. The snow lies heavy on the ground. It's no longer that light, happy snow. There is a soft tinkle, the tinkle of fine glass. Then the sharp pain of an injection into my hip. Right before my eyes are the folds of a thick apron with two pockets. My nurse.

"There," says the voice, "your last ampoule. That's it until morning."

Warm fingers take hold of my wrist and squeeze it. Far, far away someone's voice says, "Heavens. There's no pulse. She…"

She. Who is this "she"? I don't know. Maybe it's that little girl, the girl with the silky hair who didn't understand that she was Liulia.

How very quiet it all is…

PARIS, 1949

TRANSLATED BY ANNE MARIE JACKSON

ILYA REPIN

I DID NOT SEE REPIN OFTEN. He lived in Finland and came only seldom to Petersburg.

But one day Kaplan, from the publishing house Dog Rose,[1] came round with a letter from Repin. Repin very much liked my story "The Top". "It moved me to tears," he wrote. And this had made him want to paint my portrait.[2]

This, of course, was a great honour for me. We agreed on a date and time, and Kaplan took me along in his car.

It was winter. Cold. Snowstorms. All very miserable. With its squat dachas deep in snow, Kuokkala was not welcoming. The sky was also very low, even darker than the earth and breathing out cold. After Petersburg, with its loud voices, with its whistles and car horns, the village seemed very quiet. The snow lay in deep drifts and there could have been a bear beneath every one of them, fast asleep, sucking its paw.

Repin greeted us warmly. He took us into his studio and showed us his latest work. Then we sat down for a late breakfast at his famous round table. The table had two levels. On the top level, which revolved, were all kinds of dishes; you moved it round and helped yourself to whatever you fancied. On the lower level were containers for the dirty plates and bowls. It was all very convenient, and fun—like having a picnic. The food was vegetarian, and there was a lot of variety. Some of our more serious eaters, though, would complain after a visit that they'd been given nothing but hay. In the railway station on the way back home, they'd go to the buffet and fill up on meat rissoles, which would by then have grown cold.

After breakfast—work.

Repin seated me on a little dais and then sat down below me. He was looking up at me, which seemed very strange. I've sat for a number of artists—Alexander Yakovlev, Savely Sorin, Boris Grigoriev, Savely Schleifer[3] and many who are less well known—but no one has ever gone about it so strangely.

He was using coloured pencils, which he didn't do often. "It'll be Paris style," he said with a smile.

He asked someone else who was there to read aloud "The Top", the story of mine that had made such an impression on him. This made me think of Boris Kustodiev's account of how, while he was painting his portrait of Nicholas II, the tsar had read aloud one of my stories of village life.[4] He had read well—and had then asked if it was true that the author was a lady.

Repin's finished portrait of me was something magically tender and unexpected, not at all like his usual, more forceful work.

He promised to give it to me. But I never received it. It was sent to an exhibition in America and, in Repin's words, "it got stuck in customs".

I didn't like to question him too insistently. "He simply doesn't want to admit that he sold it," people kept telling me.

It would, in any case, have disappeared during the Revolution, as did all the other portraits of me, as did many beloved things without which I'd thought life would be hardly worth living.

Years later, in Paris, I republished "The Top" in *The Book of June*, dedicating the story to Repin. I sent a copy of the book to the address I still had for him in Finland. He replied warmly, asking me to send him a few amateur photographs, just as they were, without any retouching. With these to prompt him, he'd be able to recreate the portrait from memory. At the bottom of the letter was a postscript from his daughter, saying that her father was very weak, hardly able to move about at all.

I was touched by this thoughtfulness on Repin's part, but I was slow to do as he asked. Eventually, however, I did—only to read in a newspaper, the very next day, that Repin had died.

I shall remember this short, rather thin man as someone uncommonly polite and courteous. His manner was always unruffled and he never showed the least sign of irritation. In short: "A man from another age".

I've heard it said that, after pointing out the failings in a work by one of his weaker students, he would add, "Oh, if only I had your brush!"

Even if he didn't really say this, it's easy to imagine him coming out with something of the kind. Repin was modest. People accustomed to praise and flattery usually speak a lot and don't listen. Speak—rather than converse. Fiodor Chaliapin, Vlas Doroshevich and Leonid Andreyev all strode about the room and held forth.[5] Repin would listen intently to the other person. He conversed.

His wife Natalya Nordman-Severova was a committed vegetarian. She converted her husband. The revolving table was her idea too. When, overcome by jealousy, she left her husband, he remained loyal to vegetarianism. But shortly before his death, growing weaker and weaker, he ate a little curd cheese. This lifted his spirits. Then he decided to eat an egg. And that gave him the strength to get to his feet and even to do some work.[6]

His last note to me read, "I'm waiting for your photos. I'm determined to do your portrait."

His handwriting was weak. He was not strong enough to paint a portrait.

Not that I had ever really expected anything to come of all this. I've never been a collector, never been able to keep hold of things and not let them slip through my hands. When I've been asked by fortune tellers to spread out my palms, they always say, with a shake of the head, "No, with hands like that you'll never be able to hold on to anything."

There was also a portrait of me by Savely Schleifer. It too had its story.[7]

Schleifer had portrayed me in a white tunic and he'd thrown a deep blue veil over my head.

I had a friend who particularly loved this portrait. He persuaded me to give it to him and he took it to his estate in the province of Kovno.[8] A true aesthete, close to Mikhail Kuzmin, he hung it in the place of honour and always stood a vase of flowers beneath it.[9]

In 1917 he heard that the peasants had looted his house and gone off with all his books and paintings. He hurried back to his estate to try to rescue his treasures.

He managed to track down a few of them. In one hut he found my portrait, hanging in the icon corner beside Saint Nicholas the Miracle Worker and the Iverskaya Mother of God.[10] Thanks to the long white tunic, the blue veil and the vase of dried flowers, the woman who had taken this portrait had decided I was a saint and lit an icon lamp before me.

A likely story…

The palmists were right. I've never been able to hold on to anything. Neither portraits, nor poems dedicated to me, nor paintings I've been given, nor important letters from interesting people. Nothing at all.

There is a little more preserved in my memory, but even this is gradually, or even rather quickly, losing its meaning, fading, slipping away from me, wilting and dying.

It's sad to wander about the graveyard of my tired memory, where all hurts have been forgiven, all sins more than atoned for, all riddles unriddled and where twilight quietly cloaks the crosses, now no longer upright, of graves I once wept over.

1950–52

TRANSLATED BY ROBERT AND ELIZABETH CHANDLER

Chronology

1872 21 MAY Birth of Nadezhda Alexandrovna Lokhvitskaya, later known as Teffi, in Petersburg.

1892 Teffi marries Vladislav Buchinsky, a lawyer. During the following years, they live together on his family estate and in various provincial towns.

1898 Teffi leaves her husband and three small children, and returns to Petersburg.

1908 Teffi joins the staff of *Satirikon*, a popular Petersburg satirical magazine.

1909 Teffi joins the staff of the Moscow *Russkoye Slovo* (*Russian Word*), the country's best and most widely read newspaper. She often contributes two or even three columns a week.

1910 Teffi publishes her first book of poems, *Seven Fires*, and her first book of stories, *Humorous Stories*. Throughout the 1910s, she publishes a new book of stories and sketches almost yearly.

1914–18 First World War.

1917 The February Revolution. Tsar Nicholas II abdicates.

1917 7 NOVEMBER The October Revolution. The Bolshevik Party seizes power in a coup.

1918–1922 Russian Civil War. Economic catastrophe. *Russkoye Slovo* is closed down.

1918 AUTUMN Teffi leaves Moscow, setting out on the long journey—through Russia and what is now Ukraine—that she recounts in *Memories*.

1919 LATE SUMMER Teffi embarks from Novorossiisk on a boat bound for Istanbul.

1920 JANUARY Teffi arrives in Paris. During the next four years, she suffers three life-threatening illnesses.

1922 MARCH–AUGUST Teffi lives in Wiesbaden.

1922 DECEMBER–1923 AUGUST Teffi lives in Berlin.

1927 Publication of *A Small Town*, containing many of Teffi's best-known comic stories about émigré life.

1931 Publication of *Memories*.

1934 Publication of a collected edition of Teffi's plays.

1936 Publication of *Witch*, perhaps Teffi's finest collection of stories.

1937 17 OCTOBER Death of Pavel Theakston, Teffi's partner for the previous twelve or thirteen years. He had been able to offer some financial support until autumn 1930, when he not only lost most of his money in the Wall Street crash but also suffered a severe stroke. For his last seven years, Teffi was his constant carer.

1940 10 JUNE–1941 SUMMER Teffi lives in Angers and then Biarritz. She returns to Paris.

1952 6 OCTOBER Teffi dies in her Paris apartment.

A Note on Russian Names

A Russian has three names: a Christian name, a patronymic (derived from the Christian name of the father) and a family name. Thus, Avdotya Matveyevna is the daughter of a man whose first name is Matvey, and Alexey Nikolaevich is the son of a man called Nikolay. The first name and patronymic, used together, are the normal polite way of addressing or referring to a person; the family name is used less often. Close friends or relatives usually address each other by one of the many diminutive, or affectionate, forms of their first names. Lena, for example, is a diminutive of Elena (the Russian equivalent of Helen); Grisha of Grigory; and Varya of Varvara. Volodya and Volodka are both diminutives of Vladimir; and Masha and Manya are both diminutives of Marya. Less obviously, Tolya is a diminutive of Anatoly; Tyoma of Artyom; Kolya of Nikolay; and Stioshka of Stefania. Ganya and Ganka are diminutives of Agafya. There are many double diminutives; Vanechka and Varenka are double diminutives of Ivan and Varvara.

Married or older peasants are often addressed and referred to by their patronymic alone, or by a slightly abbreviated form of it.

Many of the stories relating to Teffi's childhood are set in the province of Volhynia, then part of the Russian Empire and now a part of Ukraine. At the time, Polish, Yiddish and Ukrainian were all widely spoken there, and several of Teffi's characters bear Polish names. Teffi transliterates those into the Cyrillic alphabet, but we have reverted to the original Polish spellings. Kornelia is a variant of Caroline, and Eleonora of Helen.

A Russian *nyanya* differs in many ways from an English nanny. We have therefore chosen to transliterate the word rather than translate it. A *nyanya* was typically employed first as a wet-nurse and then as a more general household servant, often becoming an integral part of the family. It was common for a *nyanya* to be more deeply and intimately involved in a child's life than his or her mother. *Nyanyas* play a prominent role in many classic works of Russian literature.

Acknowledgements

My especial thanks to Christine Worobec for her help with many questions relating to both Orthodox and folk-religious beliefs, rituals and traditions; to Veronica Muskheli and Alexander Nakhimovsky for their clear and convincing answers to many complex questions. And to all the following: Sophie Benbelaid, David Black, Ilona Chavasse, Elizabeth Cook, Boris Dralyuk, Gasan Gusejnov, Daryl Hardman, Jessy Kaner, Martha Kapos, Clare Kitson, Maria Kozlovskaya, Polina Lavrova, Sophie Lockey, Elena Malysheva, Irina Mashinski, Melanie Mauthner, Naomi Mottram, Olga Nazarova, Yulia Kartalova O'Doherty, Natasha Perova, Anna Pilkington, Susan Purcell, Donald Rayfield, Miriam Rossi, Daria Safronova, Francesca Sollohub, Jonathan Sutton, Natalia Tronenko, Elena Trubilova, Katia Volodina, Marie-Claire Wilson, Christine Worobec—and many others who have replied to questions on email forums or participated in summer schools or workshops in Pushkin House (London).

For the main part, we have followed the texts as printed in the seven-volume collected edition, *Sobranie sochinenii* (Moscow: Lakom, 1998–2005). For Teffi's articles printed in Kyiv and Odessa, we have used the excellent *Teffi v strane vospominanii* (Kyiv: LP Media, 2011). For "Solovki"—the version in *Vechernyi den'* (Prague, 1924); for "Before a Map of Russia"—the shorter version of this poem in the almanac *Na zapade* (New York, 1953); for "The Other World"—the text in *Tvorchestvo N. A. Teffi* (Moscow: IMLI, 1999).

*

An earlier version of "Love" was included in *Russian Short Stories from Pushkin to Buida* (Penguin Classics, 2005).

Earlier versions of the following were included in *Subtly Worded* (Pushkin Press, 2014): "Subtly Worded", "The Lifeless Beast", "Jealousy", "My First Tolstoy", "Petrograd Monologue", "*Que Faire?*", "And Time Was No More".

Earlier versions of the following were included in *Rasputin and Other Ironies* (Pushkin Press, 2016): "How I Live and Work", "Love", "Staging Posts", "The Gadarene Swine", "My First Tolstoy", "Ilya Repin".

An earlier version of "The Guillotine" was included in *1917* (Pushkin Press, 2017) as "Guillotine".

Earlier versions of "The Last Breakfast" and the excerpts from *Memories* were included in *Memories* (Pushkin Press, 2017).

Earlier versions of the following were included in *Other Worlds* (Pushkin Press, 2021): "Kishmish", "Solovki", "The Book of June", "Shapeshifter", "Rusalka", "Volya".

The excerpt from "Istanbul" will be published in Valentina Izmirleva, ed., *Ruin of Empires: Constantinople's Russian Moment* (Academic Studies Press, forthcoming).

Further Reading

Edythe Haber, *Teffi: A Life of Letters and of Laughter* (London: I.B. Tauris, 2019). An exemplary, highly readable and scrupulously researched biography.

Robert Chandler, ed., *Russian Magic Tales from Pushkin to Platonov* (Penguin Classics, 2012)

Teffi, *Subtly Worded* (Pushkin Press, 2014)

Teffi, *Rasputin and Other Ironies* (Pushkin Press, 2016)

Teffi, *Memories* (Pushkin Press and NYRB Classics, 2017)

Teffi, *Other Worlds* (Pushkin Press and NYRB Classics, 2017)

Robert Chandler, "Nezhivoy zver'" ("The Lifeless Beast") in *The Literary Encyclopedia* (litencyc.com).

Edythe Haber, "Teffi" in *The Literary Encyclopedia* (litencyc.com).

Valentina Izmirleva, ed., *Ruin of Empires: Constantinople's Russian Moment* (Academic Studies Press, forthcoming).

Russian Editions of Teffi

As yet, there is no complete edition of Teffi's work. The most useful collected editions are the five-volume *Sobranie sochinenii* published by Terra in 2008, the seven-volume *Sobranie sochinenii* published by Lakom in 1998–2005; and the three-volume edition published by *Rech'* in 2021, edited by Elena Trubilova.

Other useful volumes are:

1. *Moia letopis'* (Moscow: Vagrius, 2004): This contains the whole of *Vospominaniia* as well as the memoirs about writers and other public figures that Teffi intended to publish as a separate volume titled *Moia letopis'* (*My Chronicle*).
2. *Teffi v strane vospominanii* (Kyiv: LP Media, 2011): An excellent compilation of articles and sketches written by Teffi between 1917 and 1919. Many were published in journals and newspapers in Kyiv and Odessa during Teffi's last months before emigrating. Most are also included in the more readily available *Kontrrevoliutsionnaia bukva* (St Petersburg: Azbuka, 2006).
3. *Kusochek zhizni* (Moscow: AST, 2023): Devoted to Teffi's years in Paris, this includes little-known photographs, along with stories and articles from the émigré press that have never before been republished.

Notes

Introductory Note

1 Review of *The Book of June*, *Illiustrirovannaia Rossiia*, 25 April 1931.
2 *The Guardian*, 24 June 2014.
3 *New Statesman*, 13 May 2016.
4 27 November 1866. (Jubilee Edition, vol. 48, p. 116).
5 Edythe Haber, *Teffi: A Life of Letters and of Laughter* (London: I.B. Tauris, 2019), p. 20. Hereafter: Haber, *Teffi*.

PART ONE

1 Volhynia (now a part of western Ukraine) was then part of the Russian Empire.
2 From the opening of "Katerina Petrovna", in *The Book of June* (Teffi, *Sobranie sochinenii* (Moscow: Lakom, 2000), vol. 4, p. 45).
3 Teffi, *Izbrannye proizvedeniia* (Moscow: Lakom, 1999), vol. 2, p. 9.

Rusalka

1 On *nyanya*, see "A Note on Russian Names".
2 The poem "translated" by the adjutant is almost certainly Shelley's "Love's Philosophy"(1819). The second of its two stanzas reads:

> See the mountains kiss high heaven,
> And the waves clasp one another;
> No sister-flower would be forgiven
> If it disdained its brother:
> And the sunlight clasps the earth,
> And the moonbeams kiss the sea—
> What is all this sweet work worth,
> If thou kiss not me?

3 A joking reference to the custom, common to many parts of Europe, of leaving a small patch of corn unreaped—to propitiate the fertility god or goddess and so ensure an abundant crop the following year. In Russia, the ears were knitted together—and this was known as "the plaiting of the beard of Volos". In 1872 William Ralston wrote, "The unreaped patch is looked upon as tabooed; and it is believed that if anyone meddles with it he will shrivel up and become twisted like the interwoven ears" (republished in *The Songs of the Russian People* (Miami, FL: Hard Press, 2017), p. 251).
4 The hero of Teffi's story "The Limit" asserts that a *rusalka*, unlike a Western mermaid, "knows one cannot tempt a Russian soul with the body alone. One must capture a Russian soul through pity. Therefore what does a *rusalka* do? She weeps [...] If she simply sat or beckoned or something—some might not approach. But if she weeps, how can you help but approach?" (Haber, *Teffi*, p. 118).
5 Traditionally, seven women, including the bride, would help to make this large, rich, sweetened and highly decorated loaf of bread. It was presented to the bride and groom just before they married.

Kishmish

1 The Russian Orthodox refer to the first week of Lent as "Clean Week". The faithful are expected to undergo spiritual cleansing through fasting, prayer, repentance, begging forgiveness of their neighbour and taking the Eucharist. Throughout the six weeks of Lent, vegetable oils are substituted for butter and animal fats.

Love

1 He is probably limping in imitation of Lord Byron.
2 A *baba* is a peasant woman; neckweed is another name for hemp.
3 *Martha, or Richmond Fair* (1847) by the German composer Friedrich von Flotow (1812–83).
4 The heroine of many Russian folk tales, here confused with Helen of Troy.

PART TWO

1 Haber, *Teffi*, p. 224.

The Book of June

1 Tsarist Russia in many ways followed the German educational system. A *gymnasium* is an elite secondary school with a strong emphasis on academic learning, similar to a British grammar school or a prep school in the US. *Gymnasiums* for women were instituted in 1862.
2 Alexey Konstantinovich Tolstoy (1817–75) wrote lyric poems, acute satires and verse plays on historical and religious themes and subjects from legends. He was related only distantly to the famous novelist.
3 Viktor Vasnetsov (1848–1926) was one of the group of artists known as the Wanderers (*Peredvizhniki*). Many of his paintings are on themes from Russian folk tales and the oral verse epics known as *byliny*.

Shapeshifter

1 A *verst* is approximately the same length as a kilometre.
2 An organ of local government. Established in 1864, three years after the emancipation of the serfs, these democratically elected councils were central to the liberal movement during the last decades of tsarist rule. They were responsible for building schools, hospitals, roads, etc.

Solovki

1 From the second half of the nineteenth century, there was a huge increase in the number of pilgrims paying short visits to the Solovetsky Islands. *The Archangel Michael* was one of three steam ships operated by the monastery, and the voyage from Arkhangelsk took seventeen hours. The pilgrimage season started late in June and the most important feast day was 8 August, the day of Saints Zosima and Savvaty, the monastery's two founders.
2 A penance would include going to all services, a prescribed number of bodily prostrations and the repetition of additional prayers.
3 Pilgrims visiting a holy site still often buy items of clothing for their burial. During an Orthodox burial, it is customary for the deceased to wear a belt—into which a prayer has been woven—since they will need it when resurrected. Belts are symbolically important in Russian culture, suggesting order and dignity.
4 The Pomors—Russian-speaking inhabitants of the northern coast of European Russia—developed a specific culture through contact with the region's indigenous peoples.

5 Probably these women had prayed to the monastery's patron saints and vowed to send their sons there (the monastery did not accept women except as pilgrims on short visits) if their prayer was granted. The boys would serve as labourers, also receiving some spiritual teaching, for a year or two, whereupon they would return to their homes. They were not trainee monks.

6 Some recluse monks on Solovki still keep to a rule of complete silence, living alone and devoting their lives to prayer. It seems that some of Teffi's pilgrims did not understand this. It is also possible that the mutual incomprehension sprang from the use of different dialects.

7 Their walk echoes the Procession of the Cross around the outside of a church on Easter Eve and certain other feast days.

8 Considered an aphrodisiac.

9 Demons were often portrayed as shaggy, with webbed feet and twisting tails.

10 *Sparrmannia Africana*, or African Hemp, which has a delicious lime-like scent.

11 Being on the west wall, the Last Judgement was the final set of images a worshipper would see as they left the church; this makes the monks' surrender to temptation still more ironical.

12 A lightly fermented drink made from rye bread.

13 Psalm 37:45 (Orthodox numbering), which is included in the morning prayers for lay readers: "For my loins are filled with a loathsome disease: and there is no soundness in my flesh" (King James version, Psalm 38:7).

14 During the three days of their stay, short-term visitors were required not to eat meat and dairy products, so they would be ready to receive communion.

15 In the mid-1880s the poet Konstantin Sluchevsky described Pomor women as "well dressed regardless of their social and economic status, wearing long colourful *sarafany*, and beautifully decorated headwear. […] A distinctive feature of women's clothing in some parts of Pomor'e was an extensive use of pearls extracted from local rivers" (https://www.openbookpublishers.com/htmlreader/978-1-78374-544-9/ch8.xhtml).

16 In "The Sea is Our Field", Masha Shaw and Natalie Wahnsiedler write: "Sluchevsky was particularly impressed by the light and skilful movements of Pomor women in their long and richly decorated dresses as they steered their boats in rough and roaring waters" (David G. Anderson, Dmitry V. Arzyutov and Sergei S. Alimov, eds, *Life Histories of* Etnos *Theory in Russia and Beyond* (Cambridge: Open Book Publishers, 2019)).

17 The beginning of the most solemn part of the Liturgy, sung as the clergy—accompanied, it is believed, by angels—enter the sanctuary through the Holy Doors. It ends, "Let us now lay aside all earthly care."

18 Meaning "Whither". Teffi clearly chose the word both for its sound and for its meaning. It is impossible to reproduce both in English, so we have transliterated, giving the sound alone.

19 The celebration of Christ's Resurrection through the mystery of the Eucharist was believed to provoke fear among demons, which in turn could prompt fits among those in a state of demonic possession.

20 Varvara's "Ai-da!" echoes the first woman's "Ku-da!" *Da* means "Yes".

21 Normally, Varvara would not have received communion before completing her penance, but she is thought to be possessed and so is not responsible for her state. In the words of John Chrysostom, "They that be possessed in that they are tormented of the devil are blameless and will never be punished with torment for that: but they who approach unworthily the holy Mysteries shall be given over to everlasting torments" (quoted in R. W. Blackmore, *The Doctrine of the Russian Church* (Aberdeen, 1845), p. 223 n.). And so Varvara is given the Eucharist: a small piece of bread dipped in wine.

22 Saint Tikhon of Zadonsk (1724–83) was born, like Varvara and her husband, in the province of Novgorod. After serving for seven years as a bishop, he retired because of poor health to the monastery of Zadonsk, beyond the river Don. Eighty years after his death, he was canonized. Varvara imagines herself and Semyon making a pilgrimage to Zadonsk, stopping at other holy sites on the way.

Petrograd Monologue

1 *Mir iskusstva* was an artistic movement that flourished in Russia at the beginning of the twentieth century.

2 Natalina Cavalieri (1874–1944) was an Italian soprano much loved in pre-revolutionary Petersburg.

The Guillotine

1 A popular song of the time: *"Guillotin, Médecin, Politique, Imagine, un beau matin, Que pendre est inhumain, Et peu patriotique. Et sa main Fait soudain Une machine Humainement qui tuera Et qu'on appellera Guillotine."* ("Guillotin, a doctor and a politician, imagines, one fine morning, that to hang people

is inhuman and unpatriotic. So his hand swiftly makes a machine that will kill humanely, and which we will call the guillotine.")

2 The unofficial title of Charles-Henri Sanson—Royal Executioner in France under Louis XVI (1754–93). After the French Revolution, as High Executioner of the First Republic, he guillotined Louis XVI.

3 Inflation had been gathering pace in Russia since February 1917, and after the October Revolution, it accelerated still more rapidly. In 1918, when Teffi wrote this story, there was no one-million-rouble note, but it is set in the future, and her prediction was borne out in 1921.

4 In the original, the cab driver wishes the friends "gentle steam!"—a standard Russian idiom addressed to somebody about to go for a steam bath.

5 A traditional Russian drink, made of water, honey, spices and jam, served hot in winter.

Extracts from Memories

1 Known in English as *The Riviera Girl* or *The Gipsy Princess*), *Silva* is an operetta by the Hungarian composer Emmerich Kalman (1882–1953). It premiered in Vienna in November 1915. It remains popular in Hungary, Austria and Germany and was made into a successful film in the Soviet Union.

2 Valery Briusov was one of the founders of Russian Symbolism. An influential figure, he joined the Communist Party in 1920. There are several accounts of his abusing his position in the Soviet cultural apparatus to attack more gifted colleagues.

3 A green dragon with three heads who appears in one of the most famous *byliny*. He spits fire and he walks on his two back paws. See also "The Book of June", note 3, and "A Little Fairy Tale".

4 The Soviet security services were originally called the Extraordinary Committee or *Chrezvychainy komitet*, usually shortened to *Chrezvychaika* or *Cheka*. Later acronyms were the OGPU, the NKVD and the KGB; currently FSB.

5 *Novoe vremya*, a Petersburg daily newspaper (1868–1917). Under its last editor, A. S. Suvorin, it was considered extremely reactionary, and the Bolsheviks closed it down the day after the October Revolution.

6 On the *gymnasium*, see "The Book of June", note 1.

7 Teffi's younger sister Elena Lokhvitskaya (1874–1919), the closest of her six siblings, wrote both poetry and plays. In 1922, after hearing the news of Elena's death, Teffi wrote to Vera Bunina, "I feel complete

emptiness. It's as if, because of this news, a wind has passed over my earth and swept everything away. I haven't spoken, I've grown thin and grey in four days" (*Diaspora*, 1 (Paris and St Petersburg, 2001), p. 365).

Staging Posts

1 Teffi's last pre-war fictional publication (28 April 1940). Liza represents Teffi, while Katya is her younger sister Lena (see "Extracts from *Memories*", note 7).
2 *Kulich* is a spiced Easter bread, and *paskha* is a curd cheesecake.
3 *Baba* has two meanings: a peasant woman, and a particular kind of cake.
4 In Daniel 3, when Shadrach, Meshach and Abednego refused to worship Nebuchadnezzar, King of Babylon, he had them thrown into a fiery furnace. God kept them safe.
5 Masha is Teffi's elder sister Mirra Lokhvitskaya (1869–1905), later a well-known poet.
6 Peter's denial of Christ. During the Last Supper, Jesus predicted that, before the rooster crowed three times the following morning, Peter would deny all knowledge of him. Liza is attending the Holy Thursday service "The Twelve Gospels of the Passion of Our Lord and Saviour Jesus Christ"—a reading of twelve passages recounting the betrayal, arrest, trial and crucifixion of Jesus. The service also includes an enactment of Christ carrying his cross to Golgotha.
7 A famous romance composed by Yelizaveta Kochubey (1821–97).
8 This last section takes place during the Russian Civil War. Teffi had left Odessa in April 1919, on a small ship heading for Novorossiisk, the Black Sea port from which she soon afterwards set off for Constantinople (Istanbul). For a fuller treatment of this episode, see Teffi, *Memories*, chapters 17–23, esp. 23.

The Gadarene Swine

1 A violent, ultra-nationalist Russian movement that supported the tsarist principles of Orthodoxy, Autocracy and Nationality, and was fiercely hostile to both revolutionaries and Jews. Its members were drawn from a variety of social classes.
2 Genesis 7:3, where God tells Noah to take animals into the ark: "Of every clean beast thou shalt take to thee by sevens, the male and his female: and of beasts that are not clean by two, the male and his female." In the Bible, the beasts do *not* devour one another.

The Last Breakfast

1 The articles and sketches Teffi wrote during the years 1917–19 are gradually being republished in Russia and Ukraine. The most recent edition, *Teffi in the Country of Memories* (Kiev: LP Media, 2011), contains over seventy pieces. Twenty of these were published in Kyiv newspapers, mostly between October 1918 and January 1919, and three in Odessa, in early 1919.

Extract from Memories

1 Pavel Novgorodtsev (1866–1924) was a liberal political philosopher and lawyer; he emigrated in 1921 and died in Prague. Venedikt Miakotin (1867–1937) was a Populist politician; expelled in 1922, he became a professor of history in Sofia in 1928, then lived his last years in Prague. Fiodor Volkenstein (1874–1937) was a lawyer, writer and journalist; he remained in the Soviet Union. Piyotr Ouspensky (1878–1947) was a follower of the philosopher and religious teacher George Gurdjieff (1866–1949).

2 Maximilian Voloshin (1877–1932) was one of the leading Russian Symbolist poets of the early twentieth century. For over a decade his large house in the Crimea, where he both wrote and painted, was a refuge for writers and artists of all political and artistic persuasions. Voloshin's belief in the power of his words seems to have been unshakeable; his personal appeals to both Red and White officials and commanders, on behalf of individuals in trouble, and his verse-prayers addressed to God, on behalf of his country, have much in common. Voloshin believed he could affect the course of events—and sometimes he did. That he escaped arrest and execution is astonishing. See Robert Chandler, Boris Dralyuk and Irina Mashinski, eds, *The Penguin Book of Russian Poetry* (Penguin Classics: 2015), pp. 175–80.

3 In Song of Solomon 4:1, Solomon says to a woman referred to as the Shulamite, "Behold, thou art fair, my love; behold, thou art fair; thou hast doves' eyes within thy locks: thy hair is as a flock of goats, that appear from mount Gilead."

4 Ksenya Mikhailovna G (1892–1919) was an anarchist who joined the Bolshevik Party after the October Revolution. Her independence of mind led to her being sent out of the way, to Kislovodsk, where she worked as an investigator for the Cheka. After Kislovodsk fell to the Whites, she was hanged. "G" was the pseudonym adopted by her husband, whose surname was Golberg.

5 Mamont Dalsky (1865–1918) was a tragic actor, famous for his interpretation of the lead role in *Edmund Kean, or The Genius and the Libertine* (1847) by Alexandre Dumas. In his trilogy *The Road to Calvary* (1918–41), Alexey Tolstoy wrote, "When the Revolution began, Dalsky saw in it an enormous stage for tragic drama. […] He brought together isolated groups of anarchists, took over the Merchants' Club and declared it the House of Anarchy."
6 Named after Grand Duke Alexander Mikhailovich (1866–1933), the brother-in-law of Tsar Nicholas II.

Istanbul (from "Istanbul and Sun")

1 Similar to a kebab.
2 A depiction of a pile of skulls outside the walls of a city in Central Asia. Vereshchagin dedicated *The Apotheosis of War* (1871) "to all great conquerors, past, present and to come".
3 This ancient oak tree, near Hebron, is believed to mark the spot where Abraham entertained three angels, thinking they were ordinary travellers.

PART FOUR

1 Edythe Haber, "Teffi" in *The Literary Encyclopedia* (litencyc.com).
2 Haber discusses "Nostalgia" more fully in the first page of her introduction to *Teffi*.

Que Faire?

1 Fiodor Tiutchev (1803–73) is generally thought the finest Russian lyric poet after Alexander Pushkin. Avril Pyman has translated the epigram from which the speaker quotes as "Russia is baffling to the mind, / not subject to the common measure; / her ways—of a peculiar kind… / One only can have *faith* in Russia" (Chandler, Dralyuk and Mashinski, eds, *The Penguin Book of Russian Poetry*, p. 111).

A Little Fairy Tale

1 Baba Yaga is the archetypal Russian witch. Teffi's article about her—one of her last works—is included in *Other Worlds: Peasants, Pilgrims, Spirits, Saints* (Pushkin Press and NYRB Classics, 2021).

2 Leshy, the forest spirit, associated with darkness, is less malevolent than the water spirit but more dangerous than the house spirit. His role is to lead people astray—certainly not to enlighten them. From 1917 to 1946, the Soviet ministry for education and culture was known as *Narkompros* or The People's Commissariat of Enlightenment.
3 "The Humpbacked Horse" (1834) by Piotr Yershov, is a verse fairy tale. A wily but honest peasant boy captures a flying horse. In exchange for his freedom, this horse gives the boy two beautiful black horses and a little humpbacked pony. The horses are his to sell or give away; the little pony is to remain his companion. Throughout his subsequent adventures, the boy follows the pony's advice.
4 The Council of People's Commissars was elected in late 1917 at the Second All-Russian Congress of Soviets. Officially responsible for the "general administration of affairs of state" when the Congress of Soviets was not in session, it soon became the country's supreme executive authority. Lenin was its first chairman.
5 See "Extracts from *Memories*", p. 242, note 3.
6 See "Extracts from *Memories*", p. 242, note 4.
7 A female house spirit in Slavic mythology, Kikimora is sometimes considered the wife of the more important male house spirit. Usually she lives behind the stove or in the cellar, though she can also be found in swamps and forests. She is notably ugly; "to look like a kikimora" means "to look a fright".

A Small Town

1 The River Neva, which is very broad indeed, flows through St Petersburg.
2 The *Rive Gauche*—the Left Bank—is traditionally a home for students and artists.

How I Live and Work

1 One of the Twelve Labours of Hercules was to clean the stables of King Augeas. These had not been cleaned for more than thirty years, and were home to more than 1,000 cattle.
2 From November 1925 to April 1926, Teffi and her partner Pavel Theakston attended a lecture series "The Social Philosophy of Christianity", given by the religious philosopher Boris Vysheslavtsev (1877–1954). Haber's understanding is that Vysheslavtsev "condemned Communist materialism

and found the true roots of social justice and equality in Christian love and freely offered sacrifice" (*Teffi*, p. 123).

3 A common French idiom, here meaning something like "Well, can't be helped." Banine—a woman writer who was one of Teffi's closest friends during her last years—described the room where Teffi lived in the late 1940s as "crammed with an enormous sofa strewn with cushions and a motley collection of furniture, pictures, and books. Incredible chaos reigned; everything was covered with dust [...] and the photographs! There were as many of them as books; they were standing, lying, hanging everywhere" (Haber, *Teffi*, p. 191).

from "The Violet Notebook"

1 Dostoevsky's novel *The Demons* (1871–2), one of his four masterpieces, is a fiercely satirical attack on rationalism, socialism, nihilism, atheism and other ideas that he saw as dangerous Western imports.

PART FIVE

1 Haber's translation (*Teffi*, p. 179).
2 See Haber, *Teffi*, p. 190.
3 See Haber, *Teffi*, p. 198. After a relatively liberal period during the war, the year 1946 saw a renewed clampdown on the arts. The poet Anna Akhmatova and the satirist Mikhail Zoshchenko were vilified in the press and expelled from the Writers' Union.
4 Haber, *Teffi*, p. 201.
5 For a slightly reworded variant of this quote, see "Tri iumorista", in Andrey Sedykh, *Dalekie, blizkie,* 2nd edn (New York: Izd. "Novogo russkogo slova", 1962), p. 87.
6 See Haber, *Teffi*, p. 223. (translation slightly revised).
7 S. Nikonenko, "Nesravnennaya Teffi", in N. A. Teffi, *Moia letopis'* (Moscow: Vagrius, 2004) p. 14.

The Other World

1 From Alexander Pushkin's verse play *A Feast in Time of Plague* (1830). For the relevant stanzas, see Chandler, Dralyuk and Mashinski, eds, *The Penguin Book of Russian Poetry*, p. 79.
2 In Greek mythology, Prometheus stole fire from the Olympian gods and gave it to mankind.

3 Teffi's version is not entirely accurate. A Soviet publishing house did indeed intend to publish Bunin, but only a one-volume selection, and Bunin was not thought to have died. Nevertheless, the publishing house had begun planning this volume without asking permission. After furious protests from Bunin, they backed down. (*Tvorchestvo N. A. Teffi*, ed. O.N. Mikhailov, D.D. Nikolaev and E.M.Trubilova (Moscow: IMLI, 1999), p. 215).

4 Maurice Maeterlinck (1862–1949), a Belgian Symbolist playwright, won the Nobel Prize for Literature in 1911. Death was one of his central themes.

5 Ephesians 5:29.

6 Located on the outskirts of Lublin, in eastern Poland, Majdanek was a Nazi concentration and extermination camp. Due to the rapid advance of the Red Army in July 1944, it was captured nearly intact. It was the first major concentration camp to be liberated, and the atrocities committed there were widely publicized.

Volya

1 Saint Spiridon (*c.*270–348) is honoured in both Eastern and Western Christian traditions. According to the Julian calendar (used in Russia until 1918), his saint's day falls close to the winter solstice and so he is known as Spiridon Povorot or Spiridon Solntsevorot (Spiridon-Turnabout or Spiridon-Sunturn). This term was sometimes used to describe people returning illegally from exile (Olga Atroshinko, *Russkii narodnyi kalendar'. Etnolingvisticheskii slovar'* (Moscow: AST-Press, 2015), pp. 414–15).

2 Lengths of cloth wound around the foot and ankle—more common in Russia, until the middle of the twentieth century, than socks or stockings. By the 1950s, however, they had largely disappeared—except in labour camps and the army.

3 In Slavic and Baltic mythology, this magic flower blooms on the eve of the summer solstice. In different versions of the myth, it bestows a variety of gifts on the person who finds it. These gifts include wealth, understanding of animal speech and the ability to open any locked door, but they seldom, if ever, bring the finder any real benefit.

And Time Was No More

1 Quickly, quickly, quickly... He's in no hurry.

2 Adelina Patti (1843–1919) was a famous Italian nineteenth-century soprano, admired by Verdi. Fiodor Chaliapin (1873–1938) was a famous Russian operatic bass; he died in Paris.
3 The huntsman Thomas Glahn is a central character in the novel *Pan* (1894) by the Norwegian Knut Hamsun (1859–1952). Awarded the Nobel Prize for Literature in 1920, Hamsun was widely read from the 1890s until the Second World War.
4 The narrator is referring to one of Tiutchev's best-known poems, "Day and Night" (1839). See also "*Que Faire?*" note 1.
5 Teffi slightly shortens this quotation from Revelation 10:5–6.
6 Teffi is referring to the months during the First World War when she served as a nurse.

Ilya Repin

1 In 1910, Teffi's first two books were published by Dog Rose (*Shipovnik*).
2 Ilya Repin (1844–1930) was the greatest of Russian realist painters. Teffi's story, first published in December 1915, is about a fatuous man whose repeated expressions of wonder at life's everyday miracles exasperate not only his wife but also his small children.
3 All four artists emigrated after the Revolution. Teffi's *Memories* includes a brief mention of Savely Schleifer (1888–1943), a Ukrainian impressionist and modernist painter who died in Auschwitz, and a longer mention of Yakovlev. The whereabouts of these portraits are unknown; probably they have not survived.
4 Boris Kustodiev (1878–1927) was a painter and stage designer. His portrait of Nicholas II (1915) can be seen in the Russian Museum in St Petersburg.
5 Fiodor Chaliapin (1873–1938) was the most famous operatic bass of his day. Vlas Doroshevich (1864–1922) was a journalist and writer of short stories; from 1902 until 1918 he edited *The Russian Word*, the newspaper where Teffi published much of her early work. Leonid Andreyev (1871–1919) was a central figure of Russian literature's "Silver Age"; he wrote plays, short stories and novels.
6 Teffi seems unaware of the distinction between vegetarianism and veganism—perhaps seldom made at this time.
7 Teffi also tells this story in chapter 2 of *Memories*; some details differ.
8 Kovno was one of the north-western provinces of the Russian empire, now a part of Lithuania (Kovno in Russian, Kaunas in Lithuanian).

9 Mikhail Kuzmin (1872–1936), one of the finest poets of his time, was known as "the Russian Wilde". He also wrote plays and composed music. In 1906 he published *Wings*, the first Russian novel with an overtly homosexual theme; two large editions sold out at once.
10 A famous icon. The original is held by a Georgian Orthodox monastery on Mount Athos.

About the Contributors

BEE BENTALL graduated from the University of Nottingham in 2014, inspired by their love of Russian punk music. They are now an autism peer-support worker.

MICHELE A. BERDY is a translator and author who has written about the culture and language of Russia for many decades. A selection of her articles about translation problems was published by Glas in 2010 in *The Russian Word's Worth.*

ELIZABETH CHANDLER is a co-translator, with Robert Chandler, of Pushkin's *The Captain's Daughter* and *Peter the Great's African*, and of several titles by Andrey Platonov and Vasily Grossman. She does not know Russian, but has gradually, over the years, began to work more and more closely with her husband.

ROSE FRANCE is a teaching fellow in Russian language and culture at the University of Edinburgh. She has worked as a translator for many years and contributed to literary anthologies. Among her published translations are *Children of War: 1941–1945*, poems by Lermontov, and short stories and sketches by Teffi and Zoshchenko.

ANNE MARIE JACKSON is a translator and editor. She has translated works by Teffi, Alexey Nikitin and Maxim Osipov, among others. Currently residing in France, in the 1990s she lived in

Russia and Moldova, where she was shot dead by Chechen rebels in a Russian film.

CLARE KITSON came to Russian literary translation after forty years in cinema and television. *Que Faire?* launched her new career. Her first solo translation of a full-length work was *April 1917*, Part 1 of Aleksandr Solzhenitsyn's *The Red Wheel.*

AVAILABLE AND COMING SOON FROM PUSHKIN PRESS CLASSICS

The Pushkin Press Classics list brings you timeless storytelling by icons of literature. These titles represent the best of fiction and non-fiction, hand-picked from around the globe – from Russia to Japan, France to the Americas – boasting fresh selections, new translations and stylishly designed covers. Featuring some of the most widely acclaimed authors from across the ages, as well as compelling contemporary writers, these are the world's best stories – to be read and read again.

SIDDHARTHA
HERMANN HESSE

THE UNHAPPINESS OF BEING
A SINGLE MAN
FRANZ KAFKA

THE BOOK OF PARADISE
ITZIK MANGER

THE ALLURE OF CHANEL
PAUL MORAND

COIN LOCKER BABIES
RYU MURAKAMI

THE YEAR OF THE HARE
ARTO PAASILINNA

BINOCULAR VISION
EDITH PEARLMAN

SWANN IN LOVE
MARCEL PROUST

THE EVENINGS
GERARD REVE

JOURNEY BY MOONLIGHT
ANTAL SZERB

BEWARE OF PITY
STEFAN ZWEIG